THE BONE YARD AND OTHER STORIES

JOHN MORALEE

ISBN-13: 978-1502735539
ISBN-10: 1502735539

Visit www.**mybookspage.wordpress.com** to find out more about the author.

CONTENTS

The Bone Yard - 5
Nematode - 31
Open Wounds - 39
The Challenge - 51
The Shadow of Death - 63
Monsters - 87
Sickness Country - 107
The Midnight Murderer - 125
The Faintest Echo - 163
Sleeping in the Earth - 181
The Gift - 195
The Deepest, Darkest Fear - 209
The Big Favour - 231
Starlight - 251
Disconnected - 267
About the Author - 277

The Bone Yard

Some places should be left well alone.

Old Carney is one of them. Roughly half a mile from the village of Devesham in Northumberland, Old Carney is after the fork in the north road, surrounded on three sides by green meadows and ancient oak trees and the sweet smells of the country. How long it's been there is a matter for rumour and legend, but it was there in my great-great-grandfather's time. It was ancient in those days. Walking down the lane (the land slides downhill towards Old Carney like it's an iron weight dropped on a mattress) you can see the remains of the first church above the trees, the black spire a grim signpost warning the visitor: this is holy land. The lane is shaded by trees a moment later and curves left and then right ... revealing the church and the six-foot-high wall keeping out the uninvited. Dark weeds nestle in the stones and you can smell earth from the other side. Behind the stone wall is Old Carney.

The bone yard.

Good cemeteries are resting places: lush, bowling-green-smooth acres of grass with well-kept marble headstones, places families have picnics in the summer and children visit their grandparents burial plots with fresh daffodils and loving prayers.

Not Old Carney.

There's nothing nice or quaint about Old Carney.

It's just there to be avoided.

There's a mud trail that goes parallel to the stone wall, containing a gap where the top layers of stone have crumbled to expose a view of the cemetery. Rumours abound about the gap and what can be seen on the other side.

Some people say grey shadows watch the trail through the gap, looking for the curious or naive. People drawn to the gap may - if they haven't heard the rumours - take a glance at the cemetery and feel a shudder in their bowels and a light-headedness they can't explain - no - won't explain. These witnesses wander the rest of the day confused, babbling, shaking. They try to understand what they thought they had seen into some kind of sensible, rational thing - and fail. They would never say a word to another soul, for they'd sound crazy.

Some people say Old Carney is haunted and at night you can hear the echoes of the dead.

*

There are many rumours about Old Carney, but I know the truth. In the summer of 1939 many more were invented by the children of Miss Dolby's class, including me. It was in that summer I learned the stories contained some truth, though the reality was worse than the blackest fiction.

*

One day my friends and I rested on the bank of the lake, dangling our legs in the cool water. The Fearless Four: me, Joe, Brian and Alexander. We had just finished kicking Brian's football around on the field besides the lake until we had become exhausted. Joe and Alexander had won 7-3. My leg ached from a bad hack by Joe (or a good tackle from his view) and there was a nasty purple swelling developing on my shin. Brian and I were not in the best of moods.

We hated losing. Brian rubbed the mud from the ball like it was a trophy and flicked some at Alexander and giggled when it splattered Alexander's cheeks.

Alexander scowled. "You're a baby, Brian." He wiped the dirt off with his handkerchief. His father was the village doctor and encouraged Alexander in intellectual pursuits and in the ways of insulting the less fortunate working class, like the rest of us. He lifted his nose snootily and I felt a wave of loathing. Some days Alexander could irritate like an old scab. "You lost because you do not have the necessary skill and intellect."

I dipped my hand into the water and splashed him. "Shut up, Alex."

Alexander wasn't the same as us. He didn't read comic books and like Biggles. He read massive books with hundreds of pages, plain hardback covers and long-winded titles. He therefore didn't know how to retaliate like a man, with fists. "That is immature. When are you going to behave like good sports?"

I splashed him some more.

"Why you -"

Joe told us to be quiet and we obeyed because Joe was nearing his eleventh birthday and he was a good three inches taller than the rest of the Fearless Four. Joe seemed to sprout a few inches on us every week. I wondered if he bathed his feet in compost overnight. He pointed at a spider crawling on Brian's back.

"You've got a massive tarantula on you," he exaggerated.

Brian froze. Brian hated spiders. "Gerrioff!" he whined, sounding like commanding a Russian general. "Gerrioff!"

Joe trapped the spider in his hands and shook them - hard - puffing his cheeks with the concentration required.

"That will give it a headache," he grinned and opened his palm and blew the black arachnid into the grass where it vainly worked its unbroken legs in an attempt to upright itself. Brian finished it with a stick. "Rotten lousy Jerry spider!"

"And you call yourself fearless," Joe said.

Alexander, bored, put on his shoes and stretched and yawned. "Chaps, it's getting late."

It was about *six*. Joe and I looked at Alexander and thought: mother's boy. Alexander sensed this and shrugged. "I have to go home for my *dinner*."

He never said 'tea', like the rest of us, which made me hate him more.

Brian agreed with Alexander, probably because the scare with the spider made him want to go home. Mentioning food got my stomach rumbling. It had been noon when I'd eaten last and that was just a chocolate bar. I realised if I wanted a meal then I'd have to go, too. "I suppose there's no point in hanging around here, Joe."

Joe resigned himself to coming with us as we headed round the lake towards Old Carney and the way home. The lake was behind the cemetery and the only route except sneaking across the fields owned by Lord Mortimer. His gamekeepers were likely to shoot at anyone daring to cross his land. So that meant going along the mud trail and past the gap in the cemetery's wall. Brian went a dozen yards ahead and dribbled the ball and managed to collect a swarm of flies that he couldn't swat away. The heat was going out of the day and the sweat on my back was becoming cold and sticky. It didn't help I was wearing my starched school shirt and the rough cotton irritated my skin. I began scratching myself.

"Got ants in your pants?" Alexander said.

"Very funny," I said.

Old Carney grew larger and larger. We entered the shadows of the elms and oaks and automatically hushed. There was a reverence to the acres of untamed graveyard that had us believing in ghosts and evil and the bogeyman. Brian stopped dribbling. Any other wall would have been ripe for bouncing the ball off - but not the perimeter of Old Carney. The ancient stones were there to keep us *out* and whatever lurked inside *in*. Brian started tapping the football between his legs, walking like a bow-legged old man.

"Pass it back," Joe said.

Brian shook his head. "Not while we're on the path, Joe. My ball could go over the wall."

If Brian lost his ball, it would not mean just the loss of his prized possession - but a severe beating from his father for being careless. He picked up his ball and hugged it to his chest, making Joe sigh and roll his eyes.

"Come on, Brian! Kick it to me!"

"Not here," Brian said.

He walked on.

Joe shouted an insult to his back, but Brian ignored him. Joe faced me. "Do you ever wonder what's in Old Carney?" he said.

I shrugged. "Dead bodies. Lots of dead bodies."

"Corpses," Alexander said, acting smart. "The correct word is corpse. I read a book once that said the human body decays in a matter of weeks, so there will be just skeletons and rotten clothes."

"No," Joe said, "I didn't mean that stuff. I know what's in there *physically*. But I'm mean *spiritually*. They say a priest tried to exercise -"

"Exorcise!" Alexander said.

"- ex-OR-size the ghosts and he went totally, utterly insane. LIKE BRIAN! That's why the entrance is all locked up."

"It's locked because the ground's unsafe," Alexander said. "That's what my father says."

I had heard Alexander's version of the reason, too, and a little more that was the source of spooky tall-tales. Old Carney's proper entrance was near the church - but that had been blocked during the 1920s when the ground subsided during a Sunday service and quarter of the congregation lost their lives. They were swallowed by the ground or killed by falling masonry. I think God must have been having a nap that day, for the vicar and a pregnant lady were among the victims. Naturally, people stopped using the church. It and the graveyard were closed to public access because the ground was too unstable.

"Haven't you ever wanted to look around?" Joe said.

"No," I said.

"Too dangerous," Alexander said.

"Cowards," Joe said. "Am I the only member of the Fearless Four who isn't chick-chick-chicken?"

Alexander squawked and flapped his arms sarcastically.

"Huh! Maybe Brian will want to explore." Joe left us and sneaked up on Brian, who was oblivious to the conversation. He said something to Brian and it was obvious Brian said no by the shaking of his head. Joe knocked the football from his grasp and started dribbling. He began to show off - heading and kneeing the ball and juggling it on his shoulders. He was good but Brian was as nervous as hell.

"Be careful!" he begged Joe.

"Watch this," Joe said, facing away from the wall and gritting his teeth. He kicked the ball with the tip of his toe and leaned back so the ball was lifted on his foot and given spin and momentum.

The football spun over his head in a high arc and - as if in slow motion - I watched it descend, rotating like the world globe in geography lessons. It struck the top of the wall. Loose stones spat into the air and then the football bounced - going the away from us - and disappeared over the other side. The other side! I heard it land against something that rustled and cracked. I guessed its fall had been broken by twigs and bushes. I heard it roll some distance before stopping.

Joe shrugged and put up his hands. There was a malicious grin on his face. "Oops!"

Brian's face went a bright red. "Now you've gone and done it!"

There was little doubt Joe had done it on purpose. "Sorry, Brian. What can I say?"

"I can't go home without my ball!" Brian started to cry, which for a member of the Fearless Four was a major sin - but he had good reason. His father would be furious. He would belt him for losing the ball, which was his only toy. "I've got to get it back!"

"Looks like you'll have to go inside then."

"M-Me? Y-you're the one that kicked it!"

"We'll all go," Joe said.

"Hey - you two go," Alexander said. "*We* had nothing to do with it."

I nodded. I didn't want to enter the graveyard.

"The Fearless Four go everywhere together," Joe said, quoting a brand new motto for the occasion. "Anyway - the gap's only a hundred yards away."

"It's at least two hundred and fifty," I said.

Joe ignored me. "We can climb over the wall there and follow it along. The ball can't have gone far. Easy as one, two, three."

Nobody liked the sound of that - but I felt sorry for Brian. It was clear Joe was too yellow to go in alone. Kicking the ball over the wall wasn't the brave thing to do - but the coward's way. He wanted to explore the graveyard, but he didn't want to do it alone. I pictured Joe as an officer in the First World War in a trench ordering men into battle and staying safe in the shelter. There was nothing brave about that.

*

Alexander suggested we mark the wall in some way so from the other side we could tell when we got to the right place. His handkerchief was elected the object to act as marker and he perched on mine and Joe's shoulders and placed it on the wall with a stone placed on top to keep it from blowing off. While he was up there, eyes level with the top, he tried to locate the ball. "It's too dark on that side. It's like a forest."

We reached the gap. I could see browns and blacks and the hard shadows of graves, but not much more. Sunlight penetrated weakly through the trees, trees that seemed to be everywhere. Usually cemeteries have very few trees but Old Carney was the exception. Elms and oaks equalled the number of headstones. A tree planted for every soul - my grandfather's words. My heart was beating wildly in my chest. "Maybe we should leave this until tomorrow."

"My old man won't wait that long," Brian said.

He was right - unfortunately - and I knew it.

I stared at Joe. "You go first, Joe."

Joe peered through the gap. Goosebumps appeared on his naked arms and legs. They reminded of chicken skin. The next moment he put his feet on the wall and balanced there with his hands on the firm supporting slabs. He looked down. "It's a few feet drop." He jumped. There was a sound like mud struck by a hammer blow. Then silence.

"Joe?" I called.

Brian grabbed my arm, rather too hard. "You don't think he's ... you know?"

Dead. I could see my fears masked in Brian and Alexander's faces, our eyes bulged. "Joe, are you all right?"

The growling came from the gap, an inhuman sound both shocking and paralysing. I imagined a black, slick mastiff that fed on unsuspecting humans ... a real hound of the Baskervilles ... and imagined Joe thrashing in mighty jaws, jaws with too many teeth to count.

Joe's head surfaced at the opening twisted into an agonised, pleading expression. The dog must have been pulling his legs because he jerked and struggled to grab hold of the wall. Then I realised he was making the sounds. Joe stopped the dog growl and laughed. "Well, well ... if it isn't the Terrified Trio!"

"Suppose you think that's funny?"

"Yes. You should have seen your faces!"

"Idiot!"

Joe put his tongue in his cheek. "Well, what are you waiting for?"

Brian was next. When he didn't scream, Alexander and I ventured over the wall. No turning back. The grass we stood on was wet though it hadn't rained for two weeks. It smelled of mildew.

Alexander showed me a threatening toadstool bursting from the weeds, mottled pink and moist. Things *squelched* under my shoes.

I looked back through the gap at the outside world, at the blue sky, at the living world, and felt a pang of longing. Thirty seconds in Old Carney and I was home sick -

"Come *on!*"

Joe set off along the side of the wall with Brian at his side.

But I couldn't shake the image of the Hound of the Baskervilles and neither could Alexander. "Wild dogs would love a place like this," he said. "Plenty of bones."

"At least Joe will get eaten first," I said.

He nodded. "Seriously, Mike, we have to be careful where we walk. Some of this ground will be like marshland."

"Like marshland?" I said. We were in slimy water already and my socks were soaked. "Who in their right mind would bury bodies in ground like this?"

"I think it's got religious significance."

"The water?"

"Don't be stupid, I mean this whole area. It's the connection point of twenty or thirty ley lines."

Joe and Brian had veered left - away from the wall. There was an obstruction: thick thorns and wicked brambles. I stepped on a hard surface and realised I was walking on a grave. Putting the grim thought out of my mind I asked Alexander about ley lines. I had never heard about them before.

"They are a sort of magnetic disturbance where rock has a different charge from the Earth. Pre-Christian societies considered them mystical and built shrines on them." He gave me a worried look. "This was a pagan burial ground long ago when the ground was dry. The river has changed direction since and formed the lake and saturated the ground. There are probably half a dozen underground streams through Old Carney." To prove his point he dug his heel into the earth and water filled the footprint. "This land is a possible death trap."

I gulped.

We skirted around the thicket, expecting to see Joe and Brian just ahead.

But Joe and Brian had gone.

*

"I bet they are hiding to scare us," I said. "Let's just stay near the wall, find the football and get out of here. They can play around if they like."

Staying near the wall was not as easy as I hoped. Twenty feet further on, an arched headstone jutted from a mound of tall grass and nettles. There was a hole beyond where the ground had fallen away. There was a sheer drop into darkness. White roots poked from the sides of the gaping maw like teeth. I was fairly sure I could see the rotten wood of a coffin lid about six feet down, like it was slipping out from the ground. I couldn't see the bottom. It was too shaded. Sure, we could go around it, staying besides the wall, but it meant that if the soil decided not to take our weight -

Down into the blackness.

We stopped. I looked around. "Joe! Brian! Where are you?"

There was a call roughly from ahead. It sounded like Joe.

Alexander followed me around the perimeter of the hole. We had to take a crooked route between some large tombs where the ground was more solid and level. It was quite disorientating and I lost sight of the wall. Alexander had a finer sense of direction and took the lead, commenting on the Gothic architecture of the tombs and the general ambience. I thought they were grim, lonely things. Why did people want to be buried in miserable eerie places?

We passed a tomb the size of my home and I gagged at the sight of beetles and larvae nested in abundance in the dark recesses. Ivy covered gargoyles stared at me. I was getting tired. My shin bruise was throbbing. "How much further?"

Alexander said not far, which translated as I-haven't-a-clue.

"Let's turn back while still we know the way," I said.

But Alexander pointed proudly at the tiny white speck that was his handkerchief. As if mesmerised, we trailed across the ground, dodging the graves sunk low and darkly in the copse. These graves were behind the large tombs for aesthetic reasons, for they were close together and very early memorials. Some were knobbly slabs of nameless granite. Weather had worn off the names. We reached the handkerchief, but there was still no sign of Brian and Joe.

I called out their names. The silence that followed was truly foreboding. "Forget them - let's get the ball and go."

Alexander knew more than a thing or two about projectile motions, including equations of flight and range, and he reckoned the ball was no more than twenty feet from the wall - so we searched through the weeds. A ball could be lost easily in the greens and browns. "We should split up and search in a pattern," he suggested.

"We stick together," I said. "Alone is stupid." I had seen too many Abbott and Costello pictures to go wandering alone in a graveyard, especially Old Carney. I had a feeling Joe and Brian were not larking around. Brian needed his football more than a game of hide and seek. I told Alexander my thoughts.

"You know Joe," he said, "this is just a laugh to him." As if that was a good enough explanation. Always the rational one.

I poked my foot into some weeds and brushed against something that rocked and pressed against my foot. Looking closer I saw a smooth brown surface. The ball! I bent down to pick it up. And realised my error -

It wasn't the ball.

It was a long and ancient bone.

Definitely human.

A femur half buried in grass and soil.

I lurched backwards and fell on my backside, pale and shaken. Alexander rushed to my side - saw the bone and scrunched his face with disgust. He tugged my arms and I groggily stood.

"I nearly picked it up!"

"It's just a bone," he said - sounding unconvinced. "There is bound to be loose bones." He was as shaken as me - his grammar was hiding. "Are," he corrected. "There *are* bound to be loose bones."

Non-verbal understanding passed between us.

It was time to leave: football or no football.

"We can't leave Joe and Brian," I said.

"Give them a shout and if they don't respond it's their fault." Alexander wanted me to shout because he sounded like a girl when he raised his voice.

"Brian! Joe!" There was no reply so I sucked in a huge breathe and tried again. "BRIAN! JOE!"

"Try again," Alexander suggested.

"BRIAN! JOE! We're going home! You hear? Game's over!"

There was a scream so far away it was little more than a crow caw.

"God," I muttered, "that was Brian."

Neither of us believed it was a joke. There was a second cry and this one was louder, coming from where we had walked between the large tombs. I saw Brian's terrified face. He was running towards us, directed by our shouts. His mouth was a wide oval. Arms flaying. Legs pumping across the distance.

He was being *chased.*

Another thought struck like a bullet, lodging in my throat.

Something's trying to kill Brian!

"It's after me!" he yelled.

Brian leapt over a headstone, stumbled on the slippery ground, and shuffled forward until he could stand again. He glanced backwards. He cried out at what he saw and sped on blindly, crashing through thorns and bushes, falling and staggering onwards. Running and falling. Running and falling. His face was bloody - but he seemed too frightened to care about pain. A guilty thought stirred in me that I was ashamed to admit: he's bringing it this way towards *me.* And then I saw something, a greyness behind Brian. It was chasing him at a blurring speed. I couldn't focus on what it was nor did I want to because it was death. I knew that. It was death, pure and simple.

Alexander must have seen death, too, because he started to moan and pull me back - but I shook him off.

"Run Brian!"

Brian ran. His legs and arms powered by adrenaline and fear. He briefly gained ground on the grey shape, but there must have been a hole because his left leg buckled like it was trapped in a steel trap.

Krrrk.

Brian's leg broke and he screamed a raw, unrestrained scream.

And then the grey shape was on him, lifting him as easily as a football. It was like a human dressed in rags, hunched by terrible disease ... but it was something else all together. A ghost?

Something metal flashed across Brian's throat and he stopped screaming and a blood fountain spattered the ground. *Noooooooo!* He was discarded like a sack of potatoes, lifeless head tilted impossibly to expose inside the bloodied neck. Then the grey thing had no further interest in Brian. It looked at me.

It didn't need to speak for me to understand it.

It wanted to kill me next.

I turned and realised Alexander had already fled. I decided he had the right idea. I sprinted in the direction of the gap, afraid the grey thing knew exactly where I was heading and could get there first. I ducked behind a tombstone and changed route, zigging and zagging towards the darkness the elms provided. I was hoping I could hide there.

But it was waiting for me. I saw it rising up out of the dark, its teeth glittering.

Turning, I pounded across soft ground towards the church and heard the thing chasing. I dared not look back. I just ran and ran.

My foot landed on nothing solid. Feeling the ground give way, I stumbled and fell down into a hidden hole. I felt sharp brambles and stones ripping my shirt and tearing my skin. The loss of footing reminded me of toboggan rides during the winter, accelerating down a hill on a wooden sleigh. But this ride was dark and out of control and I felt panic rising inside me as I tumbled down into the dark.

I landed on my knees in total darkness. I was in icy water about six-inches deep. The second finger on my left hand was numb and the others hurt like they had been dipped in fire. I could feel flesh sliding over bone.

Above, the thing growled. I sensed its desire - no, its *need* to kill me - but it was too large to get down the narrow hole. It was up there and I down here. It couldn't get me! I felt like laughing, but tears came instead. The thing growled again and scratched at the ground. It was trying to dig down to me. I felt around, touching cold earth on all sides apart from above. I was trapped. It was just a matter of time before it got to me.

It was going to catch me eventually.

I had no where to go.

And then I heard Alexander shouting at it, calling it away. The fool was trying to save me. I tried to call out and tell him to run. I wanted him to save himself and get to the village for help … but nothing sounded from my throat except a pathetic whisper.

The thing moved away after a minute - probably to go after Alexander. I waited and expected it to return, but it did not. I didn't want to move out of my safe haven, but the fear of being trapped there if the thing returned stirred me into action.

I attempted to climb back out of the hole.

Unfortunately, the sides were too slippery and soft. My efforts just crumbled the tunnel's walls. I stopped before I buried myself. By then I could see a little in the dark. I could see the water around me. It was moving. Flowing. That meant it had to be coming from somewhere and going somewhere else. Alexander had been right about underground streams. I felt around in the dark until I discovered an opening in the ground. The water was flowing out of it. The hole was wide enough for me to crawl into, but the top of the tunnel was barely above the water level. I lowered myself into the water and crawled upstream, praying I wasn't making a bad decision. The water was icy, unaffected by the niceties of summer sun. Forty Fahrenheit, if I were lucky. I wormed my way upstream, desperately eager to find somewhere to get out of the freezing water before I died. I could smell two things: rust and methane, smells trapped in the stagnant air. They grew stronger as I went. I had no doubt the smells were from decayed bodies: at least the dark offered one respite from seeing Old Carney's horrors. I crawled on bloodied knees and elbows for thirty minutes, going where I could, bumping into low ceilings and crawling across things I knew were bones, skulls, teeth.

Then I saw a dot of sunlight ahead. Fatigue and pessimism told me it was in my imagination, but I crawled towards it. The sunlight was real and sprinkled the underground stream with a taste of life, sickening mushrooms and lichens grew from the corpses embedded in the walls. I could see the whites and yellows of human bones, but the cold had taken away my concerns. I pulled myself out of the water, heavy and numb, glad to be alive.

*

Later, much later ... I woke. I felt cheated by sleep - it was the last thing I had wanted, but my body had said otherwise. I was balled up like an embryo. The sunlight was very weak now. It was probably ten and the sun would be on the horizon, or beyond, and this was twilight's final rays. Carefully, I climbed from the hole. There were dark grey and black shapes all around and I stayed low, hunched, not daring to stand in case I was seen. The sky was the darkest blue, stars arising now the sun had left. I looked and found the church's spire for some degree of orientation, which was nearby. I was on the far side of the church in the corner of Old Carney that had dissolved back in the 1920s. The church was between me and the gap.

Somewhere, it waited.

There was a sound. It travelled crisp and clear. It was the rustle of weeds shifting. I stayed as still as a rock, hoping whatever was hunting me didn't detect me.

A silhouette flitted from grave to grave.

It was no larger than a boy.

Was it Alexander?

It was certainly not the grey thing.

I crept after him and he sensed me.

He whispered: "Who is it?"

"Uh," I said. "It's Mike. Is that you, Alex?"

"No," he said. "It's me ... Joe."

Joe! The relief was enormous and at the same time I feared for Alexander. Had he been killed like Brian? Joe moved forward. He was bloody, bruised and muddy. He had gone through some nightmare and I saw guilt for Brian's death etched in his face. He had aged a thousand years. His eyes were hollow. "My fault, Mike. I caused this ..."

"Shush ... where is it?"

"I don't know. Jesus, it was eating ... eating Brian. Oh, God. I thought ... I thought I was the only one left."

"Alexander?"

Joe motioned with a finger across his neck. "I think it got him. I heard him screaming."

So Alexander was dead, too.

"What are we going to do now?" I asked.

"I think we should hide. There's a tree I've seen with a good hiding place."

Nearby one massive elm had tipped to an impossible angle, the trunk supported by a mass of exposed roots like raw tendons anchored in the black topsoil. There was just enough space between the wide roots for us to hide inside while being protected from attack. We hid there and spoke in whispers.

"Mike, I wanted to scare you and Alexander so I forced Brian to hide in one of the tombs - the idea was to come out and scare you ... *but there was something there*. Brian said so, but I was stubborn. Then I heard it breathe. Jesus, I wet myself there and then. I mean, the stench was just ... I could hear you and Alexander going past but there was nothing I could do because I was so scared ... and I was afraid to wake it because I knew ... I knew, Mike, that it would kill me. About a minute later Brian cracked and ran out of the tomb screaming. It woke and sort of rushed past me. I don't think it saw me, but I was knocked aside like a fly. I'm sure if it had seen me it would have killed me first - but it went straight for Brian. It was so fast I ... I must have been knocked out when I hit the wall because I woke with these bruises and could hear Brian screaming at you guys. I've been hiding ever since."

"We've got to get out of here," I said. "But we can't use the gap."

"I've tried the walls, Mike, but those stones are too tightly packed with moss and mortar. I couldn't get a grip. But the two of us ... you could stand on my back and get over. At least then you'd get out alive."

"I'm not leaving you," I said. "You stand on my back and you escape."

"No. It's my fault Brian and Alexander are dead. I don't want to kill you as well ..."

"You didn't kill anyone. It did."

"It's my fault," he sniffed.

"Rubbish. You didn't know."

"I should have known ..." He reminded me of a rabbit afraid of a farmer's shotgun: eyes wide, mouth slack. His eyes were dry from crying too much. He wasn't thinking rationally. I had to do something to get us out of this mess. "Look, we either hide in here and wait for someone to come looking for us, which might not happen for days, or we escape together as soon as possible. What do you want to do?"

"I don't want to stay here," Joe said. "Mike, I had an idea but ... you see that tree near the church?"

The tree in question was an oak. Its large branches were like tree trunks themselves.

"We could climb it. There's a branch overhanging the wall. We could climb it and drop down on the other side. What do you say?"

I nodded. But a fear lurked: I was a poor tree-climber. Joe knew this.

"It's a good time to learn," he said. Joe started to move, but I stopped him. I had sensed something. I was sure the thing was out there – waiting for us to make a move.

"Hold on," I said. "We need a distraction."

I looked for a stone to throw but there weren't any nearby. There was a bone, like the femur I'd seen earlier. In normal circumstances I would not have touched it, but I was no longer frightened of dead things. I had crawled through a tunnel filled with them. All I cared about was surviving the day. There was nothing to fear except the living, so I picked it up and hurled it as far as I could. The bone struck a headstone and whip-cracked. A shadow raced across the graveyard to investigate the noise. It had been just a few yards from the us.

We broke cover and headed for the oak, but we didn't move so fast we made noise or slipped down one of the pot-holes. The time spent going across the ground dragged and I thought we would never make it. It would see us and ...

Reaching the tree, Joe asked me to go first and he'd push me up. I tried it but - damn - it was like gripping treacle.

"You go first," I said. "You can pull me up from the branches."

Joe climbed the tree, moving slowly but surely up the trunk and I waited, keeping eyes peeled for the thing. He slung his legs over the first branch and leaned down, one hand gripping the tree and the other ready to grab me. I hugged the trunk and started an arduous climb, clutching the trunk so hard my skin and the bark were one pulped mass.

And then it saw me.

Joe saw it too. The time for discretion was over.

"Come on, Mike, climb!"

"I'm trying! I'm trying!"

But it was running and it knew the quickest route. It belonged in Old Carney and we did not.

Joe reached for me, but there was a clear foot between us. "Hurry!"

"I can't!" I was weeping with the effort.

"Come on, Mike, just a bit more!"

It pounded across the distance. I struggled higher and higher.

Joe's fingers touched my shirt collar and vainly tried to grip something.

But I slipped. It reached the tree and swung at Joe, but he was too high for the talons to cut him. He shouted at it from safety - cursing it and distracting, giving me time to sprint in the direction of the church and, beyond it, the gap. Behind me, the thing tired of trying to reach Joe and launched after me.

"Get help!" I cried.

Joe dropped from the branch onto the lane outside Old Carney. He was safe. "Don't die, Mike! I'll be back!" I heard him running, but it would take an hour for him to muster some adults and get back. He would return too late.

I hurdled two headstones in quick succession and scrambled up the bank to the church. The broken ruin offered many shadows and places to hide. If I could get there then -

It struck me in the back and shoulders - fast and heavy - I went down into grass and stones and my head swam. It was worse than a rugby tackle. It was above me. On top of me. I couldn't fight something so heavy and powerful. I knew I had to play dead or suffer like Brian.

Then I was vaguely aware of being dragged by my feet into the church, too stunned to fight. I kept my eyes closed. I was dropped and rolled. A quick slash and my throat would be spill my life on the holy ground. It sniffed me quizzically ... and moved away. I could hear its slow breathing - close - but I dared a look. There was a dim amber fire lit on what was left of the altar - now a sunken slab in the floor. Six or seven grey things sat around motionless, like statues. The grey things were all dead and had been for some time. Human corpses. Skeletons in dusty Sunday clothes twenty-years-old.

And the living thing was hunched over the fire eating with wet slopping noises. Yes, it had been human. The greyness was skin unused to sunlight. I smelled pork. It went to one of the skeletons and pushed bloody meat into its mouth and then worked the jaw bone mechanically, like it had done this a thousand times.

"Ma," it said, touching the corpse. "Eee."

But the corpse would not "eee" or "eat" or anything and it became distressed.

"Ma!" It howled. "Ma?"

Strangely, I felt a pang of pity. The skeleton was its mother and it didn't understand she was dead. At the same time I felt revulsion, for the thing was no longer human. Years of enforced cannibalism had turned he or she insane: it was eating one of my friends.

There was a moan from some distant corner. Weakly: "Don't eat me!"

Alexander!

He was alive!

He sounded weak … but he was not dead yet.

The thing silenced Alexander with a slap. It preferred fresh food and had spared Alexander's life for that reason. I had to do something. Looking in my immediate area I saw nothing to use as a weapon - nothing but bones.

While it was busy devouring Brian, I brought the largest bone I could to my side. I put both hands around the narrowest end, planning to swing it like a club when it got close.

"Urrrk," I said.

It approached to investigate. Foetid breath stung. Its head was so close to mine ... I swung.

The bone hit its forehead - whack - and it roared, more

surprised than hurt. I pushed. It lost its balance and fell in the fire. The flames licked it greedily, sparks flying. The dry clothing ignited and it panicked, running from the church smoking and in pain. It didn't have the sense to roll on the ground and was probably going to douse itself in water, which would take time.

Adrenaline pumped inside me suppressing pain and fatigue. I rushed to Alexander. He was in bad shape, blood on his lips. Eyes unfocused. "Mike?"

"Get up," I said, tugging his arms. He obeyed. "Can you walk?"

He nodded. I guided him and we headed towards the gap. Alexander was a dead weight, but I wasn't going to abandon him. He could be annoying and snobby, but he was my friend. I had to save him. We had to get out of the graveyard.

Somewhere the cannibal screeched. Then it was silent. I feared it had found water, putting the fire out, which meant it would now be angry and looking for us.

I pulled Alexander onwards.

The gap loomed - so close and yet so far.

I willed us forward.

It was too late.

I could hear the cannibal coming.

*

With one last effort, I half-dragged, half-carried Alexander towards the gap. The cannibal was crossing the bone yard with leaps and bounds, leaping from headstone to headstone, snarling and screeching. Reaching the gap, I pushed and lifted Alexander over the low wall. Looking back, I saw the cannibal only twenty feet away. I grabbed the wall with both hands and jump-kicked to propel myself upwards and over. I tumbled through the gap, strength going, consciousness going. I was too tired to run when it inevitably attacked. Alexander and I were a tangle of arms and legs, lying on the trail.

The thing slammed into the wall. Its hands gripped the stones. I kicked them. It growled, retracted the hands. Its dirt grey face bared yellow teeth. It only had to climb over the wall to kill us.

But it stopped.

There was an expression in its eyes:

Fear.

And I understood.

It was afraid of our side of the gap.

Our world was as frightening to it as Old Carney was to us.

It lingered at the wall - shaking with indecision. It wanted us dead - but it was terrified of the consequences of leaving its home.

"Leave us alone!" I yelled.

It hissed ... and was gone.

I laughed hysterically and forced myself to stand. Alexander swayed drunkenly, so exhausted. I aided him up the hill. I kept looking back in case it changed its mind. But it did not. It stayed in the bone yard.

I heard a car's engine and wept with joy. Bright headlights blinded me. Joe had reached the village and obtained help. Knowing this - knowing we were going to be all right now - my legs collapsed and I lost consciousness.

*

Today Old Carney is still there, though the walls have been repaired with concrete and the gap blocked and signs placed to warn the public. It's a little part of England that will always be there. Sure, the weeds and the thorns might get longer and the wall might lose a few stones, but it will never change. Old Carney is a place that has a bad aura you can never shrug off.

I'm old now, but I will never forget that hot summer of 1939. I'll always remember Joe, Alexander and Brian.

Brian was like a brother to me. He was not smart or special, but he was part of the Fearless Four and his death was something that irrevocably changed my life. I became a doctor because I wanted to save lives after seeing Brian die.

Joe's guilt over Brian's death changed him, too. He became a vicar; the irony of that makes me smile.

Alexander used the experience in his novels and lives in the hallowed halls of Oxford, lecturing students on a subject with a multi-barrelled title.

These days I live a long, long way away from Old Carney, but it's always there in my memory, late at night, just before I go to sleep.

After we escaped the bone yard, the authorities tried to hunt down the cannibal, but they never found it. They did discover hundreds of half-eaten bodies in the ruins. They were reburied in a different cemetery miles from Old Carney. Then everyone tried to forget about the old bone yard.

Most local people think the thing starved underground many years ago. But some local people still say they hear weird noises coming from Old Carney. Like the sounds of a wild creature.

I believe them.

Nematode

The wound, like the hungry mouth of a lamprey, opened.

Kelly looked down where his navel had been only moments before. He pulled up his slick T-shirt and let out a cry of alarm as the thing wriggled its purple tail inside his abdomen, bloating him as if six months pregnant. *Oh, God, this can't be happening.* But it was happening, and the thing made wet sucking sounds as it forced its way between his organs, eager to be inside the warmth of his body. Once it had vanished, his blood started flowing like water out of a garden hose.

Kelly clutched his stomach and vainly tried blocking the blood. But it just spurted between his fingers, splattering his legs and feet, so much that he knew whatever had entered him - what was it, a worm? - was killing him, even as he staggered out of the barn and towards his farmhouse - which seemed so far away. He had to reach the phone. Call a doctor. Call a vet. He fought the pain, somehow remaining conscious, holding his stomach together as he waddled up the lane. He entered the dark farmhouse. Reaching the phone, he hammered nine-nine-nine. Come on, come on, answer, someone help me. *Police? Fire? Ambulance? George Clooney! Anyone!*

A thick, guttural slurping sound emanated from his chest, like a massive belch. It was feeding, he could feel its teeth. Then the pain passed a threshold and Kelly collapsed, unfortunately pulling out the phone line. *I'm going to die.*

Kelly was wrong. It was far worse than that.

*

Killing was the worst job in the world. Seeing it on a regular basis had converted Kelly into a devout vegetarian, but killing was the family business. He'd learnt the slaughter trade as his final promise to his dying father, Douglas Kelly. Kelly had become CEO of Bovine Products Enterprises, a semi-large company employing 230 people that killed cattle by the thousand in a complex of corrugated iron slaughterhouses. Since the BSE scare, business had been booming. The slaughterhouse killed cattle, putting a bolt into their brains on a deadly production line of a thousand a day, then sent the reluctant corpses to an incinerator plant outside of Birmingham.

He'd hated it. Kelly had found it hard to remain detached from the act of slaughter whenever a pair of big, dopey eyes stared at him. Cattle were so stupid, he felt sorry for them. He could barely watch his people drive a bolt through their brains and watch their legs give out under them. It had been hard enough for him to justify the work when the cattle was being put to a purpose - for food - but the crisis over BSE convinced him to renege on his promise. It was just killing for killing's sake. A waste. Most of the poor animals assigned for incineration were BSE free. And the ones with BSE probably circumvented the slaughter and ended up on Mr and Mrs Jones' plate anyway. So he'd quit and sold the slaughterhouse for half its real value, buying a farm in Surrey.

He'd decided to breed cows for milk.

That had been his plan, six months ago.

Funny how things had changed.

*

Kelly's cheek was stuck to the stained carpet. A strange feeling scratched at his consciousness. It was an absence of something.

Pain. Yes. There was no pain. Was that a good thing? Yes. He hoped. What an awful dream he'd had. It had seemed so ... real. Nauseous, he tentatively felt his stomach. There was a hole. He could feel it. Too big for his navel. The dream ...

When he remembered how he'd got in the situation, Kelly groaned. He rolled over and sat up, peering down. The wound had stopped gushing, brown coagulated blood now circled it. The floor was another story. About nine pints of vintage Kelly '96 had pooled around him while he'd been unconscious.

But he was still alive.

Impossible.

Unless ... unless the thing was keeping him alive.

He stood and hurried to the bathroom.

He desperately needed to go.

*

One night, the cows were restless. He could hear them all the way from the farmhouse. They sounded like screaming children. Kelly opened the gate and swept his torch over the herd. They shied away from the light.

"What's wrong?"

He'd never seen them act this way. It was as if they were scared - no, terrified. He moved among them, shining the beam on their flanks. Maybe they had a skin infection causing them distress. No. Nothing. They looked fine. But his presence just caused them more agitation. They were frightened.

The torch caught something red in its beam - a dead cow. The cow was lying separate from the rest of the herd and the other cows wouldn't go near it. Kelly felt a sick feeling in the pit of his stomach.

As he got closer he saw its abdomen had been horribly mutilated. Yet the same cow had been alive just hours earlier. During the night, someone or something must have sliced her open and removed the internal organs. Why? He had no idea. The idea repelled him. Cattle slaughtering had been happening in the US for years ... where it was blamed on anything from UFOs to the CIA. But he'd not heard about it happening in Britain. Unless the government was covering it up.

It was obvious by the extent of the damage and the precision of the injuries that no wild animal had caused the mutilation. The vet would need to examine it. And the police. Maybe there was a psychotic in the local village he didn't know about, one who got a kick out of hurting animals. Maybe the perpetrator was watching him, right now.

*

Kelly showered the blood off, sluicing it down the drain. Then he looked at himself in the mirror. Apart from the weird hole instead of his navel, he looked normal. The swelling had gone down. He was very anaemic, yes, but otherwise normal. It was little comfort, considering what the thing had done to his cows. How could something that big fit inside him? Would it just burst out, like that creature in the Alien films?

He returned to the living room and went to replug the phone.

Pain rippled up his chest, raw and excruciating pain. The pain managed to get worse the closer he got to the phone. He stopped, and the pain stopped. He stepped forward - and buckled in agony.

Kelly realised it didn't want him to call for help. The pain was a warning.

"I'm not listening to you," he muttered, dragging himself across the room.

*

"I've never seen anything like this," George McMurry said. The vet stood next to the steel table, rubber-gloved hands deep in the cow's abdominal cavity. "There's been a 95 percent loss of blood. If I believed in the supernatural, I'd say it's as if someone drained the blood like a vampire. As a rational man, I'd say this was ... something else."

Kelly said: "What about the organs?"

"Gone," McMurry said. "There's surgical precision to it, Ian. You have any enemies?"

"None I know about."

"Then you've got a problem."

"Yes," he admitted. "I'll call the police."

*

I should have called the police when I had the chance, Kelly thought, as he lay on the ground, barely a metre away from the phone. *But no, I'd decided to handle the problem myself. Then that thing had come out of the latest dead cow, headed straight for me. Like it was upgrading species.* He rolled away from the phone and the pain vanished. In the brief glimpse of it before it entered him, he'd seen it was unsegmented, like a nematode. Nematodes were pointed at both ends, with a mouth and anus, unlike flatworms which just had mouths. Its skin had been smooth and thick, dappled white and pink, almost transparent. He knew of two species of nematode that were parasites of humans, roundworms and pinworms, but it had been too big and too fast to be their big brother. George McMurry had been right - it was Something Else.

The way it had stopped him reaching the phone meant it was intelligent.

Tomorrow morning Kelly's wife would be back from London. He could not let the nematode live long enough to make her its host. He would rather die. He walked into the kitchen, switching on the phosphorus strip lights. The lights flickered on unsteadily then filled the kitchen with painful brightness. The pain did not belong to him, he sensed. The nematode didn't like light. It didn't like his intentions, either, sending white hot agony up and down his body in waves. The nematode must have tapped into his spinal column, playing his nerves like a harp's strings. He could feel it renting and tearing, plucking pain in every way it could. Black spots danced before his eyes. Oxygen starvation. He grunted and grit his teeth. "You'll ... have to ... try harder, buddy."

He walked past the oven to the counter top by the windows. There were knives in the drawers, and hanging up in racks. A spot of self-surgery sounded the best option. It could not add to his pain. Half-blind, he grabbed a ten inch carving knife and aimed it at his stomach. His skin rippled in concentric patterns, centred on his navel. The creature was nervous. With all the force he could muster, he stabbed himself.

The blade sunk in up to the handle. There wasn't even any resistance. Not a splash of blood came out. He moved the knife upwards, to where his breastbone stopped it. Nothing. His chest looked as if he'd been given a zip. He put the knife between his teeth and used his hands to grip the sides of the opening. His fingers sunk into his chest. Then he pulled back the flaps, an living autopsy, delicious agony causing him to weep. Behind the flaps of skin there was a hole. The kitchen lights shone into the red and purple cave.

The nematode was curled into a spiral adhered to the wall of the hole. His knife attack had gone through the middle, striking nothing. The nematode's black, shiny eyes looked up at him, as if to say: "You missed me."

A giddy insanity rocked Kelly. The nematode started to unwind, pushing upwards and downwards with unimaginable force. Kelly felt as it he was going to split in two. He took the knife out of his mouth and jabbed at the undulating flesh. A black and red ichor jetted out.

Now it was pushing up into his throat, determined to make its host's brain dead before he could strike the killing blow. Kelly stabbed himself in the neck, again and again. As long as the nematode was keeping him alive, he had the strength, the will-power to fight. He was relentless, cutting and hacking until the kitchen tiles were awash with white chunks, like the off-cuts in a fish restaurant. The pressure on his neck stopped. Falling to his knees, Kelly worked the knife inside his ribcage, just to be sure. Something slithered over his hand. He pulled his hand out and stared at in in horror. The headless nematode was wrapped around it. Released from his body, it was no longer supporting his life functions. He fell backwards, slamming against the oven door, head lolling against his punctured throat. Through the crimson haze, he could see a new head growing out of the nematode's bloody mass, feeding on the flesh of his arm. Razor teeth buried into his wrist. The thing was one of those worms that could survive even when cut in two.

Sheer anger kept Kelly going. He slammed his hand against the floor, stunning it and dropping his knife. Twisting around, he put his hand in the oven. Then he picked up the dropped knife and hacked off the hand, his wrist bone snapping easily thanks to the nematode's previous attack on it. Then he shut the door, leaving his hand and the worm inside. He fell against the oven door, exhausted.

The nematode slammed against the wire-glass, but Kelly's body weight prevented its escape. Still, he could not leave it alive. It was one species that deserved extinction. Reaching up with his one good hand, Kelly turned the oven on full, 220C. *It's really cooking tonight. Delia Smith, eat your heart out. In fact, eat your stomach out.* When Kelly slumped, a numbness taking over, he could hear the nematode screaming.

Open Wounds

All along the border dead bodies steamed in the desert heat, their final death throes frozen for the pale UN troops to see and be sickened by. Babies, children, teenagers, parents and grandparents drew a bloody line in the sand, a red line on the map. I could see where they had been cut down by AK47 fire or chopped by machetes or burned by flame throwers. Naively, when I saw a little girl move her arm I thought she had survived - I put down my rifle and rushed over to the mound of corpses. But once I'd stepped over the slick human parts and pulled her out of the mother's lifeless arms I realised how I'd been fooled. The maggots swimming in her open chest wound had given her illusion of life, eating away at her insides until her arm had fallen off.

Of course, I should have known not to expect miracles. Sanguro's soldiers had been too thorough and enthusiastic to leave anyone alive. He'd herded them out of the UN camps and straight to border, where his devoted men had gone to work, slaughtering innocent villagers, killing anyone who could oppose his junta. From his point of view the operation had been a complete success. Bodies were heaped upon bodies, limbs tangled into knots. A sprawl of butchered human meat a hundred miles long. I could not even imagine the number of people that would total. The excrement stench was something I'd never forget, a stain on my soul.

Sergeant Kelly swore and called me across.

"We just got word that all the refugee camps from here to Jagadisa have been razed to the ground." He spat into the sand. "Maybe half a million victims. Maybe more. Nobody's counted them.""Hell," I said.

"Close as," he said. He took a moment to compose himself. "Our orders are to check out Camp 5 - sixty klicks west of here. The Red Cross station there hasn't called in for twelve hours. We're worried." He raised an eyebrow, telling me he suspected the worst. "Anyway, you and me will scout ahead using the Land Rover. There shouldn't be trouble from Sanguro's men if we go along the riverbed marked here on the map. It's dry this time of year and it's unlikely he's mined it yet. Still, it's a dangerous mission, so if you don't want to go I'll get someone -"

"I volunteer," I said. Anything was better than staying here. And if I could save even one person from suffering at the hands of Sanguro I was up for it. I was a nineteen year old with delusions of heroism. I'd grown up watching action movies where the good guys won, and I wanted the real world to be the same. With adrenaline pumping through my bloodstream I followed Kelly to the Land Rover.

"You drive," he said, "you need the practice."

The Land Rover powered down the muddy riverbed, sloshing up the red mud so common to the region that we had nicknamed it Sanguro's blood. With the main roads mined and half the country rocky and impassable, the riverbed was the fastest way to reach our destination short of risking a helicopter against Sanguro's SAM sites. As I drove 60 mph - Sergeant Kelly studying the map in the passenger seat - I prayed the Red Cross had not fallen, that the lack of communications was explainable - a radio breakdown, a flat battery, anything. The Red Cross were doing an excellent job, but they had no defences against a man like Sanguro.

Once every generation a man is born so evil he hurts the whole world. Sanguro was that man, a man driven by an uncontrollable power lust. In the fifteen years of his reign over Kansassa, he'd invaded his two neighbouring countries, imprisoned or killed all who opposed him in his own, and defied the UN countless times. He existed on his own terms, an invisible presence I could feel in the dusty air. He had not appeared in public for several years, rumours claimed he'd been assassinated and his minions now ruled, but while driving through Kansassa's bloody landscape I knew he was alive. Killing the innocent was his trademark. If only his country had oil then something might have been done before this latest tragedy, but Kansassa was the country the world had forgotten, a Central African nowhere, brushed under the carpet of political affairs. Something had to be done about Sanguro, I knew. But in order to deal with Sanguro, you had stoop to his level. Unfortunately, Sanguro wallowed in the ninth circle of hell, smiling up at you. Waiting.

The riverbed forked ahead.

"Left," Kelly said.

"Sir, may I ask you something?"

"Of course. What?"

"If you had Sanguro in a locked room with you, what would you do?"

"Kill him." His mouth was a tight line. "Slowly. Nothing could make him suffer like those people suffered, but I'd give a good try."

"Uh-oh, Sarge," I said. "Something's ahead."

I slowed the Land Rover. Kelly readied his rifle and leant out of the window. The riverbanks were dotted with rotting corpses, skeletons and skull fragments. I felt bones crunch under the tyres, snapping and clicking. These bodies had to have been dumped when the river was full. Red mud caked them. They reminded me of

Chinese chicken. I almost laughed at the absurdity. The corpses went on and on. I was appalled to think the people downstream had swallowed the polluted water, believing it to be clean.

We drove on in silence.

We were soon used to the graveyard, saturated by the horrors. I was tired and restless and demoralised, eager to leave the riverbank. Kelly, despite being a Falkland's veteran, was as pale as a raw recruit. I was desperate to have the day end, increasing my speed over the corpse path. The wheels ejected a trail of body parts in our wake. I knew what we'd find in the camp, but I needed to be there *now.* Not in this pit. Maybe I should have been looking more carefully, I don't know. I don't think it would have made much difference. Because just one mile from the camp they ambushed us.

Damn, they were fast.

Something struck the tyres. The Land Rover veered out of my control as if the steering wheel was an afterthought. The vehicle struck the bank. The centre of gravity tilted over and over. I slammed into Kelly and saw the hole in his temple *Where had that come from?* and his brains leaking out *Oh, God, he has a family* and thought *this can't be happening* but it was happening and I was upside down and the roof was skidding along the ground and I'd never heard a single shot ...

I could smell petrol. Opening my eyes I grunted as raw pain chewed my face where glass had imbedded. Bruises throbbed everywhere. My mind felt sluggish. Where was I? Seeing the dead sergeant brought it back. I was still in the Land Rover. My face was pressed against the shattered but intact windscreen. I could see several holes typical of .22 bullets in the glass. They must have hit Kelly. I tried to move, but couldn't. The seat belt held me in place. I fumbled it loose and dropped onto the roof. Voices drifted in an alien tongue. Sanguro's men! My gun -

A khaki uniform yanked me from the vehicle. The soldier said something. I slurred my name and number. He pushed me into the mud. Hands stripped off my uniform. So they're going to rape me before they kill me, I thought dully.

For once in my life I was grateful for being wrong.

They just took my clothes and left me drinking mud.

Twisting my neck, I could see a couple of soldier's dressing a corpse while others inspected the upturned Land Rover. Their officer barked orders, they hurried up. Then he walked over to me and spoke in English.

"I am so sorry about the other one," he said. "That was a mistake. General Sanguro likes his meat fresh." He laughed and kicked my ribs. Two soldiers younger than myself approached. They carried me to a truck parked a hundred metres from the river and tossed me in the back like a sack of rice. They closed the doors. An engine started. A far away explosion told me that I didn't exist any more.

*

So I was going to meet Sanguro, but it was going to be on his terms. Alone in the dark truck, a fear gripped me worse than any I'd known. It was a solid, bowel-loosening fear. I had to escape. I hammered my fists against the steel doors until they were bloody, then crawled up in the darkness, too tired to move.

Perhaps worse than death was humiliation in the eyes of your enemy. Being naked and vulnerable made it seem more real. I'd heard war stories about Sanguro, stories I'd dismissed as the impossible exaggerations. Sanguro had once forced a rival warlord to eat the flesh of his own children, while they *lived.* In a homage to Vlad the Impaler he had spiked the heads of a hundred villagers on the walls of his palace - for no reason at all. What would he do with a British Army soldier, a despised UN enforcer?

I envied Sergeant Kelly. At least he had not suffered.

The doors opened and bright painful sunlight hit me.

The truck was parked on a verdant lawn in front of Sanguro's palace. The palace was a shadowy nightmare in front of the descending sun. Black towers and minarets spiked the purple sky. Hell's Palace.

Soldiers wearing black kerchiefs covering everything but their eyes yelled at me to get out. When I didn't respond they dragged me out kicking and punching. Suddenly handcuffed, I was led towards the vast entrance archway. It was like a viper's mouth, a red tongue of carpet leading up the steps to a profound darkness. I knew Sanguro waited for me.

I decided then that if Sanguro wanted me to beg for my life I would not. I would not give him the satisfaction. Never.

Never is a long time, a little boy's voice said. It was the voice that was scared of the dark and the thing under the bed and the bogeyman.

Sanguro was the real bogeyman.

As the darkness swallowed me whole, I screamed.

Naked and handcuffed, I was thrown into a vast chamber decorated entirely in red silks. A king sized bed was in an alcove, over which six lion heads glared. A gold world globe rested at the bed's edge, spinning on its axis. More stuffed animals were in niches

- tigers, pumas and even an entire rhinoceros. Evidently, Sanguro's bloodlust did not discriminate between species. I wondered where he was, since he had to have spun the globe.

Several layers of silk curtain billowed in front of the windows. I thought I glimpsed a figure on the balcony beyond - an awesome silhouette that could only be one man - but he was gone in an instant, leaving me to concentrate on my immediate predicament.

A soldier attached a heavy steel chain to the handcuffs, and left me alone. The chain was fastened to the onyx floor with just enough length to allow me to stand. I did so. I pulled at the chain. It would not break loose. The floor had been designed for this purpose.

Looking around, I noticed I was in the centre of a circle below the level of the normal floor by about six inches. There were small holes under my feet, like a pepper shaker. I could think of no purpose unless ... unless the holes were there to drain away *blood* and the ridge was to stop it *spreading*.

The curtains parted like a ghostly veil, hidden strings pulling them back into the walls. He was standing in the crimson light of dusk, facing the mountains. His black uniform filled my vision. He turned around and looked at me. Though his hair was greying, the streaks only served to darken his features. His brown eyes sparkled with intelligence, the skin around them wrinkling as he grinned.

"You are mine," he said. His teeth shone behind his dark beard.

"Go kill yourself," I said.

"You are a spirited man, English. I like that. You may last longer than the last one to be in your position."

Sanguro walked towards me, but stopped tantalisingly out of my reach. He could see the fury in my eyes. I would have given my life right then to squeeze the life from Sanguro, to hear his neck snap as my thumbs dug into the soft skin above his breast bone. It wasn't meant to be. Sucking in a deep breath, I saw a whip at his side. He toyed with the whip, cracking the air between us. He was Thor, God of Thunder, and I was a mere mortal.

"I will take the spirit out of you," he promised.

When he swung the whip at my chest the movement exposed the vermilion shirt beneath his jacket, showing as a gash at his throat. Like a cut throat, I thought. Then the whip struck, opening a line from breast to sternum. A warm wetness dribbled down my stomach. His second strike wrapped around my legs and pulled, landing me on my back. Laughing, he cracked the whip between my legs. Pain flared supernova bright. And he continued. A God never tired.

*

Every morning a guard sluiced my blood down the holes using an icy hose. Some would leave me curled up, shivering, but others turned the hose on me. The cold water was like acid against the red raw wounds. I was sure they put salt in to add to the agony. They kept me alive with raw meat. When I stopped eating it, hoping to die, they would just force the meat down my throat, so I had to eat it. I had little doubt the meat was human. They would not waste food on a non-human like me. Vaguely, I held on to some hope of rescue, but after six weeks of whipping and mental torture I knew this would not happen. Nobody knew I was alive. Unless they did an autopsy on the bodies found in the Land Rover - and it was unlikely given the larger atrocities - they'd never find out. And if they did - what could they do? Nothing. No, the only way the suffering could end was if I died or I escaped.

So I ate what was given, and took Sanguro's whipping without complaint, pretending to feel more pain than I did. Over time Sanguro grew bored with his human pet, the whipping's becoming less frequent. He was like a child with an old toy. He ignored me, talked with his men as if I wasn't in the room. He was often called away to the war zone - leaving me to recover for weeks at a time. I grew stronger. The steel chain was excellent for weight lifting, building my muscles, turning the raw protein from the meat into muscle. I sharpened my teeth on the bones. I turned pain into pleasure, revelling in the burning agony of my wounds. Whipping merely fired the adrenaline in my body, made me stronger. Sanguro was so blind to my presence that he did not notice the scrawny prisoner changing into a raging beast. Only I could feel and see the difference. He had stripped away my humanity, and revealed the creature under the skin. Below the purple and black scars was a killing machine, waiting for its moment.

Sanguro was Thor.

But I was Odin.

One night Sanguro left the balcony, sighing as he unhooked his whip for the night's entertainment. The whip opened a cut on my cheek, a blood splatter arcing away with the whip. A delicious pain squirmed inside me. He flicked it again. The tip of a whip could hit at several hundred miles an hour, but my eyes followed the movement as if it was in slow motion. The tip flayed my wrist. Gripping it hard, I yanked it from his hands. He was so surprised he gaped. I did not give him time to move - switching the whip handle to my handcuffed hands and copying his technique in order to bind his legs. On one knee, I pulled him off his feet and dragged him across the slick floor. He kicked at my face but his kicks were nothing. I had him, and he knew it. His eyes widened in terror. Discarding the whip, I pressed my hands over his throat, pinning him to the ground. He thought I was going to strangle him.

I was glad to disappoint.

My razor teeth burrowed into his uniform and shirt, plunging into his chest, renting a mouthful of bloody flesh and muscle, tearing it as my head whipped backwards. He screamed. I knew there would be no answer - the guards were too used to hearing screams. I swallowed the meat while Sanguro bucked under me, burying my face in the gore. His blood pulsed wonderfully. Surfacing, I stared at his rictus face, pink saliva dripping from my mouth. Sanguro could not believe what was happening to him. Leaving his chest wound for the moment, I chewed at his face - the cartilage in his nose crunched between by incisors. Moving on, I took off an ear, spitting it in his mouth. That really made him panic. He almost choked on it. A low, pitiful moan came from him.

"Kill me," he said.

"Not yet," I replied, taking my teeth to his right eye.

At dawn he was dead.

I felt nothing. No pleasure. No disgust. Nothing.

I found the key to my handcuffs in his ragged clothing. Freeing myself, I strode out to the balcony, leaving a trail of wet footprints. Sanguro's blood glistened in the cold sunlight, like war paint. In this part of Africa some believed the eating of your enemy's flesh makes you stronger. I could feel it. The red plains and the mountains were mine now. I was triumphant. There was no turning back to a normal life, not for me. I wasn't human; I was something else, the darkness evil men feared. I knew those who chose oppression would fear me, for I was the beast within them, forever hunting them as they hunted the innocent. When Sanguro was consigned to a historical footnote, I would be a legend. Parents would tell their children about me, as a warning to treat others as they would like to be treated. Not even death could kill me. I was already dead.

I jumped over the balcony and landed cat-like on the lawn, running to my homeland. Free.

Doctors will tell you the dead have no expression. It's not true. *I* am grinning.

Can't you see my teeth?

The Challenge

Lauren did not remember how she had entered the tower, but she knew there had been a life before, if only she could reach those tantalisingly enigmatic memories of yesterday. She found herself climbing smooth stone steps behind a man wearing similar grey, shapeless sackcloth pyjamas, like a prison uniform. He was one of many walking above her. Lauren was wearing nothing on her feet, just like him. He would not talk to her. Neither would the man on the step just behind her, or the people behind him. He pushed her if she so much as slowed down for a second. There was a person on every step, and only enough room for one person on a step at a time, no way to squeeze past the person above or below without crushing both. They were all walking at the same brisk, tireless pace, like zombies. She wanted to stop walking up the spiral stairway, but some instinct told her that was the worst thing she could do. The stairway spiralled up and up, with stone walls on either side. Dark green moss and lichen grew between the cracks. There seemed to be no end in sight.

"Excuse me? Where are we going?"

No answer.

She kept walking. And walking.

*

Eventually, she reached the top.

Her sudden relief turned to immediate despair.

The stairway circled the top and seemed to continue back down to the bottom of the tower. Peering over the rail down into the darkness, she could see the tiers and tiers of the outer wall of the stairway until the darkness claimed the last morsel of light. The 'up' stairway and the 'down' stairway were entwined like two ropes, reminding her of a DNA double-helix, the backbone of life. She had no doubt then that the two stairways joined up at the tower's base. Descending took the strain off her legs for the hours it lasted, but then she reached the bottom and saw there was no exit, no door leading out. She was pushed along to the stairway she had already gone up once. The people were going nowhere. So why were they doing it? Was she the only one who noticed the completely pointlessness? Now she really, really wanted to stop, but if she did the people behind her would step on her. She knew they would not stop - they could not because the people ahead would not. But she was tired, her calves were hurting, her hamstrings like taut wires, her leg muscles burning. This was insane, she knew. What was the purpose of all of this walking?

"Hey," she called to the man in front, "talk to me! Where are we going?"

He was puffing and gasping. "Can't. Talk. Must. Walk."

"Why? For God's sake, why?"

He did not answer.

"WHY ARE WE DOING THIS?"

He ignored her. Angry, she punched him not too hard. He did not turn around, as she had hoped, but he did speak one word per step. "We. Have. To. Because."

"Because what?"

He shrugged. His lank hair shone with sweat. She grabbed his shoulder. He pulled away, but she glimpsed his pale face and what she saw scared her. He was terrified. He wasn't going to stop for anyone. He would keep walking until his heart exploded.

She continued ascending and descending, following the walkers on their seemingly endless journey inside the tower. After several hours she could no longer think straight. Sweat was in her eyes more or less constantly. Her lungs felt like bags of acid dissolving inside her, eroding what was left of her body and spirit. Her feet ached, ached like bloodied stumps. If she didn't look down regularly she would have sworn they'd been worn away to the bone. Walking. Walking. Walking. The stress on her joints was unbelievable. It felt as though someone had hit her knees with a hammer. When Lauren stretched her neck to look up at the people, she saw one or two stumble and fall out of step, quickly struggling to get back into the rhythm. There was a woman six steps ahead who kept slacking. She kept tripping. Each time, the woman recovered, but only just. Her sobbing echoed; little sad gasps.

Lauren realised there was sobbing up and down the line, like background noise which had been there all of the time but she had not noticed. The sound filled the gaps between the shuffle-shuffle of feet on cold, hard rock.

Closing her eyes, she walked on. As time blurred and her fatigue and pain increased ten-fold, she focused on her thoughts. She could see the tower in her mind's eye as being the only man-made object on a rocky island in the middle of a grey sea. The tower had no windows and no doors. No way in or out. It looked incredibly ancient, but it also looked timeless. She didn't know if she had seen the tower from the outside, or if it was merely her imagination. She liked to think it was her imagination; if it was not then that meant there was no way out, but then how did these thousands of people get inside? Had someone blocked up the exit with mortar and stone?

Was this some kind of tomb? And why were they here? Had they volunteered? Had someone kidnapped them?

A scream.

Not her, Lauren realised with relief.

Her eyes snapped open.

The woman who had been sobbing had fallen. She appeared unconscious. The next man stepped on her, walked over her. And so did the next. The woman had broken their rhythm, but did not slow them. They just kept on going.

"Wait!" Lauren cried. "She's hurt! Stop! Stop damn you!"

But no one was listening.

When Lauren reached the woman she tried to lift her, but she was too heavy, and the man behind didn't give her time. The woman disappeared under his feet. Lauren yelled out in frustration, but the man barely registered her presence. She was forced to continue. The next time she reached that point in the stairway the woman was dead. She had been crushed under thousands of feet. Her bones were broken, flesh squashed. After a few more cycles there wasn't much left on the steps. Most of the woman was on the soles of their feet.

So that was why nobody stopped, Lauren thought grimly. A mad laugh spewed from her lips. She wondered how far she had walked. Miles and miles. There were a thousand steps on the stairway, she had counted. She regained a little energy every time she was going down, but the upward spiral was becoming harder and harder. It was as if the steps were stretching, though she knew it was in her mind. The steps were not becoming taller, she was becoming *weaker*. Raising her feet just a little distance was like having rocks tied to her feet. She'd lost track of the hours spent there. It felt like at least a day. She wanted to go home, wherever that was. She'd had enough.

Soon there were more bones on the stairway as people fell and died. Was it ten or eleven bodies now? Difficult to tell. The walking went on regardless. The death smell caused her to retch as others had retched before her.

Up. Down. Up. Down. No space to stop. Slipping on looping entrails. Crack. Crunch. She was crying. She was dying. Slowly. So thirsty she was tempted to drink from the bodies underfoot like a vampire. So tired she did not stop to urinate, just like nobody else did. Here there was no place for prudery, for hygiene. Only the walking.

As she walked she clawed at the stone walls, hoping to find a loose slab, a chink of light from outside. There were marks already there by other fingers. She wasn't the first to think of escape, the first to fail.

Ten bodies doubled to twenty, then forty, then eighty ... Since there just over two thousand people in the tower she wondered how long it would take for all of them to fall dead or dying. A day? Two?

Why didn't they sit down? Sit down and stop the madness.

Because they knew something she did not, that was why.

What?

She wished she could remember.

They knew it, but they were not telling.

They were keeping a secret.

She thought about the reason. And only one possible motive made any sense. Someone was testing them, and that someone would only be let out the very last person standing. It was an endurance test. A sick game. They (the owners of the tower?) were removing the weakest people. Now, thinking that hypothesis, she had a deep feeling that she had been told that earlier, outside the tower, in the vague time before. It gave her some hope - she just had to keep going until she was the last person standing. Since she had arrived *after* the others, she believed, then they would be more exhausted than she would. Heh-heh-heh. Ugly laughter, ugly thoughts. Desperation was making her wish these other people would fail.

She could imagine herself tripping the man in front.

No.

That would be ... murder

Was she that desperate?

There were more spaces in the line now. Her feet were cut and bleeding from standing on sharp bones, her blood mingling with that of the dead. The man she had talked to had fallen sometime earlier, but she could not be sure when. He was gone. Dead. There was more space for her to walk in, a full five steps. She felt guilty for being glad for the extra room.

And on it went. After a while the walking became automatic, the pain irrelevant. Her heartbeat matched the pace of her walking and the thudding of her skull.

When she was going down the stairway, she did it on her hands and knees; it was easier. It was like sliding down a chute in places, where the human carpet was slick and wet. But there was hell to pay when she started on the climb again: her legs wobbled and often buckled.

But she kept going.

Walkers collapsed more frequently, and the way was blocked by bodies in places she had to crawl over, her hands and feet sinking into pounded flesh. Face to face with the lifeless.

A memory surfaced:

The door opens when the last one walks alone.

Someone had said that. She was certain. She could place no face with the voice, but she knew the person had not been lying. There was a door, but it was locked and hidden until there was only one survivor. It was at the top of the tower, she knew. She gritted her teeth with cold determination. She would survive. The tower would not beat her. It was matter of will-power. She could go on forever, if necessary. She would not stop. She would not die. Nothing could beat her. Nothing.

Her hunger burned inside her, bitter acid eating away at her stomach lining like a cancer. Desperately, she stuffed a handful of moss into her mouth and chewed it. It was bitter and hard to swallow, but she managed it. The pain receded, slightly. It was nothing compared with that of her legs and back. The moss gave her some energy to carry on, so she peeled off more strips of it, eating it as she walked. Its limited nutrients helped a little. She prayed no one else had thought of eating it. That would be unfair. It was her idea. Nobody else's. Hers.

Nobody could walk this long, this hard, she knew. How much time had passed? A month? Easily. She knew it for a fact, not as a crazy reaction to her fatigue, her pain. She just had to count the bodies beneath her feet to know it had been that long. She had been walking for a month. It was impossible - no one could do that, not the hardiest of marathon walkers, not someone given the strongest of designer drugs - but she had done it. Was doing it. Would keep doing it. So that meant this place was beyond the ordinary world, if it existed anywhere outside of her mind, that was. She wasn't sure about anything any more. All that existed was the stairway, and the stairway belonged to her. Everyone else was a trespasser ... so beware.

*

At some point she became aware there was just one other walker left. A man just as resourceful and strong-minded and ruthless. And he was gaining on her. She could hear his footsteps.

She kept walking.

A bubble of memory rose up from the depths of her subconscious mind and expanded until it was the only thing she could think. The memory was fully formed, but, like a real bubble, to press its surface was to risk bursting it, sending it back into oblivion. But she did risk it. She had to know the truth about why she was here. Her memories flooded back. She could see her previous life through the impartiality of distance from birth to now.

She had never been satisfied. Always, she had been seeking more. Everything had seemed ephemeral, unchallenging, to a woman who could achieve whatever she set her mind upon. Having conquered the business world at an early age (still in her teens, she had reaped billions from the City, then retired to the consternation of her peers), she had moved on to tougher challenges. She had experimented with the danger sports: skiing, diving, parachuting, rally driving, mountain climbing, cave exploring, adventuring across jungle and desert ... taking each to extremes, *daring* death to take her.

Death had shied away, though it had left its scars - the shark bite on her outer thigh, the broken bones, the punctured kidney, the destroyed lovers, the wrecked marriages. Death had a way of taunting her, mocking her, humiliating her. It was like a father scolding its child for disobedience. One day, she had promised herself, I will beat you, death.

That was her ultimate challenge.

The secret of life.

But she had known the secret would not come from the science of this century, or even the next. It would come from the shady world around her, where rules were for breaking and truths were to be disproved.

There was a rumour of a man who knew the secret of secrets. He was called simply the Doorway. He had no other name. The Doorway could show her places that were hidden. After many years of searching, she traced the Doorway to a dark pit of a place somewhere in Thailand. The Doorway squatted in a stinking hut miles from the nearest village. He had been waiting for her, expecting her. He was a blind man, with eyes a milky white and skin as black as the deepest cave. It looked as though he had been waiting for a thousand years.

"Enter," he said, in English, as she peered into the hut. "Sit."

She sat down facing him. His cataract-bulging eyes studied her.

"Can you help me?" she asked.

"What do you seek?"

"I seek the ultimate challenge."

"You do?"

"I do."

"I do not think you are ready."

"I am. There is nothing else left for me."

"Very well," he said. He reached down between his legs as if seeking carnal pleasure, but instead he raised a cloth scroll onto his lap, unfurling it with a deft flick of his fingers. The text was Babylonian cuneiform, at least four thousand years old. The text surrounded a picture of an island with a tower in its centre. *The* tower. The tower reached up into the clouds. The picture looked almost three-dimension, as if she could reach out and step into the image. It made her eyes water.

"Is it real?"

"As real as any dream or nightmare," the Doorway said. It was then he explained the rules. "Many people such as yourself have come to me asking to enter the tower, but the exit will only open for one, the winner. You will have to compete against them all. And win. Only then will I reveal the secret of secrets. If you think you are ready for the challenge, then just touch the tower and you will enter. But if not, I suggest you leave now."

"What happens if I fail?"

"You will pray for death, but it will not come."

"I have always loved a challenge," she said, and she touched the tower and found herself on the steps.

*

Remembering the reason for her being there stirred her into a faster pace. The footsteps behind her receded ... and eventually she was gaining on the man. He matched her pace for weeks, occasionally slipping ahead, occasionally slipping behind, but after a time she got within sight of him. He looked back with fear in his eyes. He was afraid. She had no pity. Like her, he had chosen to take the ultimate challenge. But she would win. She would be last.

When she was just a few steps away from the man he let out an agonising cry of defeat, both hands holding his heart as he staggered and fell dead. The dying scream echoed within her until she reached the top for the final time. If the door did not open, then she would pull it off its hinges. But it did open with the gentlest push. She stumbled into a room and lay down on the floor and wept. When she felt better, she opened her eyes.

She was in the hut.

The Doorway was there. Waiting.

It looked as though no time had gone by in the real world. She wondered if the tower had been a dream, but looked at her own body, seeing the damage done, she realised it had been real.

There was something different about the Doorway. His eyes were no longer blind. They held the Earth in each socket; his right showed the planet at its creation, four billion years ago; the left showed its death as the sun expanded. Lauren wondered what kind of being he was. Was he even remotely human? All of human time was within his vision. There had to be nothing he did not know.

Lauren gathered her strength and said, "I did it. I beat them all. Now, what is the secret of secrets?"

"The secret of secrets is ... there is no ultimate challenge."

"What?"

"There is *always* another challenge. The secret of life is to accept what there is, to be satisfied with what you already have, to be the best person you can be."

"I don't understand."

"I know," he said. "I know ..."

Lauren did not remember how she had entered the tower, but she knew there had been a life before, if only she could reach those tantalisingly enigmatic memories of yesterday.

The Shadow of Death

In darkened bars and darkened alleys the dead clung to the shadows like half-remembered nightmares. Jason Frost stepped out of the black taxi and walked into the *Finnegans Wake*. It was a theme bar, the theme being 1950s Irish-Americana, not the James Joyce novel. The walls were covered with black and white photographs of hard-working men constructing buildings and making cars, their faces black with grease, oil and sweat. Frost chose a stool and ordered a whiskey from the sombre bartender. Other customers along the counter were drinking Guinness in real *glass* glasses, mostly tourists seeking a nostalgic drink in quiet company. They looked at him suspiciously, then seemed satisfied that he belonged and resumed their drinking. Frost was not Irish or American. He just went to the bar because it was dark and smoky and the customers usually kept to themselves.

He could see many dead people in the alcoves and clustered at tables, hiding from the living. Some were seriously decayed, their off-white skulls showing through ribbons of greenish flesh, but most looked almost alive, mottled by the lividity of the dying process, like boxers bruised in the ring. There was the faint odour of embalming fluid in the air. By mutual agreement, the living stayed near the bar counter while the dead stayed in the darkness. Most of the living enjoyed the ambience; it gave them a feeling of being close to the edge.

But not the drunk sitting next to Frost.

He was a deadneck, a man with a pathological hatred of the dead.

He was an American tourist sloshing beer on the counter and

on his chequered shirt, which looked like a tablecloth stolen from a roadside café. The tourist looked at Frost through glazed eyes and whispered loudly. "You see those guys sitting over there, man?" He indicated the main group of dead with his thumb. The dead were playing poker. "Zombies, all of them. You look at their eyes, man. Big zombie pupils, like a drug-addict's, you know? You know they got no souls, man. Slack-jawed dead-eyed evil flesh-eating brain-dead mothers should all be killed properly, burned up in a crematorium or something, man. Should never have been resurrected, man. Never."

The man was drunk, but there were only so many insults Frost could take, even though the drunk didn't know he was dead. So he leant across the counter, in the drunk's face.

"I'm dead, *man*. You want to join us?"

"N-no. Look, man, I didn't know. You look so -"

"Normal?"

"Yeah."

"Except for the eyes, right?"

The tourist checked his watch. "I gotta go."

Frost watched the man lumber towards the exit and out into the night. It gave him no pleasure to scare the American - Frost could feel no normal emotions. That was the primary difference, the reason the living feared the dead. The dead did not feel emotions. His body was unable to produce the normal reactions to environmental stimuli. Adrenaline, endorphins and hormones were things his resurrected self could not create. The chemical reactions necessary for feeling emotions did not happen in his brain. The alcohol he was drinking would have no effect on him - he merely drank it out of habit. He did have the memory of emotions, and he knew *how* he would have reacted to insults before his death, so he acted the same way now. It was his way of staying human, by acting like a living person. He had good reasons to drink. Today, he'd lost his job as an English teacher. Few parents wanted a dead man teaching their children. The school's governors had agreed, half-heartedly apologising as they fired him. A dead man was not a good role model, they'd said. But losing his job was not the reason why he was drinking.

"Hey, you," said the bartender. "I saw that, *sir*. You scared that bloke off. You know the rules - no dead guys sit there unless invited."

Frost shrugged. "I have a right to sit where I want."

"Not in here you don't."

Frost could have argued with the man, but he knew it would serve little purpose. The dead had no legal rights against the living. The law had not adjusted to the changes - as far as the law went you lost all of your rights once you were certified dead. He picked up his whiskey and looked for a seat. The group of dead waved him across, making a position available at their table. There were five dead men. He sat down, and thanked them.

"I'm Jason Frost," he said, shaking cold hands with each of the dead.

The dead introduced themselves.

Daniel and Frank were in the worst condition, both having died six months before the Revival Ruling passed in the High Court. Daniel had actually been buried until his family requested his revival. Daniel's face was sunken. His eyes were new implants bulging in the sockets like table-tennis balls. His teeth showed whether he was smiling or not. His lips had rotted away. He wore gloves, to keep his skeletal fingers from breaking up. Daniel moved slowly and awkwardly, as if he was arthritic. Frank was not quite so decayed. He had much make-up covering his skin blemishes, the thick cosmetics they used to use in mortuaries and movies. It looked like pink talcum powder on his cheeks. Eric, Charles and Stephen had all died in the last month, and had had the treatment as soon as they passed over. They didn't look so deteriorated, but Frost noted their eyes were dead, like his own. Big, black holes. Emotional chasms. The deadneck was right, he thought, you can tell. The dead are different.

"How long have you been dead, Jason?" asked Eric. It was the standard question.

"Since the seventh of September," Frost said. His deathday.

"F-f-f-four weeks," Daniel said. "A monk. I mean, a month."

"Yes, I thought I had a headache," Frost continued. "I was wrong. It was meningitis." He remembered the sickness, creeping up gradually, hitting hard. "I was in hospital a couple of weeks, being pumped full of antibiotics, but I died anyway. My wife Nicola held my hand the whole time. I can remember Caitlin - that's our daughter - crying as I died. She was the one who asked for the revival. Nicola agreed and used the life insurance money. The next day I was back."

"Expensive," muttered Stephen.

"Yes." Frost had been at his own funeral, an odd event. An empty coffin had been buried, and his friends and relatives had gathered around to console Nicola and Caitlin while he stood there, ignored. "Then, when I went home, they were different. Nicola was distant. And Caitlin ... she was afraid of me. I knew I had changed, that I wasn't the same me, but I tried to be the way I was. I tried to act the same, to be a good husband and father. And yet we were strangers. Caitlin didn't want me near her - she would run away.

Nicola no longer wanted me near our daughter, either. As if I'd turned into a child-molester. Yesterday, Nicola said she wanted me out of the house. She said she couldn't love a dead man. If I go back she'll have me cremated."

"It's a common problem," Stephen said. The rest nodded in agreement. "Nobody wants to make love to a corpse."

"B-b-bad ship," Daniel said.

"What?"

"Excuse Dan's speech," Eric said, "he lost a few brain cells rotting in his coffin. His speech was damaged. In life he was a solicitor, but he's okay now." Eric laughed. "You're a good bloke, aren't you, Dan?"

"Y-yes. I good block. *Bloke*."

"Dan's like a lot of the early revivals - a little slow at thinking - but he's certainly not a zombie, like those deadnecks would have the living believe. Us dead guys have to stick together."

"Damn right," Stephen said. His breath smelt like wet leaves.

"Are you a member of any of the societies for the dead, Jason?"

"No," he admitted. "I ... haven't thought about it."

"You should." Stephen handed him a pamphlet. "This is a guide to those in London."

"Thanks," he said.

"Now," Eric said, "do you know how to play three-card stud?"

*

Frost left the *Finnegans Wake* at 11.30 p.m. He was using his cellular phone to call a taxi when he heard footsteps behind him. He turned around to see the same American tourist. He was sober now, and he didn't look pleased to see Frost. There were six skinheads with him. Frost could see tattoos on their muscular arms, ugly black and red symbols, like scars. They all shared the same one: a death's-head with the black letters BLP below. In the flashing purple light of a shop-window display they looked positively evil. The BLP was the British Life Party, a fascist organisation for dispossessed and angry youths. They blamed the dead for taking jobs off the living. They also called the dead 'meat', and were known for extreme violence. Frost wondered if he could run fast enough to escape. There was an alley across the street. He thumbed 999 into his phone as he smiled at the American. He hoped the police would be quick. Perhaps he could slow down the -

"Here he is," the American said. "Take him, fellas."

They came for him. Baseball bats and flick-knives sprung out of nowhere. Frost headed for the alley, but he was hit halfway across the road, knocked tumbling and rolling. They kicked him and dragged him into the alley, where they set on him with everything they had. They swung baseball bats at his head. He put him hands up to protect himself, and heard his wrist snap and twist.

The pain was real. His nerves still sent messages; he could experience pain, though feeling it was another matter. It was an intellectual warning that something was wrong, an overload of his nervous system. His hand hung useless. He was powerless against the constant assault. He heard his ribs crack and the wet thud of a bat pounding, pounding bones. The American joined in, breaking his nose. Thick transparent biofluid splattered out like mucous. He tried to curl up into a ball, but the deadnecks were too strong and fast, too determined. A baseball bat caught the side of his head and whipped his head sideways. Biofluid filled his ears, almost deafening him. It poured out of his mouth. Biofluid was the substance keeping him functioning, without it he would die the permanent death. He could feel his thoughts slowing down as he lost the vital fluid from gaping wounds.

One skinhead plunged a knife in and out of his chest. Screaming: "Meat! Meat! Meat!"

"Open his skull, man," the American said. His voice was muffled by the biofluid. "Scoop out his brain like an oyster."

That would kill him, Frost knew.

The skinheads, charged with adrenaline, grabbed his head and kept it still. Their leader showed a flick-knife to Frost.

The next thing was a blur. The flick-knife went flying, and suddenly the skinheads were screaming and running. He heard someone yell: "Zombies! Run!" Then the skinheads had gone. The American lay sprawled on a bed of dirty newspapers. He was unconscious, and would wake with one hell of a headache. Real blood shone wet on the red bricks behind him. Daniel and Frank guarded the alley, two ghouls no living person would want to mess with. Eric, Stephen and Charles examined Frost's injuries. His body looked like it was wrecked. Eric told him to be still, Charles was a doctor. Charles's fingers probed his soft wounds.

Frost could only offer a weak smile to his rescuers.

"Us dead guys should stick together," Eric said.

Frost grunted and nodded.

*

They took him to a hospital for the dead. Unlike the living, the dead could not heal naturally. They needed repairing. Treatment was crude and uncaring; it was like a repair shop. Hundreds of dead people waited in the dank rooms of a closed-down school for help from the overworked staff. Some had probably been there for days, unable to move. Charles knew one of the doctors and used his influence to speed up the admittance process. Frost was taken by stretcher into a large room that used to be a gymnasium. About a dozen operations were going on simultaneously, half of the patients looked like vivisected animals.

Frost closed his eyes but could not sleep.

The operation lasted an hour. His broken bones were glued together, or replaced, and litres of fresh biofluid were injected into his body and head. A plastic surgeon reformed his nose and shattered cheekbones. It was like a pit-stop for a racing car, he thought, just enough to keep the machine running for a few more laps. Push it too hard and it would crash and burn.

Afterwards, he could walk again, but the experience taught him how much the living could hate the dead. The only people who could understand were the dead.

"You'll have to disappear," Stephen said. "That guy we knocked out will call the cops, I'm sure. He'll say we attacked him."

"But he attacked *me*."

"Jason, you have no legal rights against a living person. The powers that be consider us no more than furniture to be used and abused."

"Stephen's telling the truth," Eric said. "You're a wanted man, now."

"Bad sh-ship," Daniel said.

"Yeah. I know exactly what you mean."

Frost went with his new friends to their home. They lived in a derelict Odeon, among rats and dust, for the dead needed no creature comforts. The alienated just needed a place to hide. Nothing could disgust a dead man; it wasn't logical. Disgust was an emotional reaction. Without emotional stimulation he was the real Mr Spock, able to see the world perhaps more clearly than when alive. Objectively.

Stephen's prediction proved accurate - the tourist went on television and spoke to the tabloids about his encounter with 'a bunch of crazy zombies'. Frost was the suspect, described accurately by the bartender. No mention of the skinheads reached the media. Like millions of other dead people, he had to eke out an existence as an outcast.

The heat of the day was enough to keep the biofluid warm and active, but at night the dead gradually cooled down and became sluggish and, if the biofluid dropped below $4^{O}C$, shutdown. The dead did not sleep, did not dream. He used this knowledge to blank out his time, by deliberately staying indoors, in the cinema. He found he could be shutdown for twenty hours a day, if he avoided heat. It was Stephen and Eric who forced him to go outside in the sun, carrying him bodily onto the street.

"You're dead," Stephen said. "You have to get over it. You don't see Daniel moping around in the darkness, and he only has a tenth of the brain you have. You can be a something. You have to try."

During the following weeks and months he attempted to become part of his adopted family, to throw off his cloak of living, to be what he really was: dead. He spent most of his time outside, warming his biofluid in the fields far from the living, contemplating what he was. All pretences of being alive were a sham, and he tried to exist with that knowledge burned in his soul. To wallow in his deadness.

But he wanted to *feel* again.

To be happy, sad, angry, mad.

To love, and be loved.

To be part of Nicola and Caitlin's lives.

He wanted these things. He needed these things.

Though he found conversations with the dead occupied his time, there was something missing. Was it real emotion? It was. The dead could not laugh convincingly, and none could cry - the tear ducts did not function. He wondered if he was prejudiced against his own kind. Probably. His thoughts were plagued with past memories of his family, of Caitlin as a baby, learning to walk and talk. Of the first time he kissed Nicola. Going out. Holding hands. Making love.

His present existence was purgatory.

The living drew him like a moth to flame.

Often, he would hide in the trees outside Caitlin's school, watching his daughter in the playground with her friends. She looked as if the joy had been stolen from her life. She no longer played hopscotch with the others, instead she just watched, hanging back from the crowd. He wanted to go up to her and hug her - and have her hug him. But the gulf between them was too wide. He was part of the unseen now, something the living shunned, a reminder of what fate lay waiting all of them once they grew old or unfortunate.

Waiting for a glimpse of Nicola, when she collected Caitlin at the end of the school day, formed a habit. He could see the way she would sweep her dark brown strands of hair away from her eyes, catching the sunlight like gossamer threads. Green eyes flashing with life and warmth. Somewhere a man could lose himself.

"You can't live like that," Stephen said, after he'd told him about his obsession. "Get on with your life."

"Death, you mean?"

"You can't turn the clock back."

Stephen was right. The cold logic of the dead was insurmountable.

There were dead like Stephen who seemed to revel in their deadness, but there were others like himself. Eric had a living wife and two boys aged four and six. Frost wanted his family back, too.

Existence was not enough.

*

He was out sunbathing and thinking about his ex-family, when there was the fire. He returned to find the fire had gutted the Odeon, turning everything and everyone inside it to a sticky charcoal. Blackened skeletons weeping boiled biofluid lay in the bricks and wood. Five bodies were pulled out in a non-recoverable status. He was alone, truly alone.

A petrol can was found in the remains.

*

The worst thing about losing his dead friends was that he could not feel the loss. He could think about them, memories looping around and around his biofluid-saturated brain, neurones firing in response in their millions, but the detachment was always present, as a dark cloud blocking the sun. A layer of perception was gone. It was the difference between being human and being a computer pretending to be human. He knew the difference. There were only two things that mattered to him: Nicola and Caitlin.

He had to see them.

*

"Hi," he said, "it's me."

"You're not meant to call," Nicola said coldly.

"I know, but I had to." He was standing under the mock-Victorian lamp post across the road. He had a clear view of the house and the rose-gardens and the uncut lawn. Mowing the lawn had been his Sunday morning routine, but without him it was beginning to look ragged. He could see Nicola through the bay windows. She was fidgety and looking around, probably suspecting him of spying on her like a stalker. The telephone cord followed her movements like a white snake. Frost ducked behind a parked car when she approached the windows. "I want to see the both of you."

"No, Jason. I was watching TV the other day. There was a description of a dead man who'd attacked a tourist. It was you, wasn't it?"

"Yes, but -"

"Christ, you're a wanted man!"

"Forget that. The guy's lying. Besides, he doesn't know my name."

"He says you beat him up and stole his wallet."

"Lies, Nicola. Lies. You know me. The American will be going back to the States soon, so the police will lose interest. There isn't a story in the world that runs for a week."

"Jason, exactly why are you calling?"

"I'm the same man you married. I need to see you. A lot's happened and I -"

"Jesus! Why won't you listen? I hoped it would work out between us. I tried! Heaven knows I tried! I can't handle it, Jason. *My* Jason is dead. You're something ... something else. You're dead."

He could see her crying. "I'm not asking to move back in. I just want to be part of your life. And Caitlin needs a father."

"She has a mother, too," she said. "I count as well. I want to go on living, and I can't if you try to make me feel guilty for being alive."

He decided to change the subject. "What about Caitlin?"

"What about her?"

"How's she coping?"

"Fine," she said. Fine was not good.

"Does she miss me?"

"Of course she misses you," Nicola said, sighing. "*I* miss you."

"Let me come back, please."

He saw her shaking her head, chewing her bottom lip.

"Nicola?" he said.

"I can't. You have to leave us alone, Jason."

She hung up.

A man had entered the room. Frost did not know him. He was a handsome, *living* man wearing nothing but a blue towel. The man said something. Nicola nodded. Nicola kissed him, running her hands through his wet hair. He responded by hitching up her dress around her waist and lifted her off the carpet - her legs fastened around his hips as he carried her towards the hallway ... and the stairs leading up to the master bedroom. The blue towel was left behind.

Oh, Nicola, why? Why him?

You should never have revived me.

It was starting to rain.

How appropriate, he thought.

*

Standing on a bridge over a section of the M25, he considered suicide. Suicide among the dead was one solution to eternal existence - but jumping off the bridge was no *guarantee* of success. If it failed he would be a horrific mess still existing in a devastated body. A passing truck would probably just smash his bones and leave him in a filleted body. Suicide was stupid, he knew. After all, he was not depressed. That was another emotion he was also incapable of feeling. The serotonin levels in his brain mattered nothing to his state of mind. Destroying himself would solve nothing. So he returned to his car, vowing not to take the coward's way out. A sensible answer had to be available.

He went in search of emotions. Emotions were the key to winning back his family from the usurper wearing the blue towel. The top expert in the field of post-life thought-processes was the inventor of biofluid, Professor Stuart V Badenhoff. For the next seven days, Badenhoff was holding lectures at Cambridge.

*

"I believe sentience and emotion can't exist in separation. You can't be human with only a functioning brain. You need the outside world to provide pleasurable and non-pleasurable input ..."

Frost sat at the back of the lecture hall, wearing sunglasses. It was two weeks since he'd lost his friends. The BLP were getting stronger, openly destroying the dead and wrecking revival clinics. Hard-line dead and their supporters were fighting back by killing the living and making them join their ranks or die at the hands of their ex-allies. Frost was pretending to be alive, so he could move around in daylight. Professor Badenhoff was the leading figure in the new science of necro-psychology, a man the BLP and several religious leaders considered the Antichrist. He was maybe the one man in the world who could help Frost rediscover his emotions. The lecture covered the properties of biofluid in some depth, boring to the layman, like Frost. At the end of the lecture, the professor invited questions from the audience. A few tentative students asked challenging questions, then Frost stood up:

"Sir, is it possible to recreate emotions by stimulation of the cerebral cortex by artificial means?"

"A good question! I would say yes and no. Yes, it is possible. No, it isn't possible yet. If you had listened properly to my lecture you would know the biofluid I invented is incompatible with the endocrine system of a living person. That is why the living can't be granted immortality by a simple injection of biofluid, but I do foresee a time when the living and the dead will be indistinguishable. Soon the dead will just look like normal people. The problem of eye-adaptation to light is one I am currently working on in leaps and bounds. In fact, I have a theory the dead person's brain will eventually adjust to the absence of these emotion triggers by finding new pathways to produce them as time goes by, in much the same way a child's cognitive skills improve with age. Is that all?"

"No. How long will it take for this step?"

"Ten, twenty years. The time will be nothing for the dead, who after all feel nothing."

You don't know what you're talking about, Frost thought.

Two days later Professor Badenhoff was destroyed by a BLP bomb left in his Mercedes. Nothing was left of him to be resurrected.

Frost did not shed a tear.

*

And so he wandered far and wide, searching for the answers that would make him live again. Badenhoff was not the only expert. He had been the pioneer, sure, but his followers were in every university and research laboratory, working for an answer to the emotion problem. Billions of dollars, pounds, marks and yen were there for the taking, if only the strike of genius sparked. Frost spoke to experts, becoming more and more informed as he did so. What he learnt was not good.

Unfortunately, Badenhoff's ten to twenty years estimate for a breakthrough looked optimistic. Nobody really understood biofluid, with its weird quantum-mechanical properties. It was like electricity to a Neanderthal, a great mystery that didn't really belong in that time. Fifty years was more likely than twenty. By the time biofluid II was on the market, Caitlin would be grown up and Nicola remarried.

He would have lost the very reasons for living.

*

The article was in the *Fortean Times*. After he'd read it, he read it again. Then he checked the publication date to make sure it was not an April Fool's joke. It was not. There was one woman exploring the edge of science, a Californian scientist who claimed to have created positive results on 56 test subjects out of 200. She said she could make the dead *laugh* for real. The ordinary scientific community considered Dr Sarah Sifuentes a New Age crank, but through heavy use of the Internet Frost discovered intriguing anecdotal evidence supporting her claims: video-recordings of dead people smiling and laughing and reporting *emotions*. A call to the *Fortean Times* verified the reference sources as genuine. They came from the Sifuentes Institute in Southern California.

He phoned Sifuentes.

"I'll certainly try to help you, Mr Frost," she said. "I need volunteers all the time. But you'll have to signs some papers."

"Papers?"

"I have to warn you the treatment works in just over 25% of the case studies done so far, with varying results. You see, if it fails you'll have a serious chance of non-recovery."

"You mean permanent death?"

"I'm afraid so," she said.

"What's the odds?"

"Well, 84 subjects died on the operating table. 16 lost all memory functions and are in comas."

He could not feel fear. Even if he could have done, he doubted it would have altered his response. "I'll be there as soon as I can. Have the papers ready."

*

"What'll we'll be doing is passing electricity through your skull into your brain and the biofluid. This has the effect of disturbing the natural properties of the fluid, creating micro-eddies and pockets of liquid with radical neurological effects. These areas seem to do something to the brain structure."

Frost nodded. He hoped he understood. He trusted Sarah Sifuentes because she clearly loved her work. They were in the operating room, which looked more like a study. Medical textbooks lined the shelves. He climbed up on the leather couch, resting his head on the soft cushions. "Doctor, can I ask you a question?"

"Sure."

"Why are you doing this?"

"You mean is it for the money and fame?" She switched on a computer beside the couch, attaching wires to his forehead. "The answer's no."

"Then why?"

"My husband died of cancer," she said. The memory made her pause. "Tommy-Lee was one of the first people to be given Badenhoff's biofluid. It worked, but he wasn't the same man after. There was no vitality left in him. One day, I found a note on the kitchen table. It was a suicide note."

"What did it say?"

"'I was reborn without a soul. I can't steal yours.' LAPD found him in a ravine. He'd killed himself with his gun. He used all of the bullets because it was so hard to destroy enough of his brain to stop existing. He didn't want to come back a zombie."

"I'm sorry," he said.

"Stay still, please," she said. "This will take an hour."

*

"How do you feel?"

"I ... don't know."

Sarah Sifuentes led him outside. His head buzzed, motes of coloured light dancing before his eyes as the brightness disturbed his vision. The laboratory faced an arcing stretch of a white beach surrounded by thrashing ocean. It was a hot day, the sky pure white. The ocean roared. Blond surfers rode the waves a hundred metres from the shore.

"How do you feel?"

"Hot."

"That isn't an emotion. How do you feel?"

He knew the scene was beautiful. He knew it, but he could not feel it. "It isn't working."

"There are some tests I'd like to perform," she said, quietly.

*

"Well?" he asked, much later.

"The results are negative. I can't explain it. The biofluid *has* changed, but your emotions haven't returned. In other patients this led to rapid development of emotions. I'm at a loss to explain it. It's as if you're blocking the treatment subconsciously. I'm sorry."

"Thanks for trying," he said.

He wished he could *mean* his words of gratitude.

*

Back in Britain, the motorway was empty of moving traffic. Glass crunched under Frost's tyres as he drove slowly and cautiously along the hard-shoulder, giving the wrecked cars a wide berth. The lanes were crammed with burnt-out cars, some still smoking. It looked as if a gigantic accident had happened extending for several miles, but if that was true why had the motorway not been shut down?

He drove straight home.

*

He half-expected Blue Towel to open the door. But Nicola opened it. Her hair was unbrushed, and her mascara had formed deep shadows under her red-rimmed eyes.

"You," she said, a quiet accusation thrown tiredly in his direction.

"Nicola?"

She turned away. He asked her what was wrong but she either did not hear or did not want to respond. He followed her into the lounge, where she'd curled up on the sofa with a box of Kleenex on her lap. She pulled a tissue from the box and blew her nose. In the detached reality Frost was locked in, he noted a running nose was a side-effect of heavy crying. The shifting seas of consciousness broiled with disquiet.

"Is it Blue Towel? Has he left you?"

"Who?"

He remembered she did not know he had been observing her. She did now.

"If you mean *Richard* it has nothing to do with him. God, Jason, where have you been? Where were you yesterday?"

"California," he said. "Why?"

"Don't you know? There's been a riot."

There was more to it, he saw. A riot in itself was not enough to upset his wife this severely.

There was something she was not saying.

"Tell me."

"It was the BLP and your pals the zombies. The troubled started in the middle of London and spread ..."

Caitlin's school. On the road to the town.

"Caitlin? Is she okay?"

"She'd DEAD, Jason. My baby's dead, okay? A car hit her. A zombie was driving, trying to escape the BLP. My baby was killed instantly." Her eyes hardened. "Are you happy now? Are you? Are you?" She launched herself at him, punching his chest, kicking his legs. He stood there, taking it. She punched and slapped him until sweat rolled down her face, and she kept at it for another five minutes. Panting, she went to the drinks cabinet and poured herself an overfilled tumbler of martini. She gulped it down, liquid splashing her chin and clothes. "And before you ask, *Jason*, I'm having her cremated tomorrow! She's not becoming a zombie!"

Let me feel something, he thought. My only daughter is dead. My wife is on the point of breakdown. Why can't I feel the pain?

The pain should have ripped him apart, but there was nothing, just a gaping void in his heart sucking the life out of the living.

He wanted Caitlin alive. With emotions.

"Wait, Nicola. There's a doctor -"

"Get out. I don't want to hear. Get out."

"But -"

"Get out."

He left.

He phoned the hospital. "My daughter was brought in yesterday. Her name? Her name's Caitlin Frost. Yes, I'm her father. You need proof?" He read out his National Insurance number. He didn't mention he was dead. "Yes, I know she's dead. I want to see her. Where is she being kept? Thank you. Goodbye."

His thinking was this: Dr Sifuentes could offer hope - a slight chance his Caitlin could become human again. But he would have to be fast - before she was taken out of the mortuary.

First, he visited the hospital for the dead. The doctor who had treated him the last time provided a litre packet of biofluid in the naive belief it was for him.

One litre would be sufficient for a child.

*

Caitlin had been stored in ice, as was the standard procedure, even when the body was going to be destroyed. She looked so small and vulnerable on the cold metal drawer. She'd died of internal bleeding; her lungs had filled with blood. He touched her wispy hair, which was stiff and frozen to her scalp. It was matted with blood. The doctors had not bothered to put her clothes back on. They were in a plastic bag, crisped by brown bloodstains.

"I'd like to be alone with her," he told the attendant.

The man nodded and excused himself.

Looking around the mortuary, he saw no one else. Frost took a syringe from his coat pocket and the biofluid from inside. He'd seen the resurrection process performed countless times, and he set out on the task quickly, injecting the biofluid in sites on her neck and spinal column, the needle sinking in the greyish skin time after time.

That done, he wrapped her in his coat and carried her to the emergency exit.

He reached the parking spaces before she started to stir. He set her down on the grass next to his car to allow the sunlight to heat the biofluid. Slowly, the signs of life returned. Her skin goose-fleshed and her muscles twitched as the biofluid saturated her cells.

She opened her eyes. Her dead eyes.

"Dad?" No emotion. Not yet, but there was a chance of it, with Dr Sifuentes's treatment. "Dad?"

He hugged her. Squeezed.

"I'm here," he said. "Forever."

Biofluid clicked into place, forming new brain patterns. A revelation.

He felt something.

Dear God - he felt something.

Love.

Monsters

"Have you met Professor Frankenstein?"

"No, no. He works *here*?"

"But of course! He's the head of research. It's a tightly held secret, naturally. What with the war and everything …"

"The war …"

"Come, come, follow me …"

*

EXPERIMENTATION ROOM 52

There was a smell in the air like ozone at the beach. I breathed it in with relish until I realised what was causing the smell.

There were hundreds of Jews and Negroes in light-green tanks, floating in a preservative that seemed to glow. They were all wired up from head to toes with electrodes and optical cables. Blue-white flashes of electricity violently jerked the bodies. Computers recorded the information gathered with a quiet hum.

Some of the experiments involved pieces of humans somehow kept alive against the odds. I could see a man sliced precisely in half writhing in the current like a dying fish. Another was no more than a brain connected to a spinal column. There was every variation in between.

Curious, I approached the nearest tank and tapped the Plexiglas. It had to be at least twenty centimetres thick. I leapt backwards when a mottled face slammed against the Plexiglas and the eyes, such sad brown eyes, pleaded for mercy. He was a man stripped of flesh, his muscles exposed. The mouth opened and a gasp of trapped oxygen blurted out and bubbled on the surface.I knew what the man was saying. *Help. Help me.* He was no older than I was. But he was a Jew. I knew they were all subhuman, worse than animals, but –

"Dr Kessler, we don't have time to stand around gawking. Professor Frankenstein is waiting."

I blinked and focused on Dr Bauer. He had been my tutor at medical college in New Berlin. He was a plump blond man with the physical appearance of a man in his early thirties, though he was closer to eighty. He'd recently acquired the body of a brave SS commandant who had been killed on the Eastern Front, his brain ripped to shreds by a Russian headseeker.

Stalin was using inhumane methods to kill our soldiers' minds, then keeping their bodies for his own army. In 1945 the Americans had nuked Berlin and Bonn, forcing us underground. They'd expected us to give up, but then we'd stolen the atomic secrets and nuked New York and Moscow. Before more cities were wiped out on a tit-for-tat escalation, the Axis and Allied powers agreed to a ban of atomic weapons. Stalemate, of a sort.

For fifty years the conventional war had raged on at sixteen fronts in the disputed territories. The Allies controlled the Americas, Australia, South Africa, Russia … We controlled Europe, the Middle East, China and North Africa. Now it looked like we would lose North Africa …

We had to fight back. That was where the institute came in. And Bauer. He was a genetics genius. He probably knew more about the subject than Frankenstein. I'd known Bauer as witty and caring man, always with time for his students, unlike many of the doctors. His star student, I'd enjoyed dinners with his family. I'd always known he did top-secret research for the Reich … Until that moment, I had not known what his research entailed.

It looked like torture, simple torture. Somehow, I had imagined he used mindless corpses for his experiments. How naïve! I was twenty-four-years-old and I knew nothing. By calling me Dr Kessler and not Christian, Bauer was showing his annoyance with my childish behaviour.

I did not know this man at all.

He was a monster.

Keeping my disgust to myself, I followed him towards an office. I vowed I would behave like an SS officer. I was here to help the war effort. If a few subhumans had to suffer … well, that was a sacrifice to be made …

Thousands of eyes watched me.

Thousands of pleading eyes.

*

Frankenstein studied me with his two dissimilar eyes. They were both transplants – one blue, one brown. His face was the same as I'd seen in my textbooks, handsome with a touch of arrogance to the lips and eyebrows. As I shook his hand, I noticed the tiny scars around his hairline, signs he'd had his face grafted onto a different skull. His hand was delicate, like a woman's. The skin was as smooth as silk with no life lines – it was regenerated tissue. "So this is our new recruit, Stefan?" (Bauer nodded.) "Welcome, welcome! Do you like what you see?" He waved at the tanks seen through the window of his office.

"It's … different, sir."

"Different! I'll say! Quite a few newcomers lose their lunch on seeing the experiments. Personally, I think there is nothing more beautiful than the human body in all its forms. The experiments you've seen out there are fairly rudimentary survival tests compared with the cutting edge science in D Section. We're trying to see how far the human body can be reduced before it can't be resurrected. Basic stuff, but necessary. In D Section we really let rip with the latest developments. That's where you will be working in six months, after your internship. Believe me, all the things you learned in medical school are a mere prelude to what you will learn here."

"May I ask what you do in D Section?"

"You may ask," Frankenstein said, laughing. "But you don't yet have the clearance level to receive an answer. You should know that."

It was a rebuke. I felt sweat trickled down my neck. Bauer came to my defence.

"I told you he was inquisitive, Victor," Bauer said. "Christian is particularly interested in memory recovery techniques."

It had long been a problem that a dead person's brain decayed through cell death even in the short time it took to get it to a resurrection chamber. On the battlefield it was a particular problem. Cell death was reversible using Frankenstein's bio-animation therapy, but, inevitably, memories were lost. Death was not a barrier, but a hurdle. Sometimes you hit that hurdle and tripped over. When that happened, the patient often lost years of memory. It happened in thirty percent of revivals. For a man like Frankenstein it was acutely embarrassing. Having relatives and friends who'd lost years of memories, I wanted to do anything in my powers to solve the problem. I had some theories about retrieving memories from their associated memories, which was like constructing a copy of a damaged building using the architect's plans. The result wouldn't be identical to the original, but it would be as near as possible. Frankenstein probed my theories for ten minutes, then, satisfied I knew what I was talking about, he left me alone with Bauer.

The internship began.

*

"Dad?" I said. He was awake, I was sure. His chest had a different rhythm when he was awake. He was in an airy room in the Mengler VA Hospital, lying in a bed with blue cotton sheets and a rubber mattress. His eyes were open, staring up at the ceiling. Someone had brought some roses into the room to give it a better smell. I sat down. I gently propped my father's head up so he could see me – if he was awake. Sometimes it was hard to tell. Ten years ago, a Soviet headseeker had burrowed through his skull into his cerebral cortex. It had not exploded, as it was supposed to do, but it had left him in this persistent vegetative state. If he had not been a Party member, his body would have been taken for recycling. I would not let that happen.

"Dad, what should I do?"

He did not answer.

"Should I work for them? Tell me! Tell me!"

His breathing was as regular as a heartbeat. I wiped away some crusted dribble with a handkerchief. I stayed for an hour. Then the nurse came and asked me to leave. At the doorway, I looked back at my father.

His eyes ... were they pleading?

*

I cut a deep incision into the man's chest. He was drugged, but he was watching. He could feel no pain, but his eyes widened. Bauer, standing behind my shoulder, said, "Go on, finish it. It's only a Negro." I opened the chest with a steel clamp, spreading the ribs so I could get access to the internal organs. Blood oozed over my fingers. The man's eyes fluttered and the ECG readings blinked in warning. Fast. Fast. Fast. I removed the liver with a laser scalpel. Then I stitched up the man and put him in a tank.

I checked on him each day, watching his progress.

He died eight days later.

The experiment was a success.

I spent time in other labs. There was the radiation lab, where people were treated with various levels of alpha, beta and gamma radiation to test the body's tolerance. There was the cross-species lab, where people were integrated with monkeys, dogs, bears, pigs, horses. The hybrids created didn't live long. Luckily. There was the mutant lab, which contained ten thousand embryos in gestation tanks. The scientists were trying to make superhumans with extra arms, eyes, muscles ... Next door was the cloning lab, but that was shut down after a biohazard accident killed sixteen technicians. The accident never appeared in the newspapers. I was forbidden from discussing anything I saw or did inside the institute. I would have sounded like a lunatic if I had. Besides which, all employees were given random loyalty tests under sodium penthonal.

"That Jew Spielberg's made another movie that's been banned.

Honestly, I don't think anyone would notice his rotten movies if they didn't get banned. That Jew Spielberg!" Anita said "Jew" like it was his first name.

I looked up from my breakfast cereal. "What's it about?"

"What's it about? What do you think?"

"I don't know."

Anita sighed. "It's about *us*. He claims there are hundreds of 'death camps' all over the world where we kill Jews and use their bodies to replace ones lost in battle. What nonsense is that? Everyone knows the Jews have their own country paid for by German citizens like you and me. We keep the Jews! We let those animals live in good homes! And yet he – that Jew Spielberg – that lousy Jew – he has the nerve – the bloody nerve – to suggest we're lying. American propaganda doesn't even stick with the facts! Spielberg claims millions of Jews have been killed. It's ridiculous. Where's the proof? I've seen the resettlement camps on the television. The Fuhrer has been to visit to ensure they are treated well. That Jew Spielberg! Bah!"

Her tirade frightened me. I had never seen her so upset. Her spittle hit the table. Her face was all twisted and ugly.

"You don't think the death camps are real?"

"No. Of course not. Do you?"

"Well –"

"What?"

I'd seen the television pictures, too. There had always seemed something odd about them. They always showed Orthodox Jews in black clothes with long black beards. You never saw any ordinary Jews. Only the ones in black. Once or twice I'd thought they looked like Germans dressed up.

I thought of the institute. Bauer told me the people they - we - used had fatal diseases. They were volunteers. They would die anyway, he said. We were just keeping them alive a little longer.

But what if they were perfectly healthy until we experimented on them?

Was everything I knew about history a lie?

"Christian, what's wrong?"

"Nothing," I lied. "I'm just thinking about work. Today I finish my internship."

"Congratulations," she said. She leant over the table and kissed me. *That Jew Spielberg.* I pulled away. I ate my cereal in silence, looking at the woman I'd once loved, seeing a stranger.

*

SECTION D: AUTHORISED PERSONAL LEVEL 001 ONLY

Bauer patted my shoulder as we approached the steel doors and the ominous-looking guards. "Don't look so grumpy, Christian. You made it. The grunt-work is over. You've truly impressed me these last six months. I've had many students during my career, but none have your talent. I have a feeling your name will be written in history alongside Hippocrates and Galen. Welcome to the future."

With bravado, he slid his card over the door's lock. It blinked from red to green. The door opened and we passed through before it closed. We were inside a room as large as an aircraft hangar. What looked like prison cells covered one wall up to the ceiling. There were some fairly large buildings within the room. Technicians and scientists in white lab coats were crowded around monitors and computers. Frankenstein was talking with a group of SS officers. He looked angry. He dismissed them and beckoned for us to approach. "Bureaucrats! Always wanting more paperwork." He shook his head. "I see you've brought your progeny, Stefan? How did he do with the grunt-work?"

"He passed with flying colours."

"I wouldn't expect anything less." Frankenstein swivelled around and walked off. I assumed I had to go after him. Bauer didn't follow.

"This," Frankenstein said, sweeping his arms in the general direction of the cells, "is the tool that will defeat our enemies. I'll show you what my genius has created."

I had an uneasy feeling as I went into a small building. It looked like a hospital ward, except the patients were wearing helmets hooked up to a mainframe computer. There was a machine that looked like a diving bell. A man with his head shaved was sitting inside.

"What is it?"

"Everything you see here merely monitors the thoughts of the subjects. The machine you see is a cerebral analyser – it translates thoughts in computer images we can see on these screens." I watched the man's thoughts displayed. He could see us looking at him – and we could 'see' what he saw. The things he heard – our voices – came out a text messages. Another screen displayed the man's inner voice, his stream of conscious. It was mostly gibberish.

"The man is ignorant," Frankenstein said. "The machine only picks up the quality of thoughts transmitted."

I didn't believe him. I thought his machine was malfunctioning, but he was too proud to admit it. He quickly moved on, walking up to a bed with a Negro in it. The man was comatose. There was a small table next to the bed covered with syringes filled with a brown liquid and a large monitor currently displaying PET scans of the man's brain. Each syringe was marked with a number: 2.3. Frankenstein picked up a syringe and held it up to the light. "This liquid contains a virus. A special virus that affects the brain. It's RNA specific." He injected it into the man's arm. Frankenstein's attention went to the monitors. "You can see the virus enter the brain as a slight increase in temperature. See? It quickly spreads. In two minutes the virus will alter certain brain structures."

"It's rewriting memories," I uttered.

"Not only that, but it does it according to a software program encoded within the virus. I can change the software and have a new batch of the virus prepared in just a few hours. Like it or not, we've got the face the fact that the Americans have the upper hand when it comes to weapons technology. We can't win on brute strength. Our best hope is to subvert them from within. We can create slaves. We can programme assassins. We can take over their government and military with this virus."

"When will this happen?"

"Soon. The virus is still in the prototype. It is no easy task writing software that does what we want. One day I'll be able to programme anyone to believe anything. The ultimate brain-washing. For the moment we need a reliable software program. That is where you come in. You'll be my assistant. Use you knowledge of memory storage to come up with a voice-instructed command system."

"I don't understand, sir. What about recovering lost memories? This doesn't have anything to do with that."

He shrugged. "What's gone is gone. That's not my concern – or yours."

He showed me the "progress" of the virus. In several cells there were comatose patients. In the next dozen the patients were awake but blank, like my father. Each level of cells held patients on a different version of the virus. By version 1.16, I could have a "conversation" with the prisoners, but it was creepy because none of them knew their names. Identification codes were tattooed on their arms. On the top level, version 2.3 had been tested on six men and six women, all naked. Talking to them, I thought they seemed completely rational, if a little slow. They had been in forced labour camps until recently, when they'd been brought here. They seemed happier to be here because they got regular food and water. Frankenstein was smiling. "They almost pass for human, don't they? But watch this. Number 4, I want you to kill yourself by stabbing out your own eyes with your thumbs."

Number four – a tall Negro with skin so dark it was nearly blue – responded immediately by raising his thumbs.

"Don't," I said to the man and to Frankenstein.

The man stopped. Frankenstein looked annoyed. "Continue, Number 4. Only respond to my voice."

The man screamed when his thumbs burst his corneas, aqueous humour squirting out like jelly, but he kept pushing and pushing until blood poured down his chest and his thumbs were deep into his eye sockets. I turned away. I heard him fall. He was dead when I looked back. Frankenstein lit up a cigarette and spoke into a microphone on his collar. "Cell 804 needs cleaning up. Subject deceased. One Negro ready for spares." Frankenstein looked at me with his blue and brown eyes. "You! Never countermand my orders. I am your superior. I do not care if you are a hotshot. Challenge me again and I will report you to the SS High Command. Is that understood?"

"Yes, sir."

*

"Ah. Herr Kessler. You are visiting your father?"

"Yes," I said to the nurse blocking the door. "Why? What's wrong?"

"I should warn you there's been a *change*." There were tears in her eyes.

"Is he …?"

"He's not going to die, no. But … but the army came here and required replacements due to the shortage and –"

I pushed past her and into the room. My father was in the bed with the sheets drawn up to his neck. He looked normal, but …

I pulled away the sheets.

He had no arms. He had no legs.

The monsters. The filthy monsters.

Behind me, I heard the nurse sobbing.

I slumped into the chair beside the bed. I closed my eyes and thought of the times my father had played with me in the park when I was small. He had loved spending time with me away from the stresses of the war. Those few, brief times were the only times I could recall my father smiling and laughing. And now … My father was an honourable man. Yes - he was a soldier. Yes - he killed men. But he'd never killed civilians. What did that make me?

Was I a monster too?

*

Frankenstein didn't spend much time on the experiments himself. He left the software engineering to his assistants. There were six of us. Three worked during the day. Three worked at night. The work never stopped. We created new viruses, tested them and reported the conclusions like drones. I soon came to the conclusion that I was the only assistant with any ideas about how to accomplish the task. The others were good technicians, but they didn't have imagination. For them, it was a matter of logistics. They sincerely believed that by testing every possible genetic combination they'd eventually hit upon the right answer, just like Salvarsan 606 was discovered. But I didn't believe that. Salvarsan 606 was a fluke. That was working blind. It would take years – thousands of test subjects – to do it with that method. You needed imagination to solve the problem. There were short cuts. I wrote algorithms for the virus to use to hone itself to RNA by a process of iterations. The results improved.

Then I made a batch of version 2.91. I tested it on a 43-year-old Muslim. The virus left him normal in every way but one – I could instruct him to believe anything. It was beyond hypnosis – it was complete mind-control. And yet to anyone who didn't know he'd been programmed, they would never know. He could live in society with my instructions burned into his head more forcefully than the words of the Koran.

It was so disturbing I didn't write an honest report.

I wrote it was a failure and instructed the man to behave as though the virus had failed. I then moved onto version 2.92, but I kept the batch of 2.91 and labelled it as 1.13. Nobody was using 1.13, so it would stay untouched until I figured out what to do. I went to work on 2.92 just as if nothing had happened. I knew I would be executed if anyone found out my deceit. I tried not to think about the risk of having a trust test.

*

That night, after a poor performance in bed with my wife, I slipped out of bed when she was asleep. I looked through a gap in the curtains at New Berlin. The city had been built on the old Berlin after it was destroyed. Every building was huge and imposing in the night.

It was like living in a giant graveyard. Albert Speer, Hitler's architect, was building more every day. The city was expanding like a cancer. Speer used forced labour. People had died so I could live in this luxurious apartment. God knows what Hitler would do with programmable slaves.

At street level I could see soldiers on the street corners, keeping order. A Mercedes-Benz Dreadnought flashed by with a Nazi flag on its roof, on its way to the Nazi Party Headquarters. No private vehicles were allowed out after the nine o'clock curfew unless the driver had a pass. Tonight, there were none. Everyone was living in a permanent state of fear. Fear of our own government.

I went into the kitchen and made myself some ersatz coffee with ersatz milk. It tasted awful, but it energised me. I read yesterday's newspaper. There wasn't much news, but I paused over one story. Hitler was returning to New Berlin tomorrow – today now – and he was holding a meeting with the war council about the deepening crisis in North Africa. It was expected he would authorise tactical nukes. The tone of the article suggested this was a sensible option. Tactical nukes! We'd tried that and millions had died on both sides! Frankenstein as Science Minister was a member of the war council. Knowing Frankenstein, he would no doubt back the proposals: his radiation experiments had developed a new anti-cancer drug that he wanted to test in a war zone.

I dressed and went down to the basement garage. I drove my BMW out onto the street regardless of the danger of being stopped without a pass. I headed for the autobahn. There was one checkpoint between my home and the institute. I slowed approaching it. There was a young army officer checking IDs. I showed him my doctor's licence.

"You need a pass, sir."

"I'm on my way to an emergency transplant – no time for a stupid pass."

"You need a pass, sir."

"I'll tell General Rommel that should I? I have his new heart in here." I patted my briefcase – which contained some papers and a two-day old sandwich I'd forgotten to eat. If he asked to see the heart, I was really in trouble. "Should I tell him I was delayed because of some corporal?"

"Th-that's all right, sir."

He waved me on.

*

SECTION D: AUTHORISED PERSONAL LEVEL 001 ONLY

"It's late, sir. This isn't your shift."

I looked at the guard and nodded. "Forget to analyse my data. Professor Frankenstein will be angry if I don't finish it."

He nodded in sympathy. He knew what I tyrant Frankenstein

could be. "He's in there, so good luck."

I slid my car over the scanner and hurried into the room. I walked to the programming room. There was nobody about. I opened the large cryogenic refrigerator and removed the vials of 1.13 containing 2.91. I thawed it out and loaded it into a syringe. It was then I heard someone cough. I spun around. It was Bauer.

"What're you doing, Christian?"

"I think some of the 1.13 has contaminated the 2.92. I was just getting a sample."

"That's interesting," he said, "because I just re-tested you 2.91. I was going to tell Victor, but first I wanted to ask you about it. It was successful, Christian. But you reported it as a failure."

"I can explain," I said, stepping towards him. Suddenly, he reached into his lab coat for a gun. I was faster, though. I had the syringe in his arm in an instant. He struggled, but already the virus was reaching his brain. As a last effort to stop me, he fired his gun through his coat. The bullets slammed into me – one, two, three – all hits to the chest – the pain incredible – and then he stopped firing and stiffened and his face became slack. I found myself on the floor bleeding to death, but I didn't care about that. I just hoped no one had heard the shots. The walls were supposedly soundproof. Quickly, quickly, I told him what to do ...

Now was the true test.

*

Into the light again … After months of existing in the darkness, I climb up the ladder and push open the hatch. I fully expect to see the Coast Guard – or someone, anyone – but the deck of the cabin cruiser is deserted. I am alone in the middle of a blue-green ocean, a light breeze rocking the boat. I crawl until I gain the strength to stand, then I walk to the wheelhouse. I find signs of recent habitation – cigarette butts, beer cans, discarded playing cards – but no crew. There is some blood, though. It is smeared like grease on the walls and windows. I was right about the danger of pirates. They must have killed the crew and taken away their bodies, which they could either use themselves or sell the parts of the organ market. I look for boats on the horizon, fearing their return. I see nothing. By hiding, I'd escaped their wrath, but how was I going to steer this thing myself?

I look at the endless ocean, wondering which way is west. I read somewhere you could tell the direction by looking at the sun. I can't see the sun in the sky because it is so bright, a solid white sheet of light. No clues there. I study the controls with growing alarm: they have been smashed. There is no way to drive this thing without them.

Cursing, I search the cabin cruiser from top to bottom, pausing only to fill my stomach with dregs from the galley and drink clean – clean? – water from the toilet. Eating makes me feel better, but then I make the mistake of opening the refrigerator. A human head rolls out and thuds onto the floor. The shock nearly empties my stomach, but I hurry onto the deck for fresh air. I don't know why it shocked me - not after the things I've seen - perhaps it was just the surprise of it. People jump when a balloon pops - but it doesn't mean they are scared of balloons.

I compose myself. The head … I go back and look at the features. It was the captain. He looks … preserved. I take his head up the stairs and give him a burial at sea. His head sinks without a trace. The head … It reminds me I haven't seen how I look after weeks hidden in the engine room.

I check out my condition in a broken mirror in the captain's quarters. I look pale and skeletal. The death camp really took its toll. The flesh hangs from my bones. I can see every rib. The serial number on my wrist looks like a purple wound. I hold it up and read it to myself over and over, remembering.

1995-25-02-70-1110110101-172A.

The serial number is a special code the Nazis use. It can be split up into components. The first four digits stand for the year of capture, the next six are the date of birth – in this case 25 February 1970 (the Nazis hadn't thought the system would be required into the 21st century, so they'd used only two digits for the year). The numbers in binary described physical features for identification purposes such as colour of eyes, colour of hair, colour of skin, height …

The man this body belonged to died in Frankenstein's lab in a failed test. Bauer had transplanted my brain into it. He smuggled the "dead" body out of the building, then returned to give Frankenstein an injection and his instructions. I was on my way to the coast by then.

If everything had gone as I intended, Frankenstein would have infected Hitler and the whole war council and instructed them to sue for peace at any price. Meanwhile Bauer should have destroyed the lab and all records so the experiments could never be repeated. Then he had been instructed to infect as many people as he could with his special programming - I called it a conscience, something we'd all lost over the years.

Hopefully, the war is over.

I walk onto the deck and hope.

There's something on the horizon.

A green smudge.

It looks like land.

I stare at it until my vision blurs.

Sickness Country

He stepped into the smoky room crowded with eighty white men between eighteen and sixty. The uranium miners had ended their shift an hour earlier and had been drinking much of their day's wages. They stopped drinking and talking to look at him. They were surprised to see a black man in their bar.

There was something wrong about his face – it looked leathery but with smoother, lighter patches. It was mostly hidden under a black hat with a crow's feather in its brim. He had long black curly hair over his shoulders and face. He looked as though he had stepped out of the Outback, formed from charcoal and oil, his hard eyes cut from obsidian stones. His dark, tattered clothes and the feather in his hat made him look like a human crow.

In silence, he walked to the counter and put down dollars, pointing at the Fosters bottles cooling in their cabinet. The bartender clearly did not want to serve him, but did so against his will. The stranger sat down on a stool and turned to face the miners, drinking the beer without saying a word. He took a long time drinking the beer for a man who must have been out in the sun all morning. For a few minutes, the only sounds in the bar were the ceiling fans and the murmurs of disapproval. He sipped his cold beer, moisture shining on his lips. When he was finished, he stood up again, the stool creaking like the bones of an old man. His dark eyes looked at everyone in the bar. Nobody returned his stare. Smiling, he strode out into the white, white sunlight, leaving eighty men staring at the closing door.

Jake Harrison was one of them.

*

Freedom was a strange place to live. The town had a way of twisting the past and present into a blur, as if the desert heat melted reality into something trapped in a bubble. There was always a feeling of déjà vu because every day felt like yesterday. The appearance of the stranger was something different. And yet Jake Harrison knew he would see the man again. It was a feeling he had as he returned to his store after lunch. With Christmas coming, the store was decorated with sparkling tinsel and plastic trees. A cheerful cardboard Santa Claus wearing sunglasses stood by the entrance next to the barbecue equipment. Jake was looking into the till when he heard the door open. Looking up, he saw the man was suddenly there, his black clothes flapping and swishing around him as if caught in a wind. But there was no wind – just the door closing. Jake shivered – he was cold all of a sudden.

"G'day," Jake said. He wanted to be the first person to hear the black man speak. But the man did not reply. Jake watched him going up and down the aisles, picking up camping equipment – the best stuff. He selected a tent and sleeping bag made of space-age materials. "You're camping nearby, mate?"

The stranger grinned but said nothing. He carried the equipment to the counter. The man gave off a smell like charred steak.

"Are you staying in town?"

The man nodded.

"What's your name?"

He did not answer. Something else had taken his interest: the book rack. He studied it, turning it slowly, choosing half a dozen sun-faded paperbacks. The paperbacks had been in the store for years, perhaps decades. Jake was not an avid reader of fiction, preferring to read the newspapers and magazines. Not many keen readers lived in Freedom. Jake just had to look at the street to see why: satellite dishes were perched on the houses like the ears of bats. The man added the paperbacks to his purchase. Jake totalled everything at over 400 dollars. To Jake he did not look like he could pay for cigarettes, but he paid with cash from a thick roll kept in his black overcoat. Was he expecting rain? Jake wondered. Wearing those black clothes, Jake would die of heat exhaustion in five minutes.

The man left, leaving behind a cool breeze.

*

Later, Jake saw the man camped out by the roadside within sight of anyone travelling in or out of Freedom.

There was a large mining area ten kilometres from the town. It employed five hundred people – mostly white. Three shifts of workers were bussed to the site and back to Freedom every day. The Aborigines would not work there even if they were given the choice. They called it "sickness country" and avoided the quarry, which from the sky looked like a multiple meteor strike, with its concentric rings of excavation. Thousands of years ago the Aborigines had known there was something dangerous in the land, but it had taken until the 1950s for Australian and British scientists to identify the vast quantities of uranium-rich rock. It had made Freedom a wealthy town – for some. The land was taken off the Aborigines many, many years ago, when it was perfectly legal. They earned nothing from the uranium mine. Their descendants were fighting back the 21st century way: suing the company for fifty years of mining royalties. The company had hired the best lawyers, arguing it was unreasonable for them to pay. The ownership issue was a sore subject with the workers living in Freedom, who saw the Aboriginal lawsuit as a threat to their jobs. Many saw it as a racial battle: white workers versus black activists. For a *black* man to camp outside their town was bound to cause trouble.

He sat in the shade of a rock the colour of blood, reading a book. He was in full sight of everyone, as if he wanted to remind them of his presence. He sat cross-legged, relaxed, immune to the heat and flies. He was as immovable as the gum trees and spinifex growing from the red soil. His tent was erected. It was like seeing a one-man protest against the uranium mining, though he did not have any placards or slogans. He was simply *there*. When the trucks drove by dust swirled over the man, but he did not react … except to turn the pages of his book.

It was as though he was waiting for something to happen.

*

"That nigger. You sold him camping gear?"

Jake looked up from his newspaper, feeling his chest tense up as he recognised the McGregor brothers. The brothers had short red hair and small blues eyes, shaded by blue baseball caps. Their heavily muscled arms were deeply tanned red and glistened with sweat.

"Who?"

Gary McGregor stared. "There's only one - the Crow."

So, he had a nickname now. The Crow.

It was better than calling him nigger, Jake supposed. Just.

"I sell my goods to anyone who can afford them."

"Not to niggers, you don't."

"If you've got a problem with him, see him."

"Oh, we will." Ian nodded in agreement. "But right now we're talking to *you*."

"Talking to *you*," Ian echoed.

Jake glanced at the security camera watching the store. Gary and Ian McGregor noticed it as if for the first time. Gary tapped his brother on the shoulder, whispering something in his ear. Ian smiled. They would not try anything with the security tape rolling, Jake hoped. But he could expect some kind of recrimination. "Are you buying anything?"

"No."

"Then you won't mind leaving."

Gary aimed a finger at him like a rifle, making a click-click in his throat. "See you, Jake."

Jake did not move until they had gone, but then he looked down at his hands and noticed he had crumpled his newspaper into a rag.

*

That afternoon Jake Harrison picked up his son Donald from school and drove homeward in his Toyota Land Cruiser. The sky was a white glare. They entered the suburbs of white houses with tall fences. Heat-drunk dogs barked as usual as Jake went by. Donald was eleven. The boy was sipping a Coca-Cola, listening to the radio. But Jake wanted to talk, so he switched it off. They had five minutes before they got home.

"Watch for the McGregor brothers," he told him. "They're mad at me, so be careful."

"What did you do to them?"

"Nothing," he said. "But they think I did. There's this man in town they don't like."

"You mean the big Abo?"

"Yes, him, but I don't want you talking like that. I don't want you using racist words like Abo. The word's Aboriginal. Better yet, use the specific name of the clan."

"I'm only saying what Bruce Newman said. He used those words, Dad. He used the word wog, too, but I didn't."

"Maybe so, but there's no excuse." Jake sometimes caught himself saying racist words, almost like a reflex to a situation. He only recognised its harm if Donald said those words, innocently brought back from school. Then he felt shame because the last thing he wanted was for prejudice to grow inside his son like a malignant tumour. He told Donald about the man visiting the store and then the McGregors' threat.

"I don't understand why they hate him. He's black – so what? What did he say to them?"

"He didn't talk to nobody - but sure made himself heard by the silence he made. In the bar I never seen so many fellas go quiet." Thinking about the reaction of the miners when the stranger ordered a beer made him smile. He could see their house ahead. The windows were shuttered against the sunlight. Kathy's car was in the open garage. Jake pulled into their driveway and coasted into the garage. He switched off the engine, but stayed inside the car, looking at his son. "The poor fella didn't actually do anything. But he turned that bar into a graveyard with a single look. Then he just walked out.

Nobody can figure why he was sitting out there by the road. I'm curious myself. I got the strangest feeling I know him. Like déjà vu."

"What's that, Dad?"

*

Déjà vu is 1960, the same place, a younger Jake Harrison.

Jake fell in love for the first time during the summer of 1960 when he was only ten years old, but his feelings were very real and very strong. It hurt him deeply that he could not tell anyone in his family about it. He hated lying to his father, but he could see no other way of living. That morning his father was waiting downstairs with a question.

"Where're you going?"

"Out," he said, lifting his cricket bat.

His father approved of cricket and wanted him to play for Australia. "Hmm. Get back at six for dinner."

Summer was cooler than winter in Freedom, but it was still hot – eighty degrees in the shade. Jake ran through the boiling streets and met up with George behind the railway station. George had a new ball. Kicking and throwing the ball, they crossed the tracks. Several Aboriginal families living in tin huts along the dry creek. Desperately poor, the adults did domestic work and odd jobs for the whites, but they were not allowed to live near them. The black children were not allowed to attend the white schools, so they had little education. It was a common sight seeing small black children dancing naked in the red dirt. Fat black men sat in the shade of corrugated tin shelters, looking straight through the two white children. The men were drinking from whisky bottles. The

Aboriginal men were frightening, but Jake and George continued past them to the flat ground where they played cricket. Jake would be beaten if his father knew he regularly came here to see Sam and Mary Tjakamara. Sam and Mary were under a gum tree, waving. Mary looked so beautiful with her hair tied up in braids. He loved her so much. He and George sat down under the tree.

"I've got some chocolate," he told his friends. Jake gave his friends a bar each that he'd stolen from his father's store. They ate them greedily, not suspecting where he obtained them. Jake did not want Mary to know he was a thief. She would not accept it if she knew.

The four of them often played football or cricket, but it was too hot and dry. So, they talked about Buddy Holly and the Crickets and Elvis Presley. Then Mary and Sam told him their father was going to buy a derelict building on Victoria Street. He planned to open a store where things could be bought cheaper than in the white-owned stores. The Aboriginal people needed a place to shop owned by one of them. Some white-owned stores would not sell things to them because of the colour of their skin – or charged too much. Jake knew all about this. His own father thought no Aboriginals should be living in Freedom. Since Jake was old enough to walk, he had heard his father's opinions. Darkies. Niggers. Coons. Spades. Mary and Sam were none of those ugly words. One time, when he was six or seven, his father had caught him playing with Mary. His father called her a dirty coon and chased her away. His father banned Jake from seeing her again. Jake stole from his father because of this and kept his friendship a secret. He loved his father but hated him too. George believed there were places in the world where skin colour did not matter, but Jake could not imagine such a place. (A few years later George would die in a far away place called Vietnam.) Every day, Jake saw how the white adults treated his black friends. His father's drinking friends would like to see them all destroyed. It made him sad and angry.

"We are going to paint the store green," Mary said. "Won't it be wonderful?"

Jake grinned. "A green house not made of glass. Wonderful."

*

He was home for six but immediately knew something was wrong by the silence. He entered the kitchen and found his mother cowering over the stove. His father was sitting at the table in just his string vest and shorts. He'd been drinking. When he stood up, he towered over Jake.

"Gary McGregor saw you coming back from across the tracks. From Darktown. You've been to see them coons. What have you to say for yourself?"

"I –"

The slap struck out of nowhere. He felt the pain in his jaw and tasted blood in his mouth. A tooth rattled loose. His father grabbed and twisted his arm and ignored the sobbed pleas of his mother. "I'm going to teach you a lesson, boy. You're never mixing with them coons again, understand?"

The pain in his arm was excruciating. Jake nodded and nodded, loathing his own cowardice as his eyes blurred. His father released his arm, but did not banish him to his room – not yet. His father slapped him again – harder, just for good measure. The blow knocked his head sideways. Blood dripped from the corner of his mouth with pieces of his tooth in it. His head hung down, mouth dripping blood. He could feel the bruises forming and the pain of humiliation, but that was not the worst thing - the worst thing was the jarring motion had knocked the stolen chocolate bars from his pocket. One – two – three. They fell one by one onto the dark linoleum and lay at his father's feet.

His father stared.

"Don't hit him again," his mother sobbed.

But his father already had.

*

After his father beat him, Jake missed school for two weeks. A doctor should have treated him, but his father did not want anyone to know what he had done – even he knew he had gone too far. The school was told he had chickenpox (though he'd had it before). Jake lay in bed, bruised and aching, wishing he could see Mary, wishing he could tell her how much loved her.

*

One day when his father was out working, Jake heard a light knocking at the door. His mother was busy hanging up laundry out in the back yard, so Jake, hurting with each movement, went down to see who it was.

There was nobody there.

But he found an old guitar resting against the wall. There was a note fastened between the strings.

Play this and think of me.

Love Mary.

*

Jake hid the guitar in the attic among the old dusty things and learned to play it when nobody was around. It was his secret. When his hands made music, he thought of Mary. He prayed for the day when they could be together again. But he never spoke to Mary after that – his father kept too close an eye on him. He wasn't permitted out of the house unless his father knew where he was going. It wasn't possible to sneak off.

Jake thought of her whenever he saw the new store across the tracks. The shop and living quarters above were painted bright green – the only green in the town, for most of the buildings were dull white or drab brown. The greenness radiated something more than just reflected sunlight. It bathed him in a good feeling each time he looked upon it. The Aboriginal store seemed to be a magical thing, like a garden blooming in the desert.

*

Déjà vu is 1970. His mother and father were away in the city for the weekend, leaving him to look after the store, where he worked for his father as an apprentice shopkeeper, a job he loathed. Unfortunately, Jake had failed at school and could not afford to move out of his parents' house. His best friend George was dead and Jake didn't have any others. Mary was living on Victoria Street, but she was married and had a baby. The only thing that gave him any pleasure was playing his guitar.

In the humid night, he walked to his window and opened the curtains, letting dry air enter his bedroom. The streets of Freedom were dark but the sky was not. The Southern Cross was bright and clear. The stars exhilarated with their cold, simple beauty. There was no moon, which made the stars clearer, the streets darker. It was now so quiet he could hear someone running in the dark, though he could not see anyone. He sighed and stretched. He collected his guitar from the corner. He sat at the window with the guitar in his lap, the wood cool and calming, oddly comforting, like a loving pet. He thought of Mary. He was tuning it when the sound rolled down the street, waking everyone in a radius of five miles. It was louder than thunder. It was louder than anything he had heard before or since.

It was an explosion.

*

Jake ran and ran towards the smoke and flames. Victoria Street was on fire. The source of the fire was the store owned by Mary's family. Flames burned through the roof and broke the windows.

There was a crowd of half-dressed white people watching the fire, but that was all they are doing - watching. They were not helping. Nobody was going near the green building – they all seemed relieved it wasn't spreading to their homes. Gary and Ian McGregor were drinking beers like it was a barbecue.

Jake yelled but nobody heard over the roaring flames. Jake pushed his way through the people, wanting to do something, but someone grabbed him. Their face was blackened by smoke. The man pulled him backwards. "Don't be stupid, son."

"What are you doing? I need to save them!"

"They're dead already."

"No! Let me go!"

The man did not leave go.

"MARY!"

Jake heard screams as the violent flames burst through the unbroken windows, spraying glass into the crowd. Fifty feet above the ground, someone appeared at the top window. The person was unrecognisable and on fire. The crowd went quiet as the body leapt through the window and dropped and hit the street with a sound like wet meat.

*

"Jake, what's wrong?"

He was restlessly switching TV channels, trying to find something interesting in the dull pre-Christmas schedules. Kathy knew his moods after twelve years: his taciturn behaviour that evening was a symptom of something bothering him. He had told Kathy about the day over dinner. Donald was in bed, and they had the living room to themselves.

"Nothing's wrong."

"Are you worried about the McGregors?"

"Partly. But it's not that. I was thinking about the fire."

"The fire?" Kathy said.

"It happened thirty years ago. It killed some friends of mine. Mary and Sam. And the rest of their family. They were Aborigines."

"Jake, why didn't you tell me about this before?"

"I don't know." He didn't, either. There were just some things he had never talked about with anyone.

"How'd the fire start?"

Jake looked ahead, thinking back.

"It was a freak accident."

"What happened?"

"They had crates of liquor stored in the back room. You know how I keep my drinks in the refrigerator cabinets? Back then people would store inflammable stuff in cool places, like their basements. Only their house didn't have one. It probably got too hot and ignited by itself. One night, ten boxes of whisky went up like a bomb. I remember hearing the explosion and coming out into the street to see the green house blazing. A big crowd gathered around their house, but the flames were too powerful to do anything. The explosion and the smoke killed them before they could get out. Mary saved her boy, though. She carried him to an upstairs window. She jumped out, screaming because all her skin was dripping off like wax. Her fall killed her but protected the baby in her arms. I still remember the smell. Like meat."

"Ugh," Kathy said. "Do you think that man is him?"

"The baby was so badly burned it was taken to a special hospital in Darwin where it wasn't expected to live. I'd hate to think that he did survive because those burns … those burns were the worst thing I've ever seen."

*

That night, Jake took his guitar outside and played it softly. The teenage Jake had thought his older self would be a famous singer-songwriter, probably living in Los Angeles, but Jake had never gone further than Sydney. All his life this town had ruled his behaviour, ruled him. His guitar was something he played at the weekends when his store was empty, but he needed to play it now. It was the only freedom he knew. A long time ago he had written a song entitled *The Green House* that made him cry whenever he sang it. Its sad, lonely rhythms brought back painful memories. As he played it again, he peered into the darkness and thought of the stranger.

He was a brave man, whoever he was.

Thinking back, Jake remembered the McGregor brothers drinking beers while Mary's home burned down. For thirty years, the obvious had been waiting to be recalled.

They were drinking a brand of beer not available in any of the white-owned businesses. A beer only sold in one place.

"Hey! I need some service!" Gary McGregor's voice reached into the stockroom. "Hey!"

Jake turned around and stepped to the door, where he could see the McGregor brothers. The brothers were the only people in his store. Gary was flipping through a row of Christmas cards. He *accidentally* knocked several onto the floor, but made no effort to pick them up. "Ah. Here he is. Say, Jake-o, the Crow was seen coming out of here this morning. What did you sell him this time – your soul?"

Ian sniggered.

What a double-act, Jake thought.

"I sold him nothing," he lied.

"Goodonya, mate," Gary drawled. "Maybe we got it wrong about you. You tell him his sort don't belong in Freedom?"

"He got the hint," Jake lied. Lying was easier and safer than the truth. "What do you fellas want?"

"Just come to tell you we're going to make him leave."

"How are you going to do that?"

"You'll see."

Chuckling, they left.

Jake walked to the window and saw Gary and Ian McGregor getting into their grey pickup truck. There was a baseball bat on the dashboard, which Gary grabbed. The pickup truck pulled away. It reached the street corner before going out of sight. Jake rubbed the light stubble forming on his chin, thinking. Going outside, the sunlight hitting him in waves, he walked into the middle of the street and looked into the distance, where the town ended and the desert began.

He thought he could see a green house, but that was impossible.

*

Someone was running down the road, running towards him without slowing down or seeming to notice him. It was Ian McGregor. His mouth was wide open. He looked as if he was screaming, but no sound was coming out.

*

Jake walked into the bar and ordered a beer and listened to the rumours already spreading only hours after Ian McGregor ran screaming into town and confessed to the arson-murders of the Tjakamara family.

Earlier, Gary and Ian had stopped their car beside the black man's campsite with the intention of beating him. Gary strode towards him with a baseball bat, but before he could swing it something happened – the man waved his arms and said something that caused Gary to burst into flames - first his hair, then his body ignited with bright orange flames. Suddenly, he was burning like a human torch. Instead of helping to put out the flames, Ian fled. When the police arrived, they found a smouldering heap of bones.

The Crow had gone.

The bar was filled with speculation.

Some people believed the Crow was Mary's boy seeking revenge, but another rumour claimed the boy had died of his injuries. Some people thought it was a case of spontaneous human combustion.

"What do you think, Jake?"

"Me? I just think the heat got to him."

The miner looked at him strangely, saying nothing.

Back at the store, Jake looked at the receipt in his hands.

It was for a pressure pump and hose and a can of kerosene.

He burned it.

The Midnight Murderer

"Here," Newton said.

Marilyn Monroe reached over and squeezed Ben Newton's hand painfully hard when he pulled the pink Cadillac past the GENUINE MAKAH INDIAN FOOD sign and into the diner's parking lot. The Cascade Mountains loomed over the diner as a blue, green and purple ridge, like the spine of a putrefying giant. Brooding black clouds clung to the snowy peaks, promising bad weather to come. Newton could see rain about six miles off, streaking the blue sky with grey and silver. He parked between two pickup trucks, then turned to Marilyn and pulled his hand free of hers. She scowled. His fingers throbbed when he flexed them. "That hurts."

"Good," Marilyn said, squirming in her seat. "Ben, I'm not going in there."

"But this looks just like the diner in Twin Peaks. Maybe it is the diner the Twin Peaks diner was based on. We've got to go in."

"Not dressed like this," Marilyn said, pulling up the cleavage of her flimsy white dress.

"I'm starving, aren't you?"

"Yes," she said, "but I'm not going in like this."

"So take off the wig."

"And let people recognise me? No way. Find me a shopping mall so I can buy some new things. *Then* we'll eat."

"Come on - there's no one around here to recognise you."

"I grew up in Seattle," Marilyn said. "Some of my old school friends might live around here. It's bad enough having my proper clothes stolen, without people seeing me dressed as a dead movie star as part of your kinky fetish, Ben." The words stung Newton, but not for the reason she said. Newton did not like to think of Marilyn Monroe or any of the Hollywood Legends as dead, for as long as their films were being watched they were alive, in a way. His girlfriend, Angel Shapiro, did make a good Marilyn. The fake mole was a nice touch. She picked it off and flicked it onto the asphalt, ruining the illusion. He could tell Angel was uncomfortable playing the role of Marilyn by the subtle way she mentioned it every ten seconds.

"I'm sorry, Angel. It wasn't my fault the suitcases were stolen while we were ..."

"In the seedy motel?"

He felt his cheeks burning. "It wasn't that seedy." Her stony look said otherwise. "Look, why don't you just say you're going to a costume party?"

"No," Angel said. "I'll stay in the car. Bring me out some fries and a cheeseburger and a diet Pepsi. You do what you like in there, Mr Wannabe Movie Writer. This girl is staying here where no one will laugh at me. Jesus H Christ, this is *so* humiliating."

*

"This is a damn fine cup of coffee," Newton said to the waitress, in his best Kyle MacLachlan impersonation.

The waitress looked blank, clearly under the impression he was some crazy Brit who had never tasted good coffee in his entire life. The heart-shaped nametag on her pink apron stated, "Hi, my name is Peggy". Peggy handed Newton the bill and offered a weak smile, then folded her arms beneath her breasts and stared with all the warmth and friendliness of minimum wage.

"Is that all, sir?"

"Yes, thank you." Newton looked through the windows at the pink Cadillac. Angel was sunk low in her seat, trying to remain invisible. He could feel her stare. Newton looked back at the waitress. He found himself captivated by her noticeably *large* breasts ... and guilty for the thoughts they produced.

"I can see a great view of Twin Peaks," he said, grinning, but the double entendre was lost. Peggy evidently was not a David Lynch movie fan. Worse, she probably thought he was a pervert.

"You paying for the meal, sir?"

Acutely embarrassed, he paid for the coffee, fries and burger using two ten dollar notes. Peggy sloped off to the counter.

While drinking his coffee, Newton scribbled amendments to his screenplay, Night Fears, crossing out some dialogue between the hero MIKE RYMAN and the STATE TROOPER. He turned to page 77, the big-scene:

Night Fears/By Ben Newton: Page 77

Slowly, STATE TROOPER walks to the side-window and flips open his helmet. His eyes go to the bloodstains on the passenger seat. He points his Smith and Wesson at MIKE RYMAN.

MIKE RYMAN

I didn't do it, man. I didn't kill her.

TROOPER

Sir, you-all gonna step outa the vehicle?

MIKE RYMAN

Man, I've been framed!

Stop, stop, stop. He could read no more. Now that he looked at it with his critical eye, it didn't sound realistic. If he wanted a big-shot Hollywood producer to give him the time of day, then it needed to sound, well, more American, not more contrived B-movie diarrhoea. He could not believe he'd written that old cliché "I've been framed" and all those "man"s. It made Mike Ryman sound like a hybrid of 1940s and 1970s stereotypes. Newton tore the page out of his ring-binder and scrunched it into a ball, leaving it on his empty plate. *Night Fears* was intended to be a darkly sinister suspense thriller, a *Psycho* for the Nineties. (Not like that pointless remake of *Psycho* starring Anne Heche, but something good.) Unfortunately, the first draft read like a bad TV movie. It was only when he reread it the mistakes burned like magnesium flares. What he needed were genuine Americanisms, a thoroughly realistic submersion in their culture and psyche. Watching Ricki Lake and Oprah was not enough. That was the purpose of his trip, to see America warts and all, the places off the tourists maps as well as the locations of his favourite shows. He'd spent two weeks in LA, soaking up the atmosphere, visiting the studios, and learning e*veryone* had written a movie script. Now was heading up the West Coast for a whistle stop tour of everywhere and anywhere. This holiday was the reason his bank balance was deeply in the red.

Newton looked around the diner at the other patrons with his critical eye, searching for characters he could borrow from real life. Unfortunately, the diners were mostly fat truckers and fat salesmen, as unreal as the characters in his screenplay. Boring. There had to be something interesting. Two obese children sat with their huge parents, working their way through the menu. Their grunted conversation sounded like pigs wallowing in syrupy mud. Near the toilets, a man with stringy cheese hanging from his open mouth (who looked like an extra from *Deliverance*) was counting his fingers to see they were all there ... but no one truly inspired Newton's creative juices. He finished the dregs of his coffee.

A chair scraped behind him. Turning, he saw two truckers standing up. One guy poked the other in the chest, laughing. "Hell, for all I know, you could be the Midnight Murderer."

The poked man dropped his smile. "No, you could be, *Hank*."

"Me?" Hank said. "Frank, I was joking."

"The Midnight Murderer's no joke. Maybe you're him."

"Don't you go saying that. You're the one with the knife collection in your rig. Where were you last Friday, huh?"

"With your wife, buddy."

Hank balled his fists. Newton was fascinated and horrified. These two friends were going to fight over some joke gone sour. Hank swung a punch, but his friend dodged it. Frank's fist connected with Nyle's gut. Hank doubled up, coughing. Then a Makah Indian rushed out of the kitchen with a machete and stood between them.

"Frank. Hank. Take it outside. You ain't fighting in my place."

"Humf," Frank said. "It's over anyway."

Both men left together. The Indian swept his eyes over the tables. "It's all right, folks."

"Excuse me," Newton said. "Who's this Midnight Murderer they were talking about?"

"You don't know?"

"I've been on the road for the last few days."

"Some psycho's been killing innocent people all over the state.

Ten so far."

"Oh." Something twisted in his chest. "Why's he called the Midnight Murderer?"

"Because he only kills folks in the midnight hour. That's why he's called the Midnight Murderer, see?" The Indian (or was that Native American?) returned to the kitchen, where he could be heard shouting. Newton was left with the image of the machete in his clenched fist, an almost casual pose.

Newton called over Peggy and ordered a slice of pecan pie and another coffee. He wanted to stay another few minutes, eavesdropping on the diners now he had something to listen for - rumours about the Midnight Murderer. The Midnight Murderer could add flesh to his own serial killer character. He shuddered just thinking about it. The psychological effect of an on-the-loose serial killer on small town America life was exactly the information he needed. As he watched the people with renewed interest, he could not help but think dark thoughts. What if one of these people was the Midnight Murderer? Was the guy in the plaid shirt and baseball cap secretly a madman? Or the thin black man eating on his own?

"He uses a hunting knife," someone said, the words coming from six rows away.

"Uh-uhn, it's a *machete*."

"A hunting knife. Two edged. Sharp as a razor."

Newton was appalled and riveted by their ghoulish fascination in the murders. Unless he had seen Britain's morbid fascination with the trial of Rosemary West, he would have dismissed it as a purely American trait. But there was nothing like a serial killer to get people talking. He wrote notes in the margin of his notepad until the pecan pie was eaten.

Peggy brought the bill. "This is definitely your last order?"

"Yes," he said. Then he realised she was expecting a tip. "Keep the change."

"Have a nice day," she recited. "If you want anything else, talk to Maria because my shift's over."

"Thanks," he muttered. Newton drained his second coffee, which was bitter. Perhaps the diner deliberately made the second cup awful to get rid of customers, he thought. Certainly, the atmosphere had changed to one of suspicion since the subject of the Midnight Murderer had been brought up. People were talking in hushed voices.

Forcing his notepad into his jacket, he looked through the windows at the pink Cadillac. Angel was waving at him frantically, pointing at her watch. He had forgotten all about Angel. Eating the pecan pie had taken twenty minutes.

She beeped the horn and performed a mime he guessed was for the food he had also forgotten. When he was in writer mode, his mind loved to wander off the tasks he had to remember. He stood up. Angel beeped the horn again anyway. Newton caught the new waitress's attention and ordered Angel's food.

"Is that to go, sir?"

"Yes," he said. "I'll pay after using your loo."

"Loo? Oh, you mean the john? It's way over there."

"Thanks." Newton walked past a handful of customers, avoiding their stares as Angel continued pressing the horn. They looked at him as if he were the Midnight Murderer. He reached the men's washroom and hurried inside. Once through the doors, he swore. Some holiday he was having. He used the loo (john, damnit, get in the spirit of things) and washed his hands and face in lukewarm water.

He was combing his hair when the door slammed.

A trucker brushed past him. His shirt was red and black. The trucker stopped at the nearest urinal, unzipped his jeans with a grunt. He urinated heavily, then he said something and spat into bowl.

Newton looked left and right. The trucker was definitely talking to him. "Pardon?"

"Hey, boy, you ain't gonna let your girl jess beep your horn?" The trucker zipped up and towered over Newton. Newton could smell the beer on him. "What you say, boy?"

"Um, right."

"There's something wrong with your voice?"

"No, I'll sort it out."

"That accent is goddamn strange."

"I'm English."

"I'm Irish-American, boy. I'm proud of my blood. You English scumbags been treating my people like dirt for centuries."

"Not me," Newton said, edging towards the door.

The trucker swung around. Urine spattered the tiles. "I don't like English. You guys think you better than us? You think you're better than me, boy? Do you? Do you?"

"No."

"I saw you making lewd comments to my wife, boy. Peggy told me all about you and your 'twin peaks'."

"It was a joke."

"I saw you looking at her."

"Must go," he said. Newton hurried out of the washroom and through the diner to the counter. The trucker burst out of the washroom. Newton collected Angel's order and left. As he was walking across the parking lot, he heard the trucker following him, barely ten feet behind. Newton could not believe it. He did not turn to look, in case he somehow antagonised the man.

"Hey, English boy, you listening to me? I said are you listening to me?"

Newton gritted his teeth. He turned his head. "Um, thanks for the advice. I'm glad you're proud of your roots, sir."

The man kept following him.

Angel was standing on the rental's passenger seat. "Ben, where the hell have you been all this time? I thought you'd come straight out with my food, but no, you forgot. Where's my food?" She grabbed the packages as he opened his door. "Jesus H Christ, I've been beeping for you for the last ten minutes!"

Newton could see the trucker still coming towards the Cadillac.

"Hey," the man said, "is she a hooker? You got a hooker in your flashy pink Caddy, English boy?"

"He called me a hooker," Angel said. "I'm not hooker, you creep."

"Shut up! I think he's insane."

"Don't tell me to shut up." Angel looked at the trucker, chewing her bottom lip. "I think we should get driving."

"Agreed," Newton said. "Where's the key?"

"You have it."

"I ..." He remembered it was in his pocket.

"Let's go," Angel said.

The trucker reached into his jeans.

For a weapon? Newton thought.

Newton could not feel get the key out with his nervous fingers.

The trucker walked slowly to the passenger side and leant over Angel, lighting a cigarette as he did so and blowing smoke in her face. "Lady, you got a real mouth on you. Maybe I'll close it with a kiss." He stared at Newton. "You got a problem with me kissing your whore, English boy?"

"Don't touch her," Newton said.

The trucker laughed and put one hand on Angel's chin, pulling her closer.

"Get your stinking hands off me!"

Newton pulled the key from his pocket and fumbled it into the ignition. The trucker was lifting Angel's mouth towards his own. She scraped her nails over his face, and he staggered backwards. Five red lines ran down his left cheek. Blood dripped down his neck. He touched the cuts, stared at the blood and launched himself at the Cadillac - just as Newton got the car moving backwards, the tyres smoking, the brakes screaming.

"Go! Go! Go!"

They left the trucker standing in the lot with his fists in the air. He was running for his truck as Newton accelerated onto the road, trees flashing past at sixty miles an hour. They could see no sign of anyone chasing. They both whooped in delight at their small victory, then the adrenaline dried up. Delight was replaced by cold shock.

"Jesus H Christ," Angel said, "what did you do to get that weirdo so mad?"

"Nothing." Newton explained, missing out Peggy from the story.

"This was because you're English?"

"Looks like it."

"He'll probably have scars."

"Good," Newton said. "He had no right to touch you."

"You think he'll call the cops on me?"

"After what he did? No. He deserved a lot more."

Angel opened the glove compartment, took out a Kleenex and wiped her chin. "God, his hand was so greasy."

"Maybe we should call the police on him?"

"No," she said, cleaning her fingernails of the man's blood. "Too complicated."

The road curved through dark green spruce trees. Big Foot country, Newton thought. You could loose an entire nation in these forests. Newton kept checking his rear-view mirror, but the road was empty. Angel ate the food, seeming to calm down. But he could see she was shaken by the experience. He drove in silence, glancing back every few miles. There was no one following.

When the trees fell away on Angel's side - to be replaced by a dangerous drop - she launched the Marilyn Monroe wig out of the car. It sailed over the edge like a white owl with no wings, falling and falling. Newton noticed Angel's eyes were wet.

"You're crying?"

"I can't help think about what he did. I feel used. Dirty." She wiped her face. Newton reached his arm across the seats, massaging her silky neck. She relaxed, closing her eyes. "At least the creep won't know what I look like, huh?"

"Yeah," he said. "I can imagine him talking to the cops. 'Marilyn Monroe scratched my face.'"

"Jesus H Christ," she said, laughing.

"Jesus H Christ indeed."

*

Little Falls appeared out of the drizzle as a ring of log cabins down in the valley. Rain spattered the hastily erected roof of the convertible, getting louder as Newton descended on the winding and near vertical road. Then they were in Little Falls, and the log cabins didn't look so small. Angel pointed at the Little Falls Shopping Mall and ordered him inside because she was too embarrassed. Newton entered the general store and walked through the food section to the ladies clothing department. The cashier, a dark-haired woman with thick eyebrows, watched him hunt for a pair of women's Levis, a bra, panties and a blouse. He felt as if he were a Satanist out shopping for sacrificial kids for the outdoor barbecue. Paying, he explained the clothes were for his girlfriend in the car, but from the way the cashier looked at him, she didn't believe him.

"You know Paul Hogan?" she said.

"Pardon?"

"The Australian, like you."

He was about to day he wasn't Australian and tell her he was English, when he thought of Peggy's husband and changed his mind. Maybe all of the people around here were English haters.

"Me and Hoges are like this," he said, crossing his fingers and winking. "G'day, cobber."

"Uh - right."

Newton walked out to the car and handed the shopping bag through the window. "I'm now an Australian transvestite, thanks to you."

Angel inspected the clothes, holding the blouse up to the light for what seemed like years, finally saying: "This is the wrong colour. I wanted vermilion, this is scarlet."

He glared. "It's all red to me. You women invent colours blokes can't see."

"Scarlet is okay," she said, climbing into the backseat. Angel stripped off the white dress and began dressing in the new clothes. If anyone had been walking in the rain, Newton thought, they might have seen a glimpse of her naked. It was funny how she could be shy one minute, then completely uninhibited the next. Like she was two different people. A schizophrenic. A psycho.

Now he was thinking about the Midnight Murderer again.

Wondering if Angel was the killer.

As a writer, he loved to play the 'What if?' game. What if Angel was the killer? He did not know much about her. He'd met her in a bar in Portland, and they had immediately hit it off. She'd been serving drinks to drunken construction workers. A wild, sexual chemistry as powerful as any drug had passed between them as she smiled, and for once it was not just in his imagination that a beautiful woman liked him. After her shift was over, he'd asked her for a drink. She said yes. He learnt she was only doing the job to pay for college. He explained he was only at the bar as research for his screenplay. A lame excuse, he knew, but it happened to be sort of true. The drinks were a bonus. Angel hated serving leering men. He told her to quit - and she agreed, just like that. Then something excelling his wildest fantasies occurred. They spent one week locked in a bedroom, just making love all day and all night. Glorious. When he'd suggested she join him on his tour of the USA and then go back to Britain with him, she'd said yes. That was two weeks ago and they'd still not made it out of the Washington State. He had vague thoughts about marriage. He thought back to the nights of the past two weeks. They'd done a lot of drinking and smoking pot into the small hours. He couldn't be sure if he had been awake between

12.00 a.m. and 1.00 a.m.

Maybe Angel slipped out to kill someone.

Using his rented Cadillac.

Using him as transportation.

And as cover. The happy couple, driving from place to place.

It was a stupid idea, he said to himself. But ... what if?

"Ben, what are you doing?"

Newton snapped out of his thoughts. He realised he'd been standing in the rain for maybe a minute. Cold water had leaked down his shirt and soaked his socks. Angel was in the driver's seat, waiting. He shivered.

"Something wrong?" she said.

"Nothing's wrong," he lied. "Hold on, I'll just get a newspaper."

Before getting back in the car, Newton bought a copy of the *Seattle Star* from a vending machine. The boldface headline **Midnight Murderer Kills Eleventh Victim** made him feel sick. He rolled it up and put it in his jacket for reading later. He was reluctant to return to the Cadillac, but he found himself walking that way automatically. *Angel is not the Midnight Murderer. She is not. She is not. They are looking for a man.* When he closed the door and was next to Angel, the space seemed very small and hot. *How much do you know about her? Nothing. You know nothing about her. She could be like Rutger Hauer in the Hitcher, and you're driving with her. No - worse - you're letting her drive*

Soon they were out of Little Falls, driving through forest.

"Aren't you going to read the paper, then?" she asked.

"Later," he said.

She did not press the subject.

"Where we going today?" she said.

He took his guidebook off the dashboard and read it with shaking hands. According to *The Great TV and Movie Location Book '99* the diner they'd visited that morning featured in the David Lynch TV Classic. Obviously, the guidebook had serious mistakes. Newton flicked through the pages to the letter T and down to the Twin Peaks reference just to check.

"Well?" Angel said.

The location was different from what he remembered. "Damn. It looked like the right place. I think I read this wrong last night."

"Face it, you were stoned last night. I told you were we lost."

"I know exactly where I'm not." He stared at the verdant landscape of evergreens and snow-capped ridges. A white RV rushed past in the opposite direction, sending up a plume of water. "*Twin Peaks* was filmed around here somewhere."

Angel grabbed the book, ripped out the page, wound down the window and threw it into the rain. The sheet flew away and glued to the road. It was squashed under the wheels of a dirt-brown sixteen-wheeler. "There. Forget *Twin Peaks*. Now let's have a real good time."

"That book cost twenty quid."

"So what?"

"You've ruined it. It was good research material."

"I've told you to give it a break, Ben. I gave up my job for you."

"But you hated your job."

"Yes, but that's not the point. Let's just have fun." She pouted deliberately and blew out a mocking kiss. "Boop-boop-bee-boop, as Marilyn would say."

"Okay, you choose somewhere."

"I will," she said.

Newton removed the *Seattle Star* with a rustle. He watched

Angel's reaction to the headline. Her mouth opened in surprise.

"What's that about? The Midnight Murderer."

"Don't know," he said. "I'll read it out." He had to turn the second page for the details. "The FBI and Washington State police forces are seeking an unidentified serial killer. The victims have been men and women, of a wide age range and racial groups. No attempt at hiding the bodies was made. The victims were brutally mutilated in a 'blitz attack' that rendered them unable to fight back in a matter of moments. The FBI believe the killer is a disorganised psychopath."

"What's a disorganised psychopath?"

"It means he doesn't think through his crimes. He just does them - compulsively, without premeditation. Maybe he doesn't remember them afterwards either."

"Yuck, he sounds sick."

"Very."

"Does it say where the bodies were found?"

Newton scanned the article. He listed the places, none of which they had been in at the time the murderers happened.

"It's scary knowing he's out there," Angel said.

It stopped raining.

Angel stopped the car. Turned off the engine.

The sixteen-wheeler passed them, and then they were alone.

"Where are we?" Newton said.

Angel opened her door. "You said choose somewhere. This is it."

"Angel -"

But she was out of the car and heading for the trees. Spinning around, she beckoned him to follow.

He wanted to stay in the car.

But she was unbuttoning her blouse.

She danced into the undergrowth. "Catch me and you can have me!"

He was out of the Cadillac in an instant.

*

Angel did not make his search too hard. She was about four hundred yards into the forest. As he approached, he could hear her splashing in water. He stumbled through ferns and brackens, almost falling down a slope of black earth into the clearing below. A small waterfall gushed crystal clear water into a rock pool. Angel's clothes were on the rocks.

"Angel?"

He climbed down the rocks.

Angel surfaced as he arrived, her naked body shining with fresh water. "You found me!"

"You knew this was here?"

"Of course," she said. Her voice echoed. "When I was fifteen I lost my virginity to Bobby Masters right here. Bobby was useless, but I kind of remember how good the water felt all around me, like cold silk."

The rocks were slippery. Some soft, green moss was growing on them. Though the sight of Angel in the water was enticingly - hypnotically so - he was reluctant to enter the water. It looked so cold and deep. He wasn't a good swimmer.

Now she was swimming on her back with long languid strokes that sent ripples towards the bank and arched her breasts towards the sky.

Newton reached the edge.

"Come in," she urged.

He kicked off his shoes. As he removed his shirt, he sucked in the cold air. This was the craziest thing he had ever done. He looked all around before slipping off his jeans and boxer shorts.

Carefully, he entered the water. He gasped at the startling coldness. But when he started moving towards Angel the chill faded. She stood up, with just her head showing above the water. The rest of her shimmered in mirrored distortion. Her arms reached for him, and he accepted her embrace.

*

Newton lifted himself out of the pool, feeling as heavy as an astronaut returning to Earth. He lay back on the rocks, folding his arms behind his head. The sun was out, baking the rocks and drying out the rainwater. He had never felt so at one with the universe. Had the pioneers of this great wilderness made love in such romantic surroundings? Probably not. He could hear Angel shaking her arms and legs, feel the water flying off her in tiny projectiles. He rolled over to watch her. It was an erotic Indian raindance.

"What are you doing?"

"Warming myself up. Try it."

He did.

Once they were dry, they ended up making love on the rocks.

"Let's get married," he said, suddenly, surprising himself.

"Yes," she replied.

"You're serious?"

"Aren't you?"

"I am."

They kissed and held each other.

As they dressed, Newton thought he saw something move, above in the trees.

A man.

Gone as soon as he looked.

"What's up?"

"Get dressed. Fast. I think there's something watching." He could no longer see anything moving, but he trusted his senses. There had been something watching.

The Midnight Murderer.

*

"Must have been a hunter or something," Angel said. "There are bears in the woods. Maybe it was a bear. Have you thought of that?"

Newton started the car, hitting the accelerator. He was jerked back into his seat. He swept his eyes over the trees, seeing shapes in the shadows that could have been a man, could have been anything. "Let's get back to civilisation."

"You think it's the Midnight Murderer, don't you?"

His hands crushed the wheel. "Maybe."

There was a sign up ahead.

REDWOOD 3 MILES

It was one of the places there had been a murder.

*

Redwood was ten minutes from the I-90, in an area between places, not even on his AAA map. There was no police presence in Redwood, and the people he did see were old and sleeping on park benches. The town consisted of a trailer park, a 7-Eleven, a Shell gas station and a motel called the Redwood Inn. The motel was shrouded by trees that practically hid it from the road.. There were no vehicles in the lot. Just the sort of place a man killer would pick. Eight days ago the Midnight Murderer had picked an insurance salesman sleeping in room 105 as his third victim. Newton slowed the Cadillac as he passed it, then did a U-turn at the first opportunity.

"What are you doing?"

"Trust me," he said. He rolled the car into the lot. There were no lights on in the motel and it looked deserted. A sheet of paper was nailed to the door.

CLOSED UNTIL FURTHER NOTICE

Newton rubbed his afternoon's stubble. "I'm going in."

"Why?"

"It's something Mike Ryman would do. He'd try to understand the killer, not wait for him to strike."

Angel shook her head. "Ryman's a fictional character, Ben. Your fictional hero. Real people don't look for trouble. If you really did see someone in the forest - and I think it's your over-active imagination - then we should contact the cops."

"Come on, let's go." He stepped out and waited for Angel. She did not move. "Not scared are you?"

"Yes, I'm scared. Of you. This is insane. You can't break in to a murder scene."

"I'm not going to. If there's no way in, I'll forget it. But I have to try - even if it's just for my screenplay, I have to understand." And if he's following us, he thought, it's the best chance we have. He stepped out of the car and walked to the door. He tested the handle.

It was unlocked.

The owner must have forgotten to lock up.

He pushed the door open. A swollen darkness greeted him.

A car door slammed. Muttering, Angel joined him at the door. "I'm not staying outside alone. I've brought the flashlight. Call me Nancy Drew, why don't you."

Newton edged inside. Angel snapped on the flashlight, waving a shaky beam across the reception desk. Newton saw there was no one there. There was a sign on the desk. WELCOME. Newton didn't wait around; he leaned over the desk and took the key for 105 from the hook. Angel nudged him in the ribs.

"Don't say a word," Newton said, "just follow." He headed along the hall to a stairway. The top was in darkness. His knowledge of movie trivia compared it with the scene from *Psycho*, when the detective climbed the stairs, only to be attacked at the top. "Give me the torch. Thanks."

The beam flashed over the wallpaper. He hurried up the stairs. Room 105 was at the end of the first corridor. Yellow police tape blocked the door.

Angel pulled at his belt, stopping him. "Ben, you're not thinking of going in there?"

The rational part of him said no, but the writer part, the part that needed experiences for his screenplays, had to. "This is where the Midnight Murderer's third victim was found. I have to take a peek. Just a sec."

"Jesus H Christ," Angel said.

Newton carefully moved the tape so he could put it back just how he found it. Then he opened the door. A smell lingered. Faeces and detergent. Taking a deep breath, he stepped through the threshold. The flashlight sent dust motes scattering.

The room had been stripped of everything except the bed and mattress. There was the hint of a stain on the mattress. A patch of floor looked as if it had been scrubbed.

Angel grabbed him from behind. "This isn't funny, Ben."

"No," he agreed.

He was closing the door when he heard footsteps.

*

"I'm sorry," he said.

Angel ignored him and played with the radio.

"We weren't the first people to have a look, the guy said so. Besides, the money sorted it out."

Between country music and Christian Talk Radio, Angel found a news channel and turned up the volume.

" ... the police have issued a state wide warning that the Midnight Murderer could strike again. FBI roadblocks have been set up in an effort to find the serial killer, but so far their efforts have failed. Residents are asked to lock their doors and windows and be on the look-out for anyone suspicious. If possible, people should stay in large groups until the midnight hour is over ..."

Angel nudged Newton in the ribs. "Are you suspicious, Ben?"

"Very. I'm an Australian transvestite, remember?"

"What do you think the Midnight Murderer looks like?"

"I reckon he's a guy my size, with a girlfriend who talks too much."

"Very funny." She paused, thinking. "Anyway, Mr Sexist, you don't know he is a man."

"The Midnight Murderer's a man, I think." Up ahead, there was a set of traffic lights on red.

"The FBI *think* he's a man. He could equally be a woman."

Newton raised an eyebrow. "How could a 'he' be a women?"

"Don't be pedantic. You know what I mean. It's possible. I read that fifty percent of serial killers are women, it's just they are smart enough to avoid *detection*."

"Is that comment aimed at me?"

"Yes."

Newton slowed at the intersection. The red light was taking an interminably long time to change and there didn't seem to be any traffic going the other way. In fact, the road was empty of vehicles for as far as he could see.

He heard the squeal of brakes and turned to see a brown sixteen-wheeler pull up behind him, so close the cab was practically in the back seats. The same brown sixteen-wheeler he'd seen earlier. Its engine revved ominously. The driver's features were obscured by the glare of the headlights, but he guessed who it was. The truck's engine revved to a crescendo. Angel turned round on her knees and swore at the driver. The truck's horn blasted painfully loud -
and the sixteen-wheeler shunted them into the intersection.

Angel fell over into the back seats as Newton struggled to start the car.

The lights changed green. The truck pushed them forward, catching the edge of the fender. It turned the Cadillac a full 180 degrees, scraping all the paint off one side. Newton saw the scarred man behind the wheel, flipping a single digit up, then the truck hurtled out of sight.

"Angel, are you okay?"

"Uh-huh, I think so. Hurt my head a bit."

"I don't believe that guy. He must have followed us from the diner. He's something out of Spielberg's *Duel*." He stepped out and examined the rear lights, which were broken. "I hope these are covered by the insurance."

"You know what I think? I think he's the Midnight Murderer. Nobody else would follow us all day."

Newton chilled. He didn't want to think about it. But he had to agree. A trucker would know every route by heart, could have chased them on a parallel road without them knowing a thing. A pink Cadillac was an easy object to spot, too. Newton started the engine, but in his haste he caused a stall. Then he got it going.

"Damn, now what? Go back to Redwood?"

"No. Turn left. We know the creep will take time to turn around. He won't know which way we've gone."

"We have to report this now."

"Don't worry," Angel said. "I got his licence plate. Find a pay phone and I'll report the him."

*

But there was no phone box on the road. Endless trees lined a road little more than a dirt track in places. He could drive little faster than forty, and only then for short stretches. There were pits and fallen spruce in their path. "Maybe we should turn around?"

"And have him waiting for us?" Angel said. "There has to be

somewhere if we keep going."

*

But there wasn't somewhere. There were no side roads. It was as if the road had been designed to take the unwary driver to an excursion to No Where and keep them there until they ran out of gas.

The sky turned purple, and then night was upon them. The car snaked along the edge of a ravine at under thirty, its headlights sweeping over the edge and into blackness. The gas tank was in the low to empty. Newton was reminded of Dennis Weaver being chased by an anonymous petrol tanker along lonely stretches of desert highway, suddenly appearing just when he thought he was safe. The comparison made his grip on the wheel tighten.

DAUNTON POP 348

Newton was pleased to see the lights of civilisation sparkling between the trees. A fuzzy yellow glow grew larger. It was a bar, a garage and a few cabins. Angel pointed out the phone booth outside the bar. He pulled over into the garage lot and parked facing the bar. He looked for signs of the sixteen-wheeler among the pick-ups and trucks, but he could not see it.

Angel searched her purse and located some change in her handbag. "Watch me in case some maniac comes along."

Newton nodded and watched. She was safely inside the booth before he leant into the back and pulled the top up, securing it fast. With the Midnight Murderer still loose, he didn't want somebody creeping into the back seats. He'd seen too many horror films to be suckered like that. By the time he had finished and filled up the gas tank, Angel emerged from the phone booth and was smiling. She crossed the road. "I've just talked to the sheriff."

"And?"

"He caught the guy doing eighty miles an hour. He's in custody. His name's Wayne Kenson. Apparently, he's got list of convictions a mile long for dangerous driving. The sheriff is going to send a deputy out to take photos of our car so he can charge him with it and maybe get him for the Midnight Murderer as well, if there's any proof. He says we should stay here and he'll have a car sent out which should get here in an hour or so. Meanwhile, I want a drink. You're buying."

Newton had wanted to visit a real American bar to soak up the ambience for his screenplay, so it was with trepidation he entered the bar. It was loud and crowded and just the way Mike Ryman would have liked it. It looked as if all 348 of Daunton's people were inside. They picked a couple of stools at the counter. Angel wanted a white wine spritzer, Newton drank coke. Secretly, Newton took out his notes and observed the people and their culture. Culture consisted of people sitting on stools watching MTV, drinking Buds and shorts. They got talking to some Microsoft workers based in Seattle, young executives spending the weekend on a drinking and fishing binge in the mountains. Jocks played nine-ball pool and talked about the kind of football you needed shoulder pads to play. Newton challenged a cocky jock to a game of pool and lost. Angel challenged the same man and won with four balls left on the table.

"He let you win," Newton said to grate her nerves, "because you're a woman."

"Want to play me?" she countered.

"No," he said, laughing. "You'd only get upset."

Angel wandered over to the bar, spoke to some guys and returned with some hand-rolled cigarettes. "Want some grass, Ben?"

"Now? Are you crazy? With the cops coming?"

"Aw, we just helped convict the Midnight Murderer." She lit one up, inhaled. "I just need one to relax. Nobody's going to bust us around here." She offered him the cigarette. The marijuana smoke was sweet.

"Not now," he said, though he was tempted.

"Suit yourself," she said, drawing a second drag.

*

"Deputy Rawlins," the cop said, taking a seat at their table.

Newton's stomach churned, he could see Angel's eyes were dilated and she was far too mellow.

Deputy Rawlins did not notice because he seemed too interested in her breasts.

Angel giggled the whole way through her statement, taking six tries to get the license number right.

"She's had a long day," Newton said.

"As long as you are driving, sir." The cop touched his mirrored sunglasses and tipped his cowboy hat. "Folks, you be careful, okay? Remember the Midnight Murderer is out there. Don't be a victim, be a survivor."

"We won't," Newton said. "So you don't think this Wayne Kenson is the killer?"

"We're investigating him, but it looks like he'd got an alibi for at least two of the murders - his wife. She could be lying, of course. We'll investigate that and keep him in custody for the crimes we can already get him for. Anyway, there's no harm in being extra cautious, sir. The Midnight Murderer could still be out there." Rawlins left, his white shoes squeaking on the sawdust floor.

Newton listened for the siren but was disappointed by the silence. The cop had managed successfully to put him in a bad mood, leering at Angel.

Angel lit another cigarette, holding it in front of his face. "You look like you need this."

*

Nicely buzzing, Newton half-carried Angel outside, where she was sick on the bonnet of a green Bronco.

"Ben ... I love you. I really, really do."

"Just don't vomit in our car, babe."

They stumbled to the Cadillac. Newton checked the rear seats before he lifted Angel in, then he got in the front. He was edgy for some reason. Maybe it was the cop's warning. Maybe it was because he was dog tired, like Dennis Weaver was after tricking the bad guy over a ravine. Maybe it was the grass. Newton hoped the owner of the green Bronco would understand about the vomit, but right then he needed to find a hotel and crash out for the night. While Angel lolled drunkenly in her sleep, he had time to consider things. If he were writing a script, the Midnight Murderer would not be someone as obvious as Scar Man. A thought sneaked up on him like Jaws chasing Roy Schneider. He almost steered him off the road.

Deputy Rawlins had been wearing *trainers*.

"Angel, wake up!"

She moaned in her sleep, but stayed unconscious even after he shook her.

He ran the encounter with the cop back in his mind. Yes, the white shoes had been trainers. No real cop wore trainers. So, he was a fake cop. A fake cop could move around just like the real ones. Newton thought about going back to the bar and calling the real police. But what if the fake cop was waiting? No, better to continue. He checked the rear-view mirror, saw nothing behind.

Maybe the fake cop was driving with the lights off.

After all, hadn't the trucker managed to follow them all day?

He hit the accelerator.

*

The motel glowed purple as though it were radioactive. A neon sign advertised vacancies. There had to be a phone inside, Newton told himself. He just hoped Norman Bates wasn't the owner. He parked as close as he could to the office and rocked Angel awake. Her eyes were unfocussed; he couldn't get any sense out of her. "Stay in the car, Angel."

She nodded, trying to pull herself together.

He ran to the office and found the screen door locked. He rapped his fist on the glass. A light switched on and the owner peered out, holding a shotgun. He was an old man with a post-cancerous voice that rattled in his throat like Jack Palance's. "What you want?"

"Can I use your phone?"

"All the rooms have phones. You want a room?"

"No -" The man turned away. "- yes, a room would be good."

The man unlocked the screen door. He kept the shotgun on

him. "Can't be too careful with the Midnight Murderer loose. Take the money out real slow." He accepted cash. "There's an extra fee for towels and I expect you out by ten tomorrow morning or I charge for two days. You want the porn channel it's five dollars extra."

"I think we'll make it up ourselves."

The owner winked as Newton went back to the car, coming outside to watch Newton help Angel out of the car. She had sobered up a little more, but her blouse was a mess and stunk of vomit. The old man stared at her with his groin. "You want help with her?"

"No." Newton guided Angel towards the motel room. The motel owner got bored, slung the shotgun over his shoulder and went back to his place.

The door opened into a small bedroom with another door leading to a presumably smaller bathroom. There were flowers on the dresser - plastic orchids - and next to them the phone.

Newton dragged Angel to the bed and sat her down. Then he grabbed the phone and stabbed nine-nine-nine. He waited for it to connect. A recorded voice told him the number did not exist. Of course, he was in America not Britain.

Angel sat on the bed stripping off her blouse while he tried again, this time hitting nine-one-one. He listened to it ringing, six, seven times. He suddenly remembered he had not locked the door. Stretching the cord to its maximum, he crossed the room. He bolted the door, secured the chain and pushed a chair under the door handle. He closed the curtains, just to be sure. No need to advertise their location. Angel staggered into the bathroom where he could hear her gagging in the sink.

"County Sheriff's office, can I help you?"

"Hello, I believe I may have seen the Midnight Murderer."

The dispatch officer sounded bored when she asked him to describe the incident. Evidently, he was not the first call of the night. He told her what had happened at the bar. She said she would investigate the matter by contacting Sheriff Morton as soon as he got back from an incident. She took the address. Then she hung up on him.

*

Newton heard Angel in the shower, screaming that it was too cold, then too hot, too cold. He closed the bathroom door so he could listen for the phone. He paced the room and checked the windows and doors a dozen times. He heard the shower stop and a deep thud.

"Angel?"

There was no reply. Steam billowed under the door like the fog in John Carpenter's horror movie. For once, Newton wished he had not seen so many films. He did not want to open the door. Did the bathroom have a window the Midnight Murderer could have entered through? He didn't know. What if the Midnight Murderer was in there, in there with a knife to Angel's throat?

"Angel?"

"Ben ..."

He pushed open the door and saw Angel on the floor, naked, blood in her hair ... his heart pounded and he twisted to face the door, expecting someone behind it. There was no one. He turned back to Angel and walked across the soapy floor. Angel opened her eyes.

"Ben, I slipped."

"Thank God," he said. "I mean ... thank God you're all right."

He had trouble getting her to her feet. She had bruised her head on the shower stall, but it was a minor cut to her scalp, just below above her ear. She sat on the toilet lid and touched her scalp. "Ow! Jesus H Christ! There are some Band-Aids in my handbag."

"Where is it?"

"I brought it in with me. Under my clothes."

He went to the bedroom and found the handbag. He rooted inside blindly, touching lipsticks, tissues, Tampax, a spare toilet roll ... eventually he felt something cold and metallic which cut his fingers. Angry, he emptied the handbag on the bed.

His eyes widened.

It was a knife.

A knife with an extremely sharp blade.

"Ben?"

He spun around. Angel stood at the doorway wrapped in towels, steam billowing around her. She was looking at him oddly.

"Yes?" he said.

"My head is bleeding, remember? And bring my toothbrush and the Colgate."

"Of course ..." He gathered the Band-Aids and dental junk and walked to the bathroom, sticking a plaster on his own wound as he did so. "Babe, can I ask you something?"

She grabbed the plasters and stripped the cover off one. "Yes, but first put this on."

When he pressed the plaster on the wound, she gave a little wince and pulled away. "What do you want to ask?"

He wanted to ask why there was a knife in her handbag, but he thought of the blitz attacks. "Nothing."

"You're a strange one," she said.

"Uh-huh." He returned to the bedroom. After making sure Angel wasn't looking, he picked up the knife, turned it over in his hands. It could easily cut a throat, or worse. He looked at the phone and thought about using it again. What if it was just protection? What if it wasn't? What if she had not called the police when she said she had, but had called the fake deputy, her accomplice in crime? That would explain why she was so desperate to get him to smoke grass before the cop arrived, then afterwards. Maybe she'd not been inhaling, and had just put her fingers down her throat to make herself vomit. What if? What if? He put his hand on the phone and hesitated. There was paranoia and there was *paranoia*.

"You need proof," he said, watching the bathroom door. Nevertheless, he put the knife in his jacket for safekeeping. He switched on the television, looking for news on the Midnight Murderer, or on the trucker supposedly caught earlier. All three - Angel, the cop and Scar Man could be in collusion. He could hear Angel running water into the sink as she brushed her teeth. He wondered if there were razors in the bathroom.

The wall clock read 11.55 p.m..

His watch read 23.55.59. Now 23.56.00. Four minutes.

"Phone, ring damn you."

He stared at the phone.

He stared at the bathroom door.

And at the entrance.

He waited.

And waited.

The Midnight Hour

Newton peered through a gap in the curtains. He could see the headlights of the Cadillac were on. He could not remember if he had left them like that. Had someone had switched them on? He could see no one outside - though the quadrangle was mostly in shadow, so that didn't mean much. The car battery would be dead in the morning unless he went outside.

He felt the knife in his pocket. It offered little comfort. "Angel, I've got to go out to turn the headlights off. You'll be okay?"

"Yeah," she said from the bathroom.

Cautiously, he unlocked the door and looked out. He could see nobody around. He stepped out and locked the door after him. Then he dashed towards the car. As he got closer, he realised there was something wrong. There was something out of place. He approached slowly, taking time to look under the wheels in case the Midnight Murderer was hiding beneath, telling himself as he did so it was ridiculous. There was no one there. He checked the interior - no one - and deactivated the headlights, then he circled the car. He studied the trunk from a distance with the flashlight. There was damage where Scar Man had rammed it.

And it looked as if someone had levered the catch. The way the metal was marked it had to be someone who had been hiding inside.

Hiding inside.

The man in the forest.

Waiting for midnight.

With the knife in his right hand, he popped the trunk open with his left.

It was empty.

Now it was empty. Which meant -

"Angel! Get out of there now!"

He ran back to the motel room. He found the door open and the lights off. He stopped outside, breathing hard. He shone the beam through the door. The room looked empty. He entered, flashing the light on the bed, curtains, phone. The phone was making a strange undulating noise. It had been taken off the hook. There was a tool bag on the carpet.

Newton shone light on the bathroom door. There was blood on the handle. He kicked the door aside and saw Angel.

"No," he whispered.

She came towards him clutching her throat, blood bubbling between her fingers, spattering her chest and the floor. She stepped forward and tumbled into his arms. Her blood was hot, soaking him. There was nothing he could do to stop the flow. There was just too much. Her lips moved silently, blood dribbling from the corners, then her eyes became fixed, lifeless, and she stopped moving and was a weight dragging him down. He held her, hoping against hope he could save her. But she died in his arms.

The bathroom light came on.

The Midnight Murderer stood in the doorway, calmly wiping the killing blade clean with a towel.

Newton had never seen the man before. He was a muscular man, very hairy. He was naked from the waist up. A beard soaked crimson hid his face, but his brown eyes shone.

Angel slid out of Newton's grip.

The Midnight Murder looked at Angel's body and then at Newton. Newton stepped back, raising the knife.

"Touché," said the Midnight Murderer raising his knife,

advancing.

Newton's rage exploded. He launched himself at the Midnight Murderer, his momentum carrying them into the bathroom. The Midnight Murderer brought his knife down, down into Newton's shoulder, tearing the muscle and skin and causing him to cry out. The Midnight Murderer yanked the blade free and plunged it again, going deep, striking bone. They collided with the wall so hard the tiles cracked behind the Midnight Murderer. Newton hacked his own knife across the Midnight Murderer's arm. The killer lost the knife as blood spurted from his wrist.

Newton started to feel his own pain.

Roaring, the Midnight Murderer scratched at his eyes, clawing rents in his cheeks. Then they were fighting for control over the knife in Newton's hand.

Newton grabbed the Midnight Murderer's head by the chin and rammed it against the wall. He repeated it while the Midnight Murderer flayed wildly, desperately clawing with his dirty fingernails for something vital. One final thrust whacked the killer's head into the tiles. Newton heard the Midnight Murderer's skull crack, smearing the wall deep red. He continued pounding the killer's head against the wall until his strength ran out.

Newton dropped the Midnight Murderer to the floor.

The Midnight Murderer did not move.

He heard the wail of sirens.

Too late, he thought. Angel's dead.

Newton kicked the Midnight Murderer's face to a pulp to make sure the killer was dead, then he picked up Angel's body and carried her out into bright, flashing blue and white lights.

*

There were five police cars and twenty police officers outside with their guns trained on him. A TV van pulled up and its crew started filming. A helicopter hovered over the motel, casting a circle of bright light on the lot as powerful as the summer sun. Deputy Rawlins aimed his gun at him. Newton rested Angel on the ground and held up his wet hands.

"The Midnight Murderer's dead."

"Not until after your trial, you sicko."

Newton protested his innocence, but his words were drowned by a swarm of police. Deputy Rawlins handcuffed him and forced into a police car. Cops squeezed in beside him, and two jumped in the front.

"There's another body in here," someone said from the motel. "Must be the girl's boyfriend."

"I'm her boyfriend," Newton said.

"Shut up," Rawlins said. "Tell your lies to the jury."

"I am telling -"

"You kept the boyfriend in the trunk," Rawlins growled. "You then played a sick game with us, taunting us with the girl. Making her call the cops. The FBI told us all about the sick games you guys play with victims. We already have someone who saw you go back to the Redwood Inn. And I bet there are other witnesses."

Newton sat grimly as the car passed the TV cameras. Tomorrow his face would be in every American home. In a week, someone would have written a screenplay about him and got the interest of a major Hollywood producer. His own screenplay would be used as evidence for the prosecution.

He could see photographers taking pictures of Angel.

He turned away.

"What about forensic evidence? Check the guy's hair, fingerprints and DNA against any found at the crime scenes. You'll see I'm telling the truth. He's the Midnight Murderer, not me."

"You know you didn't leave any," Rawlins said. "You scrubbed the crime scenes clean after each murder."

Newton looked at the deputy's trainers. He laughed because there was nothing else he could do.

"Don't tell me your usual boots have a hole in them?"

"Yes. What's it to you? Keep your eyes looking straight ahead or I'll mace you in the face."

Newton looked at his stark reflection in the rear-view mirror.

There was blood on him. The blood was scarlet. Or was it vermilion?

Did it matter? Red was dead.

He wondered what Mike Ryman would do in this situation.

A sarcastic one-liner.

But in real life, there was nothing he could say.

The Faintest Echo

The day after Billy died I went insane.

Leaving Abby with her mother, I drove back to the farmhouse. The farmhouse squatted beneath the brooding Highland peaks, waiting. Our home for the last few years, it now looked ugly and sinister, as though its true nature had finally been uncovered. I entered the kitchen with a hammer. Hunching down under the sink, I felt around in the darkness until I was touching cold metal. I burst the water pipe with one blow, hitting the pipe again and again until I was knee-deep in water. I loathed the pipe; I wanted to destroy it totally. It had lurked in the farmhouse for ninety years, pumping lead into the drinking water. That lead had killed my boy.

Growing exhausted, too tired to feel angry, too tired to feel anything, I waded out of the kitchen, carrying the length of pipe. I dumped it on the gravel path. Then I went around the farmhouse and pulled the rest of the pipe free from the stone wall.

I should have felt some satisfaction, but I did not.

I trudged across the muddy field, until the farmhouse was out of sight. I tossed my keys in the mud and stamped on them, burying them. I could feel tears building up, thinking about Billy in his red wellingtons, splashing in the mud, squealing with delight.

"Look at me, Daddy! Look at me!"

I could almost hear him.

I thought that if I turned round I would see him.

But he was not there.

I returned to our Land Rover and drove down into the valley, hoping never to see the farmhouse again.

*

But it was a buyer's market. And nobody was buying a farmhouse ten miles from anywhere. Abby and I could either live in the farmhouse or leave it empty, though we could not afford another home. Returning was inevitable. It was like coming back to the scene of a crime. The lead pipes may have been replaced with plastic, but the memories were fresh. Abby was still wearing the sunglasses she'd worn at the funeral.

"Come on," I said, "it won't be that bad."

"Right," she answered, dully. She had been taking Valium, again. I went round and opened the passenger door. Abby held the Valium bottle tightly, as if it warded off evil spirits. I helped her out of the car, though it was hard to get hold of her because she was so limp and resistant. While prising the bottle from her hand, I gently closed the door behind me. I guided Abby into the farmhouse and struggled up the stairs to the master bedroom. As I tucked her in bed, she instantly fell asleep, then I carefully removed her sunglasses and set them on the dresser.

"I love you," I whispered, leaving her to rest.

The door to Billy's room was partially open, as it had been left. A Pokemon poster drooped from the wood, its upper tacks unstuck. I fastened the poster in place and entered the room. It smelt of crayons and plasticine. On the floor, Billy's Lego dinosaur models lived in a prehistoric landscape. His bed was unmade. I looked at the bloodstained pillows.

And I could hear Billy retching, retching in the night.

I took the pillows downstairs and hurled them in a bin bag. To take my mind off things, I did some cleaning up. Afterwards, I retrieved our laptop PC from the car. I had to get back into a working mode - to do something than think about Billy - so I put the computer on the kitchen table. Abby's uncompleted thesis was the first document I saw listed on the directory. I felt my chest throb, wondering if she would ever be able to write another word, if she would ever be the same woman I'd married. I moved the trackball down to Microsoft Access. I was an accountant for a number of small firms. It was the core of our finances while Abby worked on her doctorate. Unless I put some work in to update the data, I'd lose my clients, lose the house and lose my wife to Valium. Despite the sounds of water grumbling in the new *plastic* pipes and the freezing cold air seeping through the stone walls, I managed to get some work done.

*

A nightmare woke me at the table, where I'd fallen asleep with my face buried in my arms. The laptop's screen was blank. With anger, I realised I'd left it on all night and the batteries were dead. Looking at my watch, I saw it was 5.30 am. I'd slept through till dawn. I couldn't sleep any longer without getting a headache later, so I went outside and stretched my muscles in the frigid air, taking deep gulps. I walked to clear my head. I headed towards the northern hills. It was a stiff climb but I didn't feel it in my legs. In fact, I was a mile from the farmhouse before I was out of breath. Down in the northern valley the mist drifted lazily. Through gaps in the mist, I could see sheep clustered in one of Angus Seamore's fields. Billy had liked to count them, even identifying them individually. I walked along the high ground, going nowhere particular, just walking through the brutally beautiful landscape.

Suddenly a wind howled around me, billowing my shirt and trousers. I felt it pull at my right sleeve, like a small child tugging for attention.

(Like a small child?)

There are moments when you know something is going to happen that will change your life. I had that feeling as I looked down at my sleeve.

And saw Billy. Alive.

I couldn't believe it. It had to be some other boy, not our Billy. Our Billy was dead. Yet the small boy clasping his blue mitten into my hand and tugging urgently was Billy. It was impossible. But it was real. It *was* Billy. I didn't feel as if I was dreaming, surely I would know that.

"What? How? Billy?"

Billy was staring up at me with his pale green eyes. He looked confused and scared.

"Dad, I want to go hooooome. *Now.*"

I had no answer. It *was* Billy. There were no mistakes. I recognised my own son – this was not my imagination. Before I could ask questions, Billy set off towards home.

With tears in my eyes, I chased him, afraid that if I didn't keep my eyes on him he would disappear like the morning mist.

*

"Abby, wake up." She moaned and pulled the duvet over her head. I pulled it back, shaking her. "You've got to wake up, Billy's alive."

She opened her eyes then and sat up. "Don't joke. Please."

"I'm not," I said. "Billy, can you come in."

Billy stood at the door, obviously bewildered. "But I want to play, Dad."

"*That* isn't my baby," Abby said, quietly, curling herself into a ball. "This is a dream."

"No, it's not." I was so excited my voice sounded like a teenage girl's at a rock concert. "He's real! I found him over by Angus's farm. He doesn't remember how he got there, but it's a miracle."

I beckoned Billy forward. He stood by the bed. Abby reached out her hand and touched his face.

"He's cold."

"Of course he's cold. He's been outside."

"But ... but ... Billy?"

"Mum? What's wrong?" He started to cry. I patted his head and told him there was nothing wrong, that he could go and play.

Abby's reaction wasn't what I expected - I expected her to be happy, to accept Billy's reappearance as a miracle. But she looked at me as if I had brought a rat into the house. "That thing is not my son."

"Talk to him. See for yourself."

"No. Billy's *dead*. This is a cruel joke or something."

"But you saw him. It is Billy."

She got out of bed and peered down the landing at the boy playing Jurassic Park. "No, no, no. That thing is something else. A ghost. A demon. Something evil. I can feel it. Get it out of here."

I wanted to slap her for being so suspicious.

I put my hands on her shoulders. I could feel her body shaking. I spoke softly. "I think that I somehow brought him back by thinking about him, wanting him back so much. Thought translated into matter. I don't know, but the fact is he exists and he is our son."

"Roger, I'm telling you whatever it is it's not Billy. I would know. A mother knows these things, feels it. You've invited a demon in our house!"

Billy heard that and started to cry. "Mum, I am real I am I am I am!"

"There, there," I said. "Mummy didn't mean it." He fell into my arms and I hugged him, lifted him off the ground.

Abby scowled at me with a sudden hate I'd never seen before.

Abby didn't come downstairs until noon. She was wearing the sunglasses. She sat drinking Nescafe, facing Billy and me, not saying a word. She stared at Billy. I opened my mouth to say something but nothing emerged. If Abby was going accept Billy was real, the next move was up to her. There was no explanation for such a miracle. Billy finished his Alphabetti Spaghetti with tomato stains on his chin. Abby got out a Wet-Wipe and rubbed it off. He put his small hand on hers, she didn't move away this time.

"Mum? Don't look so scared and sad."

"I'm not," she lied. I could tell she had taken another Valium. Her pale fingers rubbed behind her sunglasses and came away wet. "I'm not."

"Billy," I said, "there's something you have to understand. Something happened - something bad - and we are both a little shocked. There are some things we don't understand. What Mummy and Daddy need to know is what is the last thing you can remember before you were on the hill?"

Billy's face scrunched up, thinking. "You flewed the kite, Dad. You said it was my go ... and then ... the kite ... the string ... the string snapped. The kite flewed up. I wanted it to come back but it flewed higher and higher and there was nothing I could do. And you said you'd get me a new one but I don't want a new one I want the old one 'cause we painted it. Then you were sort of gone and then you sort of came back. Only you were wearing different clothes and looked sort of sad."

I looked at Abby. "I lost the kite three months before *it* happened."

"What's it mean?"

"Billy, are you sure that's all you can remember?"

"Uh-huh," he said. "I was scared."

"Roger," Abby said, "I'm going to take him to the doctor's." She paused and whispered so Billy couldn't hear. "I want him checked out to see if he really is Billy."

It was a good idea - except I wasn't going to let her drive, not in her condition.

"I'll do it," I said.

"We'll do it," she said, eyes flaring. She didn't trust me any longer.

*

"Where're we going, Daddy?" Billy tugged at the child seatbelt, squirming. "School?"

"No, not school," I said. I looked in the rear-view mirror at my family. Abby removed her sunglasses.

"We're going on a short trip," she said.

It sounded like a threat. It was then I realised she blamed me for the lead poisoning. As if I'd chosen the farmhouse deliberately. Now she blamed me for ... for what? Bringing him back? I didn't know.

I did a U-turn and steered the Land Rover along the dirt road towards the B road at the bottom of the valley.

"My tummy hurts," Billy mumbled.

I looked at him and saw he had changed. His face was pale and he was clutching his stomach. Abby went to him, flashed a look at me. "He's sick! It's the lead poisoning again! God, drive the car to a hospital!"

I did the fastest driving in history.

"No! No!" Abby cried.

Billy vomited blood in a terrible whoosh I thought would never stop, spattering the seats, spattering Abby. Her arms were slick with it. She screamed. I almost steered off the road and into a pine tree. I had to get Billy to a hospital. Maybe he could be saved. I had to try.

"He won't wake up," she shouted. "Hurry, damn you! Hurry!"

Dark twisting roads, endless and nameless. It was the same as last time, looking for the connection to the town as the night fell like a velvet curtain. Rain came from nowhere, turning the road to a slippery nightmare and making the windscreen blurred. The wipers fought back, losing. Abby couldn't get Billy awake, and she was screaming at me to go faster, go faster, as if I wasn't going as fast I could already, the speedometer waving at sixty as I took a corner, the mountains looming like clashing Titans.

Ahead, caught it the yellow headlights, was a sign and a fork in the road. To the left: GLEN IVERSTON 6 MILES. There was a hospital at Glen Iverston. Looking in the mirror, I saw Abby clutching Billy in her arms, rocking him.

"Don't die don't die don't die don't die ..."

DON'T DIE. I could hardly see for tears. I think the car was going eighty, my foot pressed to the floor, the wheels grinding the ground.

Then the rain vanished and it was daylight and Billy was no longer in the back and Abby wasn't covered in his blood and -

"STOP!" she screamed.

*

Hell, my ribs hurt. The air-bag had saved me from worse than bruises, but Abby had a bruise on her head where she had struck the front seat. She wouldn't let me examine it to see how bad it was. I'd come off the road, braking hard, narrowly avoiding the black HGV coming the other way. It had been taking up most of the left lane as well as its own. Now that we had stopped, I could see the HGV thumb-size in the distance, apparently unconcerned it was a danger to innocent drivers.

Abby groaned and touched her reddened temple, wincing.

"Billy ..."

Unspent adrenaline sweated through my body as I tried to understand just what had happened before the near-accident. It seemed unreal, as if someone else had been driving. One second Billy had been dying in the back seat, the next he wasn't there. In fact, there was no sign he had been in the car. No blood. Nothing. Of the inexplicable downpour, there was no evidence. The windscreen was completely dry.

Abby sobbed, quiet, tiny gasps, looking at the empty seat, no doubt seeing what I saw. Nothing. "No! He ... was ... here. My poor baby. Roger, w-what's going on?"

"I wish I knew," I said.

*

The farmhouse was deathly silent except for the tick-tock of the grandfather clock in the lounge. I handed Abby a mug of tea before switching on the television, just to break the tension. Neither of us felt like speaking, so we held hands. For a brief time we had believed in miracles, and the dispelling of our belief left us in an emotional vacuum. I'd gone around checking every room, hoping to find Billy hiding in some corner. I'd even opened the kitchen cupboards, as if he could have climbed up and crawled inside.

"This is the six o'clock ..."

Abby jumped up, pulling as her hair the way she did when exasperated. "Roger, am I losing my mind? Six hours can't have passed."

She was right - we'd only just returned. (I knew after what we'd gone through we could make mistakes, but to lose six hours wasn't possible.) I looked at my watch. It was quarter to two, fitting in with how long I felt we'd been on the road and back at the house since we decided to take Billy to the doctor. The grandfather clock showed the same time as the television. A four hour difference.

"What time have you got on your watch?"

"Ten to two," she said. "It's running slow. I don't understand how -"

"We've lost time. When we were on the road it was dry one second, raining the next, and a few minutes later it was dry again. Why? Something happened to time. It was as if we were repeating the night Billy died."

"So what happened to him? Why did he just disappear like

that?"

"Hold on," I said. I went into the kitchen and plugged the laptop into the wall. Abby followed. "What are you doing?"

"Bear with me," I said, typing. "Look at the date."

"September the first ... the day Billy died."

"Unless someone reset the clock, this is no accident. I think we're in some kind of time loop."

"That's not possible," she said.

"Can you explain what just happened?"

"No." Abby was holding her ears and squeezing her eyes shut. "I don't want to listen to this. It's crazy. You're crazy. I'm crazy. Everyone's crazy."

"But it happened. You can't deny it. There's something strange about this area." I moved towards her, setting our mugs on the coffee table before holding her in my arms. It felt good to hold her. "For a moment Billy was alive again. I promise if there is some way to bring Billy back, we'll find it."

"Angus must know about this phenomenon," she said. "He's lived here all his life. He must be able to tell us about it."

"Let's talk to him," I said.

*

We drove over to his farm, but we did not find him there. In fact, all we found was a stone cottage in a terrible state. Nobody could live in it. It looked like no one had been there for fifty years. There wasn't even a sign of the sheep I'd seen yesterday.

"I don't understand this," I said. "Where the hell is he?"

*

Back at the farmhouse, we went through the local history books. Abby grabbed my hand as she found an old photograph of Angus Seamore.

"It says here Angus Seamore died in 1949."

*

That night the moon was full and the stars clear as diamonds in a display case. We watched them through the open curtains, dreaming of miracles. The moonlight gave the land a bluish hue, in which I could see the black silhouettes of the mountains. I wondered how old the mountains were, how many millions of years had it shadowed this tranquil Neverland. Everything I could see was so old, so ageless. Could it be possible there were places where time obeyed different rules?

*

The mist was heavy in the small hours. Together, we stood on the hill as the sun crept over the horizon. We were waiting. Our hot breaths formed vapour like a dragon's smoke.

Abby muttered: "Do you really believe Billy will reappear?"

I hoped so, but so far there were no signs. But then, as time approached two in the morning, I sensed a change in the atmosphere – an electricity of expectation, building and building.

There was a figure in the mist.

"Billy?" we gasped.

No, it was too big. The disappointment hit me like a brick. It was an old man in a heavy sheepskin coat. As he stepped forward, supporting his body with a walking stick, I recognised Angus Seamore. He greeted us merrily, quite unaware that in our time he was dead.

"Angus? What are you doing here?"

"Looking for Monty. He's a wee black lamb, he's gone missing. Have you seen him?"

"No," I said, harshly. I didn't want Angus to ruin the chance that Billy would appear. I liked the old man, but right then, I was worried his presence would interfere with whatever magic was in the air.

"Right you are," Angus said. Whistling, he merged with the mist. A few seconds later I glimpsed him down in the valley – an impossible distance to travel in that time. He'd found Monty. "Angus is caught in this time thing, too. I bet he doesn't even know he's dead."

"Should we tell him?"

"No," I said.

"God, I wish this made sense."

I felt a tugging of my sleeve.

"Daddy, can we go home?"

*

We all went back to the farmhouse. We ate a breakfast of toasted waffles and syrup - Billy's favourite. We were so pleased to have him back for the third time it was as if we too had been reborn. Billy acted as if it was just an ordinary day, though he asked why Mummy and Daddy were smiling so much. We didn't dare risk losing him again, so we stayed in and near the farmhouse that day, treating him to ice cream and Mars Bars. Then Abby and I took turns playing games until Billy was so played-out he was ready for bed. After tucking him under the sheets, we both sat on the bed and read him Mr Men stories, enjoying his delighted, wondrous expressions. He fell asleep happy, looking so peaceful. We kissed him goodnight and went downstairs, feeling complete.

"What do we do now?" Abby asked. "Billy's alive right now, but what if he dies again?"

"We just have to be careful, I guess."

Over the dark winter months that followed we gradually got back to living as if he had never died. Abby completed her thesis and I got a large contract that would give us a steady income for years. But we were afraid that if we took Billy away from the farmhouse everything would revert to how it had been. (He only had to wander a few hundred metres from home and he started complaining about his stomach, but improved one hundred per cent once he returned.) We could not risk taking him far beyond the bounds of the farmhouse.

Billy knew there was something wrong with him, that he could never leave the farmhouse. Ever.

Abby wanted to tell her parents about Billy, but I convinced her it wasn't a good idea until we understood if his reappearance was permanent. "Imagine the situation if the press got wind of a story like this, huh? No, we can't tell anyone until we understand it."

"But Billy can't stay here forever without friends and school and all the normal things a kid his age needs to be happy. He gets bored playing on his own. He feels trapped. He wants to know why he can't go to school, thinks it's his fault. Soon this place will be like a prison, and he'll blame us."

It was true. There had to be a way of making Billy's reappearance permanent. Keeping him alive like this was heartbreaking, but at least he was alive. But then one day Billy ran off to play by himself. I was on my computer at the time and Abby was in the town, buying groceries. I heard his scream too late. When I ran outside, I followed his muddy footprints down the road, where they stopped suddenly, as though he had vanished completely. He was gone again. But this time, when we went up to the hill late that night, Billy did not appear. He did not appear the night after that – or the ones after that. He was dead again.

*

During the months of Billy's confinement, I had performed some experiments on the valley. I used a two dozen identical watches, which I placed in locations around our home. There seemed to be no effect on the watches most of the time, but at certain times of day, usually in the early morning, the watches would be lose their synchronisation. Some would be hours ahead; some would be hours behind. By charting the changes on a map, I was able to trace the effect. There was a definite pattern, centred on the hill where I had first encountered Billy. That was the focal point. When I threw a tennis ball over the hill, I saw it stop in mid-air and return back to me.

"It's like a geyser of time," I explained to Abby. "It's not always there, but when it happens, time can run backwards or forwards within its influence. You wouldn't be aware of it if you were inside the effect. Billy is and was alive in another time – the time he was at the hill when the geyser erupted. The farmhouse seems to be a place where the time is running normally. But he can't physically exist outside the valley without snapping back into the events that already happened. He's only alive near the farmhouse. He may still be alive in another pocket of time. The faintest echo of his living self."

"So he's trapped here forever?"

"I don't know. I don't see why he can't be brought out of the time-effect alive. It must be something to do with paradoxes – he can't be alive and dead at the same time. There has to be some reason why it doesn't work, though. I've worked out the phenomenon reaches a peak in two days time. Time at its centre will be running backwards very fast – but only for a few minutes. Then the geyser will be barely active for years and years. I have an idea, Abby. I hope you won't object, but I want to dig up Billy's body. I want to bring it home."

*

With the shovel on the passenger seat, Abby and I left the farmhouse with heart beating a staccato rhythm. The time-geyser would be active that night between 2.04 and 2.07 – then our chance would be over. Billy's grave was in a quiet part of the cemetery, far from the church and the prying eyes of witnesses. I had once placed a wreath on the headstone and read the epitaph, over and over.

WILLIAM ROBERT RAMSEY

1993 - 1997

LOVED AND LOST

BUT NEVER FORGOTTEN

*

Feeling like Burke *and* Hare, the pulse in my forehead throbbing, I dug deep into the soil, working feverishly to make a hole in the frozen soil. Abby watched out for the sexton and anyone else who might object to what we were doing. Deeper down the soil was moist and crawling with worms and beetles, crumbling from the sides practically as fast as I piled it up. I worked for three hours, past the point when my arms and back were red raw with pain. Smeared with dirt from head to foot, I hit wood as the light was fading from the sky. It had taken longer than I expected – far too long. The coffin was child-sized - four feet of solid oak, caked with earth. As I hauled it out, I noted it was heavier than I expected, as if rooted to the ground, but I managed. Abby could not look at it.

I carried the coffin to the Land Rover. I slid the coffin onto the back seats. I wanted to check its contents, to see if Billy was inside and somehow breathing. But I knew if I did look - if I saw a decayed body, bloated by expanded gases and congealing juices - there would be no way I'd have the energy to continue.

"We'd better hurry up," Abby said.

The engine started with a growl of disapproval.

I drove like a mad man, Abby urging me on.

It was almost two already

Cornering too fast, the coffin slid off the back seats and wedged in the leg space. There was an awful smell, a death smell escaping from it. *Keep you eyes on the road,* I thought. *Don't think. Do. But –*

What if we were too late?

We had ten miles to go.

I kept driving. My watch read two when I could see the dark farmhouse ahead. I drove up the hill towards the site where the effect would be strongest as the seconds ticked by. It was a minute past two when I braked near the top. I parked and Abby opened the door for me. I carried the coffin to the top of the hill. One minute left. I placed it in the exact location where the effect would be strongest, hoping and praying it would work. Then I ran down the hill, getting in the Land Rover before we were caught in the time-geyser. We drove down to the farmhouse. The mist encroached upon the hill and everything was still.

It was now 2.04.

We waited three minutes.

We checked the house for Billy.

He was not there. He had vanished.

Had it gone wrong?

Nervously, we went back up the hill on foot.

I could see the coffin.

We approached it.

"Look in it," Abby whispered. She stood behind me as I slid off the lid. We both stared into the coffin at the little body within.

Billy was inside. He sat up, bewildered. He was fit. He was well. He was whole again.

He gave us a big, big smile.

Sleeping in the Earth

Patrick Bane shuffled out the rear of the prison truck bound by handcuffs chained to leg irons. He was wearing the bright-orange clothes he wore in prison. He had not shaved today, or yesterday, and his chin looked dark and rough. He was smiling, his teeth shining in the cold light of morning. His long hair – hair that had not been cut in fifteen years – bristled in the wind coming down from the mountains. He made a joke about it to the six guards, but nobody responded. They were too busy looking around the unfamiliar area, into the deep woods beside the road, their Ithaca 12-gauge shotguns held down but ready.

I sat at the wheel of my Chevrolet Neon, watching them. I was half-expecting the media to show up, but so far things were going as planned. Personally, I didn't think releasing a convicted serial killer so he could locate where the bodies were buried was any sort of plan. That was why I'd volunteered to act as a backup to the search team. When I'd caught Bane in 1985, I'd certainly never thought something like this would happen. Sure, he was going back to jail, but the whole deal made my skin crawl. I felt as though it was my responsibility to ensure nothing went wrong. I had no doubt Bane would try escaping if the opportunity presented itself. He wasn't doing this as a favour for the victims' families - that was for certain. He would try something … and I'd be waiting.

I touched my .44 automatic for luck, then opened my car door. My partner, Frank Herschel, got out his side. We both slammed our doors at the same time, walking towards the group. Frank offered a cigarette. I accepted."Nervous?" I asked.

"Like I'm visiting the dentist for an exploratory."

*

Two guards were taking spades out of the truck. I saw Bane staring at me. He was grinning. "Don't you trust my word, Ben? Should I turn around so you can shoot me in the back?"

I ignored him. I wasn't going to rise to the bait.

"This is a big mistake," Frank muttered.

"I agree."

"So why is he being let out?"

"It's election year. The governor needs the bodies found just as much as the families. He was the DA who put Bane away, remember?"

"No," Frank said. "I was only ten in 1985. You keep forgetting I'm not as old as you. I'll still be in my twenties when you retire, buddy. I don't know a thing about what he did. Tell me."

"It was a big story. During the summer of 1984, Bane kidnapped and murdered at least six teenage girls. I caught him because I staked out the grave of his first victim, Victoria Smith. He went there on the anniversary of her death. He was still carrying the murder weapon, a knife he'd brought back from Vietnam. There was blood from several people on the blade. More evidence of the murders was found in his cellar – gruesome mementoes of the killings. But we never found the bodies, just pieces of the heads, like ears and noses …"

I whispered as we walked behind the search team up a trail into the woods. Two men flanked Bane, two went ahead, two stood behind. Wisely, they had not undone the leg irons, as Bane requested. Nobody was that naïve. He had to stoop and shuffle.

As he directed the search team along the paths, Bane kept looking back, grinning.

I was highly tempted just to blow his brains out. I had my .44 out, down by my side. The safety was switched off. I was growing more certain he was just leading us nowhere, hoping for a break to escape. The woods offered so many hiding places for a man like Bane. A trapper and Vietnam veteran, he knew the woods better than anyone. I watched Bane and the pine trees, constantly scanning for any signs of trouble. Bane called back to me, "Hey, Ben, you're not going to join my fan club?"

"I'm happy where I am."

"Scared I'll bite you or something?"

"Tell me something, *Patrick*."

"What?"

"How's prison?"

He stopped talking to me after that.

"Touchy," Frank said. "He's not too friendly, is he? I liked what he said about my being a bodyguard, though. I see myself as a tough version of Kevin Costner. Maybe he's not such a bad psychopathic cannibal serial killer after all."

"Yeah. He's up for the Nobel Peace Prize. Right after Saddam Hussein."

"How far is it?" the leader of the search team asked Bane. His name was Roach.

"About another five minutes at this pace. Maybe if you undid my feet I could move faster?"

"Nice try. Where is it?"

"I'll recognise where when I see it."

"Yeah, right," I said to Frank. Frank gritted his teeth.

Bane continued shuffling up the trail.

Frank was bored. "So. What happened after you caught him?"

"At his trial he tried to get off by using some of the prosecution witnesses in his defence. Two out of the eleven witnesses who'd seen him kidnapping the girls said he was much taller. It was an explainable discrepancy – they only saw him for a few seconds from their moving vehicles, which makes it hard to estimate someone's height. But he wanted to make the jury wonder if there was the slightest doubt."

"It didn't work," Frank said.

"No. It wasn't enough for reasonable doubt, not with the forensic evidence and the other witnesses. Next, his lawyer tried to make the jury believe I set up Bane for everything, including the bodies in his house. It was a ludicrous defence thrown together at the last minute. The jury voted unanimously for his conviction. He was sentence to death. He still claimed absolute innocent until last month, when his fourth appeal failed to even reach the court. Suddenly, he changed his mind. Not only did he admit his guilt, but he confessed to three other unsolved murders. He offered the governor the location of the nine bodies in exchange for a life sentence. Of course, Bane said he would have to look for the site himself because after fifteen years he couldn't recall the place without being there."

"I don't like this, Ben. Have you seen that movie *Seven*? There's this bit when the bad guy, Kevin Spacey, takes the cops on a wild goose chase ending with –"

"Yeah, I saw it. Bane's leading us into a trap. That's how it feels."

"So what are we going to do?"

"Be prepared for anything. For all we know he could have hired one of the guards to free him."

"Maybe he hired you, Ben. Or maybe he hired me …"

I grinned at him. I had thought of that. That was why I'd done a background check on my new partner. Everything he'd told me checked out. He was the third son of a large Catholic family. He was married to his childhood sweetheart, Caitlin. They had two kids, aged one and three. I had been to his house a couple of times to see them.

"Uh-oh," Frank said. "Where are they going now?"

The entourage had left the official trail and was going up a grassy path. Bane led the team between some large pines. I could hear the sound of running water. It made me want to find a bathroom. But I continued. Frank and I maintained a vigil on the group.

They reached a glade, where Bane stopped. He made a big deal out of sniffing the air and looking around. "This is it."

Roach said, "You buried them in the open?"

"I tried digging in the woods, but I hit iron-hard roots every time. You need a lot of space for a mass grave. Besides, I did it at night with the full moon above – this was the only place I could see what I was doing without a flashlight. I knew the grass would grow over it, but I wasn't guaranteed that in the woods."

"Where exactly?"

"Now, that's the question. Where exactly?" Bane stepped forward and pointed to a mound near the far edge of the glade. "There. I remember now."

It did look as though the grass was longer.

Grass grew longer if the ground under it was deeper.

Maybe it was the right place.

The men with spades rounded on the location, treading carefully. I could appreciate their caution. It could have been booby trapped with a mine, knowing Bane.

But nothing happened to them.

"Should we dig, sir?" one asked his boss, who was standing beside Bane.

"Be careful. Bane, if there's anything in there …"

"Boy, you are paranoid, Roach. I'll dig if you like."

"No," Roach said sharply. "You stay cuffed at all times. That's how the governor wants it."

Bane shrugged.

The two men probed the ground, then sunk their spades into the earth. They were soon making black heaps around a shallow pit.

"Deeper," Bade said.

"How much?"

"Deeper."

I looked at Frank. He shook his head.

"There's nothing here!" a man protested.

"It's deeper," Bane said. "I worked on it for hours. Wait a second – maybe it's to the right over there –"

He had his guards looking right just as he jumped left. I yelled out a warning, bringing my gun up. Bane landed on something that caved in. He fell down a concealed hole, leaving the guards grabbing the air, looking confused.

That was when the shooting started.

The four men standing close to the hole were cut down by three or four shotgun blasts coming from the opposite edge of the woods. Frank and I dived into the long grass before we were targeted – but the killer turned his attention on the men at the so-called burial site. They had dropped their spades and were struggling with their shotguns as they were hit at close range. Blam. Blam. They went down, screaming. The top of one man's head jerked sideways, blood spraying. I fired where I'd seen the flashes, Frank shooting his 9mm Beretta in a more or less continuous spray. The killer stopped shooting to reload, but I could see the blur of his camouflaged clothing moving anticlockwise. I shot at him, but he ducked behind the trees and sprinted away.

"Frank, I'll get Bane. You nail that guy."

"With pleasure." Frank covered me as I ran to the fallen men. They were wearing Kevlar vests under their windbreakers, but they'd been shot in the neck or face. They were all dead. I grabbed a flashlight and a shotgun, tossed another to Frank, who was making a radio call for backup at the same time as reloading his Beretta. Frank ran off into the trees as I lowered myself into the hole. I landed on my feet in a dank tunnel. It was some kind of storm drain. Smashed plywood, grass and soil were under my feet, pieces of the false ground. Water was running through the tunnel from somewhere up the mountains. It chilled my feet, making my shoes heavy. I looked in both directions, but couldn't see Bane. I assumed he'd head downstream, perhaps letting the slight current carry him along on his backside, like a water chute. That was the way I went. If he'd gone upstream then there was nothing I could do. I dashed down the tunnel for a hundred yards, slowing when I came to a tight bend. I shone the light ahead, edging forwards with my shotgun raised. He wasn't waiting. I could see a light in the distance. I could hear splashing and a metallic rustle. I fired at the sounds. The shotgun roared. The blast echoed in the tight space. Bane cried out, then he was scrambling out into the daylight. I fired again, but missed.

I got to the end of the tunnel only twenty seconds later. The tunnel unloaded its water down a steep bank into a river. Bane was slipping and sliding towards it. His shoulder was bleeding.

I aimed at his head and pulled back the trigger.

Finding there were no more shells.

Swearing, I dropped the shotgun in favour of my .44. It was empty, though. I found a fresh clip in my pocket. I dumped the empty one, slammed in the loaded one then aimed.

But Bane had gone.

I climbed out of the opening and steadied myself on the bank beside the entrance. I looked for him. Where was he? He couldn't have gone far – he was still in his leg irons and handcuffs.

There he was. In the water. He was in a black dinghy moving fast in the current. Already, he was a small target. I tried aiming, but I couldn't aim *and* keep my balance. It was like standing on ice. My bullets struck the water. Bane was using a paddle to take himself into the faster water.

"See you in hell, Ben!"

I fired regardless.

Bane flinched, but he wasn't hit.

He was getting away.

I ran up the bank and along the cliff's edge, ducking and dodging tree branches. Something whipped into my vision, cutting my forehead, but I didn't slow down. I just blinked away the blood and speeded up. Bane was now at the far bank. He stood up and hopped onto the rocks like a kid in a sack race. Then – perhaps sensing his vulnerability – he dived forwards, saving himself from my bullet in his back. He crawled out of sight.

I looked down the river, seeing a place where the banks almost touched. I hurried down the mossy rocks and leapt across. Sheer determination helped me avoid a dip in the water, but I landed hard, losing my footing. Then I was up and running again, running to where Bane had disappeared. His blood was on the rocks. I followed it up the bank. The ground was soft and wet. His footsteps were easy to see.

I thought about him being prepared for me, but frankly I didn't care. I had my weapon fully loaded, and he was handcuffed and unarmed. I knew what a coward he was. When Bane didn't have the element of surprise or superior strength, he was nothing.

I chased his tracks through the woods, but after a short distance the ground became hard and the trail ended. I stopped and listened. My heart was thudding. My breathing was ragged. But I could still hear the rattle of his chains. I followed. The trees were claustrophobic. I came out of the woods onto a narrow road. About fifty feet ahead, parked in the darkness, was a black flatbed truck. Its engine was running. Someone was behind the wheel. He was camouflaged, his face blacked up with boot polish. I glimpsed medals on his jacket. We locked eyes for an instant, then he lifted a handgun as if saluting. Before he could aim, I plunged behind a tree. We exchange fire until I needed to reload. He stopped firing too – I peeked around the tree to see why. Bane was hopping towards the passenger door. The driver shook his head and pointed at the rear. As soon as Bane was on the back, the truck drove off, the tyres spewing up dust and pine needles. I raced after it, unloading every bullet at Bane and the driver. Bane lay down behind the panel, keeping his head down. I smashed the licence plate, hit the roof, and shattered a taillight. One tyre exploded, but the truck kept going, vanishing around a curve. When I reached the curve, my lungs burning, the truck wasn't in sight, but I could smell the exhaust fumes.

I called Frank on my radio, but he didn't respond. I hurried back the way I'd come, worried Bane's partner had killed Frank. By then, a couple of local police had arrived at the glade wondering what the hell was happening. A medic was treating the only surviving guard. I was surprised the man was still alive. I went up to the deputy and told him to contact the sheriff. "My partner's in the woods. He could be injured or dead. Get someone to look for him. I'm going after them before they get too far. Set up roadblocks to the north ASAP. The killers are in a black Ford pickup. The licence is ..."

*

Soon after, I was driving on the road where I'd seen the truck. Roadblocks had been set up at the main junctions, so there was a limited number of ways for it to go. The road wound up into the mountains, with too many trees close together for it to slip into the woods. There were a few rough tracks here and there – but I could see the tyre marks in the dirt, so I couldn't lose it. After a few miles, I saw the truck by the roadside. It looked as if the burst tyre had proved fatal. Both doors were open. It looked abandoned. I didn't take any chance, however. I parked right behind it and blasted it with a 12-gauge before proceeding. I looked underneath. I saw no one hiding. Then I checked the cab. It was empty. However, I could see a body on the bed of the truck covered in a tarpaulin. Blood was all over the bed of the truck, leaking out from under it.

I could not tell who it was from this angle.

I swallowed tightly, approaching.

I had a dark thought about the truck. Why had Bane's partner not wanted him in the front of the cab?

Was it because he'd captured Frank?

Had Frank been in the passenger seat?

Had Frank been on their side?

I got a part of the answer when I pulled away the tarpaulin.

The body was Bane's.

I suspected a trick, but Bane was quite dead. My bullets had not killed him, though. He'd been gutted, his internal organs exposed. His arms and legs had been chopped off. His eyes were staring down at the viscera. He looked surprised.

Whoever his partner was, he had killed him to protect his own identity. There was a cold-blooded logic to it.

There was no sign of the mysterious other man.

*

Frank was missing. Blood matching his type was found by a tree, but no body. The woods were searched for days, but neither he nor the killer was discovered.

The FBI were put in charge of the investigation, but I was given the job of assisting them. The FBI were working two theories. They thought Frank had either been working with the suspect, or he was an innocent victim. I believed the latter. I had to believe Frank was innocent for to believe otherwise meant trusting no one. His wife begged me to find him, even if he was dead.

I promised her I would.

I looked into Bane's background, obtaining declassified records that simply hadn't been available in 1985. I learned about his time in Vietnam as a nineteen-year-old. I learned about his sergeant, too. He was called Joseph Michaels. He and Bane had been as close as brothers. Michaels bore an uncanny resemblance to Bane, only he was taller. Michaels had taught Bane how to kill on a series of dangerous missions. For this, they were given medals. They were told to kill more. Bane was promoted from private to corporal. Under Michaels tutelage, Bane would go into villages and kill young girls, girls he believed were deliberately impregnating themselves to create new VC soldiers. Michaels liked to defile the bodies, but because the men were only killing Vietnamese peasants, the Army didn't investigate the claims or pretended it never happened. Basically, it was covered up. The men only stopped their killing campaign when Michaels supposedly died during the Tet Offensive and Bane was wounded. But in war truth and lies meant nothing.

Michaels was alive.

They'd merely returned to America to continue the slaughter.

*

I was at home when I got the phone call.

The man said: "Carson Ridge. The cabin."

That was it, the whole message.

I knew it was Michaels.

I dreaded what I would find.

*

The cabin was little more than a derelict shack. FBI helicopters swarmed over the cabin, sharpshooters leaning out of the sides. A SWAT team surrounded it. Even the bomb squad was present. They were expecting the serial killer to be inside, but I knew he was long gone.

"I have to go in first," I told the agent in charge. He studied me for a while, then nodded. He clearly didn't want the responsibility; he was glad I volunteered. I put on a flak jacket, then approached the cabin. I looked in the only window, but I could see nothing. I crept to the door. I studied it for a time, looking for signs of a trap, such as a tripwire. I saw nothing. I didn't think there would be any traps because Michaels *wanted* me to be a witness to his crimes. Besides, he could have killed me anywhere. I had to test the door. It was unlocked. *Inviting me inside.* I pushed it open and shone my flashlight into the dark. I recoiled. I could see bodies. Lots of bodies. They were in rows, as though on display. Each had been recently exhumed from the ground. Some were more preserved than others. They were all young girls. I felt sick, but I stepped into the doorway.

There was a man tied to a chair at the back wall. He was gagged.

It was Frank.

He looked in a bad way, but he was alive.

I stepped forward and groaned as I shone light on his face.

Dear God, Frank …

How …?

Why …?

Frank's his eyes had been gouged out.

There were two dark, red caves blinking and blinking.

The killer hadn't wanted any witnesses who could describe him. So he had removed the only witness's eyes.

Again, it was the cold-blooded, logical thing to do.

A message was written on Frank's bare chest in deep, savage knife gashes:

NEXT TIME IT'S YOU!

The Gift

As Rachel searched for the unpaid telephone bill among the bills and receipts Dominic kept in his desk drawer, she found a receipt for £600. She would have thought nothing of it except the date on it was from only last week, but she had no knowledge of it. The £600 had been paid to a company called Black & Sons. Dominic had not mentioned spending £600, which was usual with purchases over £100. Rachel wondered if he'd paid for a surprise holiday, but when had a travel company had a name like Black & Sons? There was a phone number listed on the receipt and she considered calling it, but thought it was best to wait until Dominic arrived home.

For the rest of the afternoon, Rachel looked after the baby and worked on the lyrics for a new song she was writing for her fourth album. Royalties from the first three albums had paid for her house, the BMW, Dominic's Porsche, the holiday home in Majorca. The record company was expecting the new material to be ready for studio-time in three weeks. They wanted twelve songs, but only nine were composed to her satisfaction. She really needed to work on the last four. But she could not concentrated when something else was on her mind. Spending £600 was no big deal, but what had Dominic spent it on? Rachel really hated surprises, he knew that, so it would not be a holiday, especially not now when she had a deadline. She stared at the receipt until curiosity sent her to the phone. She entered the number and listened as an old man answered. "Good day, this is Black & Sons. I am George Black. How may I help you?" She could tell he was old by his fragile voice. He sounded eighty or ninety, perhaps in a wheelchair. Rachel was often right about visualising a person from only their voice. "Hi, I was hoping you could help me.

I'd like to know what Dominic Carpenter purchased last Wednesday for £600?"

"I can't give out customer information," he said. His tone was haughty. "I'm sorry. Mr Carpenter stressed the importance of it remaining secret."

"He wouldn't mind you telling me," she said. "I'm his –" She nearly said "wife" but something made her change it to "- secretary". She paused, thinking up an excuse. "Mr Carpenter is away and I need information for his tax records. You know the Inland Revenue." She felt guilty for lying to an old man, but she could not help it. "Please tell me what he bought."

She heard him sigh, as though bored by her. "It was a gift for his wife, I believe. I really can't say more than that, I'm sorry. I shouldn't even be saying that."

"But what did he buy?"

"I can't say."

"Well, maybe you can tell me what business you are in?"

Another sigh, as heavy as the weight of the world. "I am a stonemason. It's been my family business for over 150 years. My sons David and Nathaniel will take over when I die, but for the moment I remain the best stonemason in the country, with no exceptions. Now, I am rather busy. I hope I've helped. Goodbye."

He hung up on her.

After that call, she could not concentrate on her writing at all. What gift could Dominic have bought from a stonemason? It bothered her. Her birthday was not for another five months. There were no dates of special significance coming up, either. She desperately wanted to ask Dominic about it when he came home, but what if he had gone to great trouble buying her a special gift in secret and she ruined his surprise? It would be like the time she accidentally found out about the dinner reservations for their fifth wedding anniversary. Dominic had not been able to enjoy the dinner once the surprise of it had been ruined. But what if she showed him the receipt and casually asked him about it? He would have to say something.

*

It was seven p.m. and dark when his Porsche drove up the driveway. The Porsche's headlights made the heavy rain look like liquid mercury. Rachel watched him through the windows as he parked it in the double-wide garage. She waited in the kitchen, making coffee. He entered the house wearing his black raincoat over his dark suit. His hair was thick and wet, his cheeks flushed by the cold. Rain dripped off his nose. He gratefully accepted an Irish coffee, after dropping his briefcase in the hall. We're just like a married couple in a 1970s BBC sitcom, she thought. Only we don't kiss as much. She had noticed the affection between them had noticeably reduced since Angela's birth. She thought she was the one supposed to be having post-natal depression.

He sipped at his coffee, saying nothing, taking it through to the living room. She followed.

"Honey, what did you buy for £600?"

Dominic saw the receipt and froze. He put the coffee down on a coaster and turned to face her.

"Where did you find that?"

"It was in your drawer."

"Hell. I didn't want you to find that. I bought you a little gift. Something for your birthday. Now it's ruined."

"It's not ruined. I don't know what you've got, do I?" She looked at the receipt as if for the first time. "What's Black & Sons?"

"Black & Sons is a jewellers."

"A jewellers."

"Yes. A jewellers."

It would have been a believable answer if she had not already known the truth. Why was he lying? Rachel did not ask. If he wanted to surprise her with something unusual, she could not spoil it by persisting. But she did not like him lying. His reaction to what to her seemed a harmless inquiry was frightening. The way he had frozen when he saw her with the receipt in her hand, it was almost like she had caught him committing adultery. She had a horrible thought then – what if had bought something for another woman? A gift for his mistress. That could be why he wanted to hide the receipt. *He had a mistress.*

"Something wrong?" he said sweetly.

"No. I'm fine. How was you day?"

"Tough. The suits in accounting demanded another budget cut. Like the art department can just snip away at our budget. I'll be making adverts with crayons and Plasticine if they keep cutting."

Dominic was an artist working for the London-based ad agency Image Perfection. He hated it. Rachel had met Dominic at the Metropolitan Creative Arts College when they were young, driven optimists. She had wanted to be a professional musician and Dominic had wanted to be a famous artist. When they graduated, they vowed to achieve their dreams together.

Her musical career had exceeded her expectations, but his had not been so lucky. New art was not easy to sell, even in London, and a reputation as an artist was very hard to build. Not every artist could be paid for dissecting cows. Dominic had been unemployed for years during the 1990s while she supported him. Demoralised, he went into advertising. He was now a commercial artist, but he no longer did it for his own pleasure. It was just a way of earning money for him just so he did not feel as though he were a drain on her. Though he had never said it, she knew he resented earning less money than she did.

Dominic's father had been the sole wage-earner in his own family and Dominic sometimes felt embarrassed by his reliance on her. Dominic had not want to have any children until he had fulfilled his dreams. But for a few years she had worried about what if he never did?

She wanted children before it was too late. When he kept saying "let's wait a little longer", she grew restless. How long could she wait? She was in her forties. Her biological clock was screaming for a baby. And so she had done something bad - she stopped taking the pill without telling him. She was sure he would be angry for a while but forgive her eventually, once he saw how good having a baby was.

She got pregnant almost immediately, almost as if her eggs had been stockpiling in readiness. It was something she did not regret, but she knew having a baby had distanced them. She had told him the truth, which he had accepted by immersing himself in his work. He loved the baby, she knew, but he had difficulty accepting what she had done.

To make up for it, Rachel had approached the subject of him quitting the ad agency so he could concentrate on his art, but that had further humiliated him.

No, he would not quit the ad business because that would feel like an admission of failure. He was a father now, he said. He had responsibilities to provide for his baby. Sometimes he said he felt caught in a trap. Occasionally, Rachel wished her success had never come – at least not first. Dominic's opinion of himself depended on how other people perceived him. Seeing the anger in his eyes, the contempt and loathing he had for the work he did, she felt sick.

What if he blamed her for it?

Had he started an affair to pay her back for her success?

His lie about the £600 started her worrying.

The only answer to it was to find out what he had bought with it.

That was why she got the address of Black & Sons from the Yellow Pages. It was twenty miles from their home, in a small village.

The next day, she packed Angela into the baby seat in her BMW and drove to the address. Angela cried most of the way. Rachel had trouble finding the address using her RAC map, but eventually she did. She parked outside it, looking. Her hands gripped the wheel so hard her knuckles throbbed.

Black & Sons was a small factory-shop with a large window display of gravestones.

That was all they sold.

*

Rachel drove home in a daze, trying to think while Angela screamed and screamed. She parked outside the garage, took Angela into the house, changed her pungent nappy, then went looking for the gravestone.

It could be somewhere in the house, she reckoned. She would not – could not – rest until she was certain it was not lurking in some corner of the house. She went from room to room without finding anything. She saved the attic and cellar for the last places. Nothing. She sighed with relief, but then remembered one place she had not checked. The garage.

It was normally so dark in the garage she didn't noticed what was at the back. She took a torch into it and shone the light over Dominic's tools and her gardening equipment, unused since the weather turned into a Siberian winter.

There was something in the dark covered with a tarpaulin.

Her torch illuminated a large rectangle resting against tins of paint and varnish. It was as wide as her arms fully outstretched and just as tall.

From a distance it looked like part of the wall. But now she could see what it was – a gravestone like those seen in the window. She touched the tarpaulin and felt how cold it was. She tapped it – stone.

Hating herself for doing it, she undid the tarpaulin and pulled it off.

The dark marble gravestone towered over her.

There were words engraved on it. Words that made her chest tighten. She could hardly keep the torch steady as she read them.

HERE LIES

RACHEL CARPENTER

BELOVED WIFE AND MOTHER

BORN 1969

DIED 20

*

"Why is there a gravestone with my name on it in our garage?"

"Ah. I knew you would freak, that's why I didn't tell you. But I can explain."

"I'm listening."

"I was talking to this guy the other week. He'd recently lost his parents in a car crash. He was devastated, but one thing gave him comfort – the fact they had a beautiful memorial, a headstone carved by a true master. He actually showed me a photograph. And I was impressed, Rache. The thought of a loved one being remembered that way, with something so brilliantly made, it got me thinking. Particularly when he said the guy who did it was close to dying himself. The guy had gone back to have his own gravestone engraved. It'd given him enormous peace of mind knowing it was ready for when he passes on. By buying it now, he didn't have to worry about his relatives being able to afford one later. It was a real bargain. So, I thought, why not buy one for my dear wife? I wanted to surprise you."

"Oh, you surprised me. Gave me a heart attack, more like."

"You're upset?"

"How would you like to find a gravestone with your name on it?"

"I'd like it if it was as good as yours."

"You got one for me. You didn't buy yourself one?"

"I don't care what I'm buried in. I do care how you're buried. It was supposed to be a gift for your birthday."

"Dominic, get it out of the house."

"What?"

"Take it away."

"You're been irrational. It's just a slab of marble. It's not like a coffin."

"I don't like it. Will you get rid of it or shall I?"

"Okay," he sighed. "Consider it gone."

*

Dominic kept to his promise, for the next time she check in the garage there was nothing. And yet she had a sneaking suspicion he had given in to her wish a little too easily. After all, he had spent £600 on something she'd asked him to throw away. Would she have thrown away something she liked if he didn't like it? Not without a huge fight.

So, though the matter had been settled, Rachel felt no better. She started sleeping badly, waking from nightmares in which she was buried alive. Her work suffered as a consequence, which resulted in greater stress.

The gravestone was all she could think about.

She could not forget it. She searched the house again. It wasn't there. But the house came with acres of thick woodland, several stone outhouses, and a stables for a dozen riding horses. The previous owner, a drug-addicted earl with more debtors than friends, had taken the horses with him. As a non-rider herself, she had not visited the stables since the property was bought ten years ago. She had considered converting it into a guest-house – or perhaps a studio away from the house. She never went there. But it was only four hundred yards up the lane.

Her instincts told her to look.

*

"No," she moaned.

Cold air whipped around her as she stared at her name. The stables was gloomy, but the solid blackness of her name RACHEL CARPENTER deeply engraved into the marble literally pulled at her eyes. A sickness hit her, and she staggered out into the lane, shuddering, crying, head reeling, fear and anger and confusion rippling through her mind. She could feel the waves of conflicting emotions pounding against her skull. HERE LIES RACHEL CARPENTER. She was powerfully sick then. It steamed on the ground, grey and lumpy, like brain tissue puked out. Oh, God, she had never felt so violated. The betrayal and disgust physically hurt.

Dominic had lied to her. Again. He had kept it hidden.

She closed the doors to the stables, hands trembling as she attached the padlock, locking IT inside. She hurried to the house. She called the ad agency. She told him there was an emergency. She begged him to come home immediately. When he asked what was wrong, she hung up the phone. She did not answer it when he rang back.

Almost an hour later, he pulled up outside in his Porsche. She stepped outside.

"What's wrong?" he said. "Is it Angela? Is there something wrong with her?"

"Angela's fine," she said. "It's that – that thing. What is that *thing* doing in the stables?"

"Hey, calm down. I can't believe you made me drive all the way home for that. I did what you said – I moved it out of the garage."

"I asked you to take it away."

"I can't take it back. It's engraved. There are no refunds. What's the harm of keeping it in the stables?"

"It's creepy, Dominic. I want it destroyed."

"Destroyed? You didn't say destroy it the other day. That's extreme, Rache."

"I said get rid of it. That didn't mean keep it in the stables -"

"But we don't use the stables, Rache."

"Destroy it," she said.

"What?"

"You heard. Get it out of the stables and destroy it. I want to see you take it away right now. Or I'll start screaming."

"I'll need to call the guys again."

"Do it."

"They'll take some time."

"I'll wait."

Over an hour later, two big, muscular men arrived in a grey van marked Black & Sons. Dominic unlocked the stables and led them to the gravestone, while Rachel kept an eye on it from down the lane. The men had to be the old man's sons, she guessed. It took the two men to lift the slab into the van, walking very slowly, their faces dripping with sweat. Neither looked pleased to be moving it. She felt guilty for acting like a scared little girl, but she hated the gravestone too much to let it stay. They drove away. Dominic walked back down the lane towards the house, shaking his head. "There. It's gone. They'll smash it up for you. Are you happy now?"

She was happy now.

"Thank you," she said.

She approached Dominic to kiss him, but he drew away, storming into the house as though she did not exist.

*

The next morning, Rachel looked out her bedroom window and saw the gravestone.

It was at the far end of the garden, where the grass met the trees. The gravestone had not been there the night before. The stonemason's sons must have erected the dark-grey tombstone while she and Dominic slept. In the winter light the grave cast a shadow almost reaching the house. She felt as though it was reaching for her. She stepped further back into the bedroom.

"Dominic ..." she said, but of course he was not in bed. It was nine o'clock and he would have gone to work when it was still dark. He would not have seen the gravestone. Was he avoiding her? Had he told the men to do that? It seemed so spiteful and cruel, she could not believe Dominic would tell them to do that. But the gravestone was there, lingering at the bottom of the garden.

Someone had done it deliberately. The engraving was in shadow, a wall of blackness, but as the sun rose over the woods, the white light heating up the garden, she could read the epitaph and feel the downy hairs on her arms stand upright.

HERE LIES
RACHEL CARPENTER
BELOVED WIFE AND MOTHER
KILLED IN COLD BLOOD
BORN 1969
DIED 2011

The date had been completed. And it was this year! No, no! This wasn't happening. Killed in cold blood? Rachel pulled her velvet nightgown around her tighter, but she was aching with biting coldness. She dressed quickly, then grabbed her phone. She was tempted to call the police, but first she dialled Dominic's number.

It wasn't connecting.

No. She'd dialled wrongly in her haste.

Try again. It rang. He picked it up. "Hello?"

"This isn't funny, Dominic."

"Rache? What are you talking about?"

"The gravestone. Killed in cold blood? Is that how you feel about me? You want me dead? You hate me that much for Angela?"

"I don't know what you're talking about. I don't hate you."

"The gravestone. In the garden."

"What? I swear I don't know anything about it. You're telling me the gravestone is back?"

"Duh. Like you don't know."

"I told those guys to dispose of it."

"I'll dispose of it myself. With a hammer and chisel."

"Wait!"

"No," she said, hearing the doorbell ring. "I'm not discussing this with you. I'm hanging up now."

"But –"

She hung up. The phone started ringing again. She took it downstairs with her, but she didn't answer it. Let him wait a few minutes, she thought, as she walked down the hall towards the door. There was someone standing outside, a hazy figure through the glass. Probably the postman. Her phone stopped ringing. The figure was ringing the bell again. Now her phone was ringing again. As she put her hand on the latch, she glanced down at the newspaper on the mat. It was the local Gazette. There was a picture of an old man on the front page.

VILLAGE MOURNS DEATH OF MASTER
STONEMASON
GRIEVING SONS BURN DOWN SHOP
WHO WILL WRITE THE EPITAPHS NOW?

She opened the door – too late recognising the men. Big and strong, the two sons were standing there, waiting, one with a hammer, the other with a chisel, both with weird, sadistic grins.

"We make home deliveries now."

The Deepest, Darkest Fear

Temple had not heard her voice in eleven years, but he knew it immediately without her saying her name. It was Montana, pronounced Mon-tar-nah, not like the state. There was something desperate and urgent in the tone of her voice. He would never forget Montana Doland's gentle Southern accent if he lived to be a hundred. Every night, he heard it whispering to him in his dreams, its aching sadness charged with deeply hidden sensuality. Montana had a voice like butter, like a breeze on a hot day. It was the voice of a Southern Belle who had sought happiness once but had long forgotten what it was like. He held the phone to his ear and walked with it outside where his wife would not overhear. It was dark and cold on his sun porch, the moon and stars already out, bright and clear in the summer night.

"Montana?" he whispered.

"Temple, something awful has happened."

He could hear her soft exhalations as she said the words all parents dread:

"Our son is missing."

He was silent.

"Temple?"

"I hear you. I'll be there in five minutes."

Temple went inside for his sheriff's jacket and car keys.

*

Temple was a deputy when he fell in love with her.

He was assigned as protection for her husband Nelson Dolan

and his family when an ex-employee called Trey Ramirez made some threats after he was fired for drinking at work. Trey Ramirez was a jailbird with a history of violence so his threats had to be taken seriously. He'd smashed up Nelson's office and sprayed the walls with I'M GOING TO PAY YOU BACK. An arrest warrant was issued but nobody knew where he was. The fear was he would attack Nolan or his wife or his baby daughter. Temple guarded the Dolans for three months.

At first Temple and Montana tried ignoring their mutual attraction, but as weeks turned into months they spent more and more time together – alone. She was a lonely woman – what she jokingly referred to as a business widow because her husband worked 24-7. Her husband had lost interest in her sexually after she had her first baby, Angela, who was sixteen months old. They still made love – but rarely. It was not enough for Montana.

Temple was drawn to her like nobody before or since. They began their affair one weekend when Nelson was in New York. It started in a motel room and moved on to anywhere they could meet in secret. Their affair ended two weeks later when Trey Ramirez was captured breaking into the house. Temple was a hero for saving the Dolans, but it ended his assignment - and his romance. They both knew it was wrong, but he could not regret it. His love had been real. Their romance had only lasted two weeks but it felt like a lifetime of joy. They made love only seventeen times, but that was six times more than Nelson and Montana had done in a year. One of those times made Montana pregnant. Bradley was his child, but nobody except them knew. As far as the rest of the world was concerned, Nelson was Brad's real father.

Temple had moved on by marrying Judy, a nurse who worked at

the county hospital. He loved Judy … but when they made love he thought of Montana.

*

The Doland ranch was a soft glow among the low hills of Green Vale County until Temple drove around the final bend and then the ranch appeared in all its glory. It was huge and white and cost nine million dollars to build in the 1980s, when Nelson Dolan shifted his business offices to Green Vale County. Light was coming from a floodlit lawn that any pro football team could have used for practice. The lawn was luminous green, with a marble fountain in its centre, where a waterfall cascaded down a bronze sculpture of an oil pump. The sculpture was so accurate the pump went up and down. Nelson Doland had made his money in oil and loved the display of his wealth. Every light in the ranch was on, which made it seem like day as he drew up beside the entrance. He walked to the white doors and rang the bell.

Nelson Dolan opened the door, frowning as he saw the sheriff standing there. "Oh. It's you, Sheriff. I was hoping it was my son. What brings you here?"

"I called him," Montana said, walking down the hall to join them at the door. Whenever Temple saw Montana in town, he felt a pulse of electric lust between them – a feeling never lessened with time. Even now at a moment of crisis he could not avoid the rush of attraction. Her reddish-brown hair flowed down to her shoulders like polished mahogany. It was thick and wild and brought memories of its cool brush against his skin. She was dressed in a blue cashmere jacket, white pants and boots. Her green eyes were wet. "I told him Brad's missing."

"Five hours is hardly missing," Nelson said.

"He's only ten years old."

"I went hunting by myself when I was ten."

"That was fifty years ago."

"Forty years," Nelson said.

"The world is more dangerous these days," Montana said. "Isn't that right, Sheriff?"

"It is, unfortunately. Can I come in?" Temple asked. He wanted to interrupt the domestic argument before it exploded again.

Nelson nodded. The three of them walked into a massive living room with big oil paintings on the walls. Nelson was a millionaire with several oil fields in East Texas. He usually wore a grey suit as well as diamond-studded Stetson and alligator shoes, but at home he wore sweaters and Levi's and looked pretty normal. From his expression Temple could see rage and worry twisting inside him like a jagged knife. A man like Nelson would never admit he was frightened by anything, but the disappearance of Brad was every parent's greatest fear. Montana sat down on a large sofa while her husband poured himself a whiskey. There was a family picture opposite Temple of the Dolan family. It showed Nelson, Montana, their twelve-year old daughter Angela, and ten-year old Nelson Bradley Dolan Junior. In the picture they looked happy and radiant as they stood in the sunlight outside their stables. Angela had her father's dark hair and mother's green eyes, but Bradley had lighter hair and blue eyes. Temple recognised himself at that age. Anyone seeing the two of them aged ten lined up would think they were twins.

"Tell me what's happened, please."

"Sheriff," Nelson said, "it's quite simple - my Brad's disappeared."

"He should've been home hours ago," Montana said.

"Montana is real worried. He'd never stay out this late. My boy wasn't raised that way. We've told him to tell us if he's going to be late."

"Have you called his friends, sir?"

"I called Jimmy Ewan, his best friend," Montana answered. "He said he hasn't seen Brad after they left school this afternoon. Brad was riding his bike home on Richmond Avenue. That was at four o'clock. It takes only ten minutes to get here."

"But he didn't show up," Nelson added.

It was 9 p.m. now. Five hours later. "Why didn't you call me sooner?"

"We would have," Montana said, her voice cracking, "but we didn't know he wasn't home."

"Nobody was here?"

"I was out at the oil fields," Nelson said.

"I was shopping," Montana mumbled.

"It's not our fault," Nelson said. "Our help was in the house – Martha and her husband Stephen - but neither noticed Brad hadn't come home. The useless bastards. We only found out when we got back at eight."

"I was horrified," Montana said. "I should have come home earlier, but I never thought ..."

"Montana called me on my cell. I came home straight away. We've been calling his friends for the last hour. I even went driving along his route. Nothing. He might have gone to play at a friend's house, but unless he had some friends I don't know about … you see the situation."

"I'd like a list of his friends. I also have a question. It's not a nice question, but I've got to ask it. Is there any reason why he could have run away?"

"No," Nelson said.

Temple could not read Montana's expression, though he sensed she had things she could not say in front of her husband. For the moment she shook her head.

"He wasn't angry or upset?"

Montana sighed. "He was happy this morning."

"Okay. He's never done this before?"

"Never," she said.

"You haven't seen anyone suspicious?"

"No."

"Had any weird phone calls?"

"No!" Nelson shouted. "Look – we would tell you if we knew something." Nelson paused, finishing his whiskey in a swallow. "Give me a straight answer. Do you think he could have been kidnapped?"

"Let's not jump to conclusions."

"I'm a millionaire. Conclude."

"There is a chance, yes."

Montana put her hand to her mouth, sobbing behind it.

"What if it's that maniac Ramirez?" Nelson rounded on him. "What are you going to do?"

"I doubt he's out, considering the kind of trouble he was in. But I'll check. I'll also contact my deputies and have them canvass the streets. I'll also talk to Brad's friends in person. I'll have a description of Brad distributed ASAP. I will find him."

Montana walked with Temple to his sheriff's cruiser.

"That thing you said about running away?"

"Uh-huh?"

"It could be what's happened."

"Why?"

"He could have learned you're his real dad."

"Is that possible?"

"He's a bright boy. He could have figured it out. Maybe that's why he's disappeared?"

"Maybe," he said.

And maybe it was a kidnapping.

Maybe Brad was dead.

"I'm scared, Temple. It's like this is God's punishment for what we did."

God has nothing to do with this, he thought. "Kids do irrational things, Montana. I'm sure he'll turn up soon enough."

She nodded as though wanting to believe him.

He got in his cruiser and drove away. He switched on his radio and spoke to his best deputy, Al Greenberg.

"Al, I need a check on the whereabouts of Trey Ramirez. Is he out of prison? Contact me as soon as you find out something."

*

Jimmy Ewan said the last time he'd seen Brad was on the corner of Strawberry Street and Richmond Avenue. Temple parked and walked up the street with his powerful flashlight sweeping the sidewalk and bushes. There was a tall picket fence behind some bushes running the length of the block and continuing onto the next block. He moved slowly, not wanting to miss anything. It took him twenty minutes to cover the block, then he moved on to the next. He'd gone 500 yards when something silver reflected by the fence. He could not see what it was for the bushes. He approached it from a side angle, pushing his way through the green leaves and whip-snapping branches. He shone light down on the silver object. It was a piece of smashed mirror. Looking down, he saw the spokes and wheel of a blue bike. The bike had been dumped behind the bushes.

Temple closed his eyes and felt the blood rushing into his body and a sickness in his stomach. It could be some other child's bike, he thought. It could be someone else's. Not that he believe it. Opening his eyes, he saw it again, the blue bike. Thrown over the bushes by someone evil.

He called his discovery in.

"Are you all right, Sheriff?"

"Just get some people here," he barked. His mouth was dry and tasted bad. "Now."

He was tempted to lift the bike from its position, but there was the danger of contaminating evidence.

Nothing would be touched until the area was sealed off.

But that didn't stop him working while he waited.

Heartsick, he searched for the body he was sure he would find.

*

"Judy? It's me."

"Have you found him yet?"

"No. We're looking, though. I found his bike. Looks like a kidnapping."

"God, it must be terrible for his mom and dad."

"Yes," he agreed.

"Temple?"

"Yes."

"Everything okay?"

He wanted to tell her the truth. Perhaps if he'd been talking to Judy face to face he would have done it, but something stopped him. He could not betray Montana like that. She'd chosen to stay with her husband, and he had to respect that, despite his own desires.

"I'm tired, is all."

"You sound it. When are you coming home?"

"I'm staying up until the FBI get here. I won't be back tonight."

*

"At least there's no body yet. The kid could be alive."

Temple wasn't sure which deputy said that, but he prayed it was true. It certainly looked as though Brad had been kidnapped on his way home and his bike had been hidden in the bushes by the kidnapper.

But nobody had called the Dolans.

They'd agreed to a having their phones tapped.

Montana and Nelson were waiting for a call.

In a kidnapping the FBI had jurisdiction – but they could not get there until tomorrow morning, by which time Brad could be dead – if he wasn't already. The FBI's nearest field office was over a hundred miles away, so they could not help right now, when they were needed. At the moment the responsibility was all his. It was ten p.m. and so far he had no witnesses and no suspects. He was hoping some forensic evidence could be obtained from the bike, but that would take days to process. Days he did not have. Every minute mattered in a kidnapping.

Al Greenberg arrived in his cruiser. He was a big man in his early forties with a white crew-cut. He walked towards the crime scene with a long sheet of paper in his hands. "I've got bad news. Real bad news."

"Spit it out."

"Some guy's been hanging out by the school. Brad's friends have seen him three, four times over the last month."

"Description?"

"5'9, muscular, black greasy hair, long sideburns, acne scars. Seen driving a grey van."

Temple's hands clenched. "That fits Trey Ramirez."

"Yeah. I know. The guy hassled the Dolans."

"More than hassled. He would've killed them if I hadn't caught him. He got ten to fifteen at Angola for his crimes. Have you found out where he is, like I asked?"

"You're not gonna believe it. Ramirez was released two months back. He's been quietly living in our town. We should've been informed, but some jerk forgot to tell us. Freaking bureaucracy makes me sick. Anyway, his address is listed here. It's the trailer park. We gonna pick him up?"

"Let's go." Temple ran to his car. He juiced up the gas and zoomed through the dark streets at twice the legal limit. Al Greenberg followed. Al wanted to get back up, but Temple said no. This was personal. He could feel the anger throbbing behind his eyes, his heart thudding. He speeded up until he was at least two blocks ahead of Al.

"Al," he said into the radio, "I want you to look for the van. I'm checking out his trailer by myself – understand?"

"I don't think going alone is wise."

"Just do it."

The trailer park was dark and quiet. Slowing to a silent crawl, he drove past rows of aluminium RVs looking like overturned beer cans. Trey Ramirez's trailer was beside a heap of car parts and trash. The dirty metal shone in the moonlight. The windows were dark, the curtains closed. There was no grey van visible, which bothered him. Maybe Ramirez had skipped town with the boy. The boy? Not just a boy - his son. Not that Ramirez would know that. He would assume he was kidnapping Nelson's son. His trailer looked like something dead that had clawed itself out of a grave – its walls were muddy and covered with obscene graffiti drawn by Ramirez. Temple parked a few trailers behind it and approached on foot, weapon out. He trudged through dried mud and foul-smelling pools of water. Somewhere in the distance he could hear a radio playing a song by Sheryl Crowe. He stopped at the side of the trailer. He was wearing Kevlar in case Ramirez was expecting him. But as he peered through a gap in the curtains, he wondered if he was too late. It looked empty. But then he saw a faint light – the glimmer of a small black and white television glowing in the dark. And then he saw a shadow moving. He ducked down and crept along to the door.

He would give Ramirez no warning.

Temple kicked the door and pushed his way inside. He stepped into darkness. There was a man in the bed watching TV. Ramirez. He opened his mouth when he saw Temple standing over him, a gun in his face.

"Move and you're dead."

"Hey, I ain't moving. I ain't done nothing."

Temple hauled him out, dragging his half-naked body outside into the moonlight, where he cuffed him and pulled him towards his cruiser. He could smell beer and sweat. Temple shoved him in the back and slammed the door. He went back to the trailer but found nothing to tell him where Brad was. He returned to the car. Then he drove out of the trailer park and headed away from the populated area, turning off a road into nowhere.

"Remember me?"

"You were the deputy."

"I'm the sheriff now. I took you down once. I'll do it again the hard way unless you tell me where you've taken the boy."

"I don't know what the hell you're talking about."

"I know you've been watching the boy. There are witnesses. That's all the evidence I need. There's no trial this time. The only way you are going to live until tomorrow is if you tell me where he is. Right now."

"Where is who?"

"The boy."

"What boy?"

"Nelson Dolan's kid."

"I don't know what you're talking about."

But his eyes looked down.

Ramirez knew who he was talking about.

Temple stopped the car. He turned off the engine.

"This is where you get out."

There was nothing around. Just the stars overhead and miles away the lights of the town.

Ramirez's eyes were big and white in the mirror.

Temple opened his door and walked to the rear. He pulled Ramirez out and told him to walk into the dark.

They stopped after a hundred yards. The road looked small from here. The ground was rocky and uneven and could not be seen from the road.

The perfect place to bury a corpse.

Temple undid the cuffs. Ramirez rubbed his wrists. "What's this?"

"Get on your hands and knees and dig."

"What?"

"Dig yourself a grave."

"I ain't doing that, man. Come on – what do you want?"

Temple punched him in the stomach. He doubled up and threw up and lay on his side, sucking in ragged breaths. Temple hit the sole of his foot with his night stick. He screamed.

"Dig," he said. "Or talk."

"I didn't kidnap nobody."

"Dig," he said, kicking Ramirez in the knee.

Ramirez started digging, getting dirt under his fingernails, blood on his palms. "I swear I didn't do nothing."

"You were seen at the school."

"Okay, okay! I was there. I did think about doing something like kidnapping the kid. I spent ten years inside for Dolan and I wanted him to pay me for it. But I couldn't do it. My beef was always with Dolan. He's the guy fired me. For ten years I wanted to get revenge, but when it came down to doing it, I couldn't. In prison I had a long time to think. It wasn't worth it. I have a job now. I want to live a real life."

He was sobbing, his tears falling in the dirt.

"What did you do today?"

"I was working all day. I've got a job driving a forklift. Ask my boss."

"What's his name?"

"Steve. Steve Vanson."

"What time did you finish?"

"Eight."

"Liar. Where's you van?"

"My van? It's in a garage. There's something wrong with the motor. It needs fixing."

*

Deputy Danny Cooper was the only deputy in the sheriff's office when Temple came in at 10.35. He was manning the radio, keeping the sixteen men under Temple's command organised via a computerised map. The red dots on the map were the police cruisers. He did not say anything about the fact Temple had driven his cruiser out of signal range for fifteen minutes, but he did raise an eyebrow at what he brought in with him.

"What happened to him?" Cooper asked.

Temple was dragging the half-conscious Trey Ramirez through the doors of the sheriff's office and towards the cells. The man was bleeding onto the blue floor. Temple said nothing until he had Ramirez locked up. Then he faced his deputy.

"He walked into a door, Danny."

Cooper chuckled. "The door have fists, sir?"

"This is Trey Ramirez. I'm keeping him in lockup until his story's checked. He says he was working all day, giving him an alibi if true. Always claims his van is getting repaired."

"You think he's the guy?"

"I'm not so sure now. We did some talking."

"After he walked into the door?"

"Yeah."

A light lit up on the computer display. Cooper pressed RECEIVE. Greenberg's voice came through loud and clear. Temple answered.

*

Her name was Lydia and she would be 92 in August. She needed to talk to the sheriff, he had told Greenberg. Temple was now in her house with a drink of tea in his hands listening to her story.

That afternoon she'd been sitting on her porch petting her Scottish terrier when she saw a boy on a blue bike. She knew him because she watched out for him every afternoon. She watched him ride by her house at four o'clock. He kept pedalling down the street until he was out of sight.

That would not have been significant but her address was 560 Richmond Avenue – two blocks beyond where the bike was found. Unless she was mistaken, Brad had ridden past. Lydia had stayed on her porch until five before retiring for a short sleep. During that time she had not seen the boy come back. It was unlikely he had gone back – which meant someone else did, leaving his bike to be found afterwards.

Brad had arrived home.

*

Montana opened the door.

"You're back. Have you …?"

"No."

She smiled with relief. "Then there's still hope. What are you doing back here?"

"The help. I need to talk to them."

"You think they are involved?"

"I don't know what to think yet."

Temple followed her down the hall. He passed the living room, where he saw Nelson sitting by the fire with a glass in his hand, his eyes focused on the flames. Temple continued up some stairs, Montana announcing their arrival at a closed door. The door opened and a man and a woman stood before Temple, both looking nervous, as though he would arrest them and deport them.

"The Sheriff has some questions for you."

"We want to help," said the man. His wife nodded. "We love Bradley like our own kids."

"What were you doing at four?"

The couple held hands. "We here."

"Yes, but what were you doing?"

"We here."

"Did you not hear Bradley come back?"

The woman spoke in Spanish, crying.

"What did she say?"

"Nothing," her husband said.

"She said sorry," Montana said.

"We not here," the man said.

Temple wondered if they'd been doing something that would

have got them fired.

"Mrs Dolan, can you give me a few minutes?"

"Oh. Surely. I'll be downstairs with my husband."

He waited for her to go.

"Look, anything you tell me is confidential. I won't tell Mr and Mrs Dolan. But I need to know why you didn't hear Bradley. A young boy like that would make a lot of noise when he got home."

"We not here."

"Yes, but why?"

"We not hear. We have afternoon off."

"You did not *hear*?"

"Is what I say."

"So where were you?"

"We at home. Is bad?"

"It depends. Why did you go home when you should have been on duty?"

"Mrs Dolan say this morning, 'Have day off until six'. So we do. Then later she say we not understand – we suppose to be here. But is not our fault. She say it. We not understand."

"Mrs Dolan told you to take the day off?"

"Yes."

*

She wasn't in the room with Nelson.

"Where's she gone?"

"The garage. She wants to look for Bradley herself. I told her we should stay here, but she won't listen."

Temple hurried outside. He ran towards the garage, where he

found Montana driving out a red Porsche with the top down. She pulled it onto the driveway. He blocked her way, standing in front of the car. She braked. "Temple, get out of the way. I've got to look for my baby." She revved the engine.

"Not now," he said. "Stop the engine."

She turned it off.

"Get out."

"What?"

"Get out, Montana."

She opened her door and stepped out.

She looked over his shoulder.

Nelson was behind him.

He had a gun.

He staggered as he walked.

"What's the gun for?" Temple asked.

"Something's going on I don't like," Nelson said. "I want the truth. What's going on, Montana?"

"He's trying to stop me looking for our son."

"Is that true?"

"Yes – because she already knows where he is," Temple said. "She's responsible for his disappearance."

"What?" Nelson said. "Are you mad? She's his *mother*."

"She has a secret Brad must have found out. She was probably frightened he'd tell you. She was afraid you'd divorce her. She couldn't risk that. She loves the money, you see. A divorce would ruin her lifestyle."

"Secret?" Nelson looked at Montana. "What secret?"

"There's no secret. He's obviously lost his mind."

"We had an affair," Temple said. "Brad's my son."

The shame of it disgusted him.

"NOOO! He's out of his mind," she said. Nelson, I didn't want to say this – but he made a pass at me earlier. I've also seen him following me in town. When I turned him down, he promised he would make me sorry. I think … I think he's killed Bradley. That's why I was driving away. I was going to get some help. He's insane."

She was convincing.

Temple would have believed her if he were Nelson.

He pointed the gun at Temple.

"Did you kidnap my son?"

"He's not your son."

"No."

"Would I lie to you about that with a gun pointed at me?"

"Montana?"

"Shoot him, baby."

"If you shoot me she'll tell my deputies you made Brad disappear. She'll get them to believe it. You'll go to prison."

"Where's my son?"

"Bradley came home, Nelson. He found his mother waiting. She knew he'd found out about the affair we had ten years ago. She had to shut him up somehow. Maybe she tried to scare him into silence, maybe she planned something worse. She did something, anyway. Then she needed a way of making it look like a kidnapping. She dumped his bike hoping it would look like a kidnapping, but she didn't figure on an old lady seeing him on his way home. She has him in the trunk of her Porsche. She wanted to dump his body somewhere but was afraid it would be discovered and DNA or something would connect her to the murder. In a day or two she would have made some excuse to visit drive her car and used it to take the body somewhere it could be dumped." He paused. "The only question is has she killed him already?"

"He's trying to trick you, honey. Don't listen to him."

"Montana, shut up! I can't think! You – sheriff - open the trunk. Don't even think of reaching for your gun. Montana, give him the key."

Temple took the key and unlocked the trunk. It opened as he stepped back.

"If there's anything in there," Montana said, "he must have put it in to set me up."

Temple looked into the trunk.

There was a black plastic bag in the trunk space.

It had a body inside.

"No," Nelson said. "My son!"

And he blew out his own brains.

Before he hit the ground dead, Montana was scrambling for the dropped weapon.

Temple pulled out his .45.

"Touch that gun and you're dead," he said.

She turned to look into his eyes. Her hand was inches away from the gun, but she made no move towards it. She lifted her hand away. Her voice became low and husky. "This can end any way you like, Temple. We could say Nelson found out Brad wasn't his son, so he killed him. You and me – we could be together. I'm now a rich widow. What do you say? You and me – like it's meant to be? Yes or no? Our little secret?"

She was panting, sweating, waiting, a sultry smile forming in her mouth and eyes. The body in the trunk meant nothing to her - neither did her husband's lying by her feet. He hated her. And yet he could feel his body responding to her as though compelled by fate.

"I'll tell you what I say."

And he told her.

With a kiss.

Of a bullet.

*

"What a bitch," Al Greenberg said. "What did you do next?"

"She was reaching for the gun," he told Greenberg. "So I had to shoot."

There were in Temple's cruiser. Greenberg was driving him home to Judy. Temple had told him the whole story of his affair with Montana and filled out the paperwork, but the deputy was asking for the details. If he suspected the real circumstances surrounding Montana's death, he did not say. Greenberg had been surprised to find out Bradley was Temple's son. It would surprise a lot of people.

"Well, it's over." Greenberg turned into Temple's driveway. "Tough call, but lucky."

"Very. I was standing there, shocked like you wouldn't believe. It was then I heard the gasping from the trunk. At first I couldn't believe my ears, but then I pulled the bag apart and found him alive. What did the doctor say?"

"He's gonna be okay," Greenberg assured him. "His mother gave him a nasty skull fracture with the tyre iron we found in the trunk, but he's a tough kid. He'll survive. Guess he takes after his father. Speaking of that - how are you going to break the news to Judy?"

"Gently," he said. "But right away. No more secrets."

The Big Favour

When Lana asked me for help, I could not say no. Though it was after my normal bedtime, I got up and drove the five miles to the Two Hearts Motel. As I pulled past the neon sign, the eerie green clock on the dash of my car showed 11.32 PM. I parked in the lot beside a custom Ford pickup truck. I could feel the cold night air as I stepped out and looked around at the apartments.

Lana appeared in the darkness of the doorway of number seventeen, wearing a white bath towel that made her look ghostly in the moonlight. Her mouth was a dark line, her eyes hidden in shadow. She beckoned me to come in.

"What's going on?" I asked her, but she did not reply.

I could not see anything inside the room until my sister closed the door and switched on the light. It was a typical cheap motel suite. There was a chair, a closet and a TV chained to the wall. A door led into a tiny white-tiled bathroom smelling of pine-scented bleach, but I didn't look there. I stared where Lana stared – at the bed.

My first reaction was shock.

I could not believe what I was seeing.

The naked man was lying on the bed, his face and neck covered in glass and blood. More blood had soaked the sheets. He looked very dead and the blood looked very red.

"Is he ...?"

"Yes."

"Did you ...?"

"Yes," she said, very quietly. "But I didn't mean to, Susan. It just happened."

"Who is he?" I asked."It's Ken."

Now I recognised him. He was the foreman of the construction company owned by Lana's husband, Dean. I had met him at a Christmas party. Ken was married and the last person I'd expect to find dead in a sleazy motel room.

"What happened?"

Lana didn't reply. She started crying like a little girl. "You ... have ... to ... help ... me."

"Okay, okay – but I need to know how this happened. Start at the beginning."

It took a few minutes for her crying to subside. Lana told me everything in a low, barely audible voice.

"Ken asked me for a drink a few weeks back. It was a night Dean was out of town. The kids were staying overnight with their friends. I was bored and lonely so I agreed. Ken seemed like a nice guy. We got talking and started sort of seeing each other after that. Nothing serious. We kissed and fooled around like a couple of teenagers, but we didn't go all the way. It was exciting to feel wanted. Dean hasn't wanted me like that since I had Jess."

"What happened tonight?"

"Tonight we were going to finally make love. He picked me up after work in his blue pickup. We booked the room under false names. Mr and Mrs Johnson. We started drinking champagne and fooling around. It was fun at first, but then I started thinking about Dean. Ken wanted to make love but I changed my mind. It felt wrong, like it was one step too far. I didn't want to cheat on Dean. I told Ken. Ken got mad then. He pinned me down and tried to ..." She sobbed. "I wanted him to stop - but he wouldn't. He wouldn't. It was like the drink turned him into another person. I said "no" but he wouldn't listen. He was going to rape me. I had to stop him. So I hit him with the champagne bottle. It was the only thing I could reach. I just wanted to knock him out. Get him off me. But the bottle broke and somehow the glass cut his throat and ..." She touched her own throat as she recalled it. "You should have heard the horrible gargling noise." She shuddered. "Suddenly, there was blood everywhere. On me – on the sheets – on the walls. By the time I pushed him off me, he was dead. It was an accident, but nobody would ever believe it. Look at the mess – would you believe it wasn't murder?"

"You need to explain this to the police the way you've just told me. They'll understand."

"The police? Are you serious? They won't believe me. They'll think I murdered him – or the very least manslaughter. Either way, Dean will find out and he'll never want to see me again. He'll divorce me and take away my children. My life will be over, Susan. Don't let them put me in prison. You have to help me. You're the clever one. The schoolteacher. Please help me. Please."

I should have said no, but she was my sister.

"Did anyone see you with Ken tonight?"

"No – apart from the guy in the motel office. But I was wearing a hat and a scarf. I'm sure he didn't see my face."

"Okay. That's good. When were you expected home?"

"Uh – uh – uh - before midnight. Dean thinks I'm at your place. Ken was going to drop me off after ..."

"Is there blood on you?"

"No – I showered after I called you. Couldn't stand the blood on me."

"What about your ordinary clothes?"

She shook her head. "They're over there."

"Okay," I said. "Take off that towel. Then put your clothes back on. Drive home in my car – but don't speed. Leave it parked at my house."

She nodded vigorously. "What're you going to do?"

"Don't worry. I'll take care of everything. Just don't say anything to anyone about Ken. You didn't see him tonight. You spent the whole night with me, watching old movies."

"What movies?"

"I don't know! Something you've seen before."

"What about *Titanic*? That's a long one. I know it by heart."

"Okay," I said. "Now get going."

*

By the time Lana left in my car, I'd formulated a plan.

The first thing I wanted to do was move the body out of the room, but it posed various problems. Ken was a big man compared with me, so I knew I'd have to drag him out. I would have to bring his pickup as close to the door as possible, then move him to the vehicle unseen.

I found Ken's keys attached to his jeans. One was for the pickup I'd seen outside. Ken had also been wearing a denim jacket and a baseball cap. I put them both on as a disguise before leaving the room. When I pressed the button to unlock the vehicle, the alarm made a beep I was sure anyone within a thousand miles would hear. Beeeeeeeep! Quickly, I opened the car door with the sleeve of his jacket to avoid leaving fingerprints. Once behind the wheel, I started up the engine and moved the pickup closer to the door.

I returned to the motel room for the next part of the task. I nearly gagged at the smell coming from the dead man. Nobody had told me dead bodies loosened their bowels. Feeling sick, I wrapped Ken in the bloodied sheets before dragging him towards the door. He was just as heavy as I feared. I had to yank him several times by the feet. His body left a streak of blood on the carpet.

I turned off all the lights and opened the door. Across the street, I could see the orange glow of the street-lights and the black silhouettes of apartment buildings where some lights were still on, though all the drapes looked closed. I could see nobody around but I didn't want to take a chance because occasionally a car would pass on the highway and the headlights would illuminate the parking lot. I waited for a lull in the traffic noise before I dragged the body to the car as quickly as possible, hoping nobody would see me. I ducked down when I heard a vehicle. I had a horrible thought it would pull into the parking lot, but it flashed by. Lifting the body, wrapped in the blood-soaked sheet, wasn't easy. He kept slipping. I got his head and shoulders into the back first, then somehow pushed the rest of him into the back. I covered him with a tarpaulin. I could not see him, but it looked obvious to me there was a human body underneath. I tried to make the shape look less human.

My heart was pounding every second, cold sweat pouring down my face. The body was out of sight – for the time being. Then I went back to look at the motel room.

God, what a mess. The blood was a huge problem. There was no way of getting it all cleaned up without leaving invisible traces. No matter what I did there would be hairs and other forensic evidence left behind. It was impossible to clean the room so no evidence of Lana or my presence would be present. But then I realised it was only a problem if it could be seen. It didn't matter if it could be detected by forensic science providing nobody knew a crime had been committed there.

I started cleaning up with what was available in the bathroom – soap, hot water and towels. The blood washed off the walls and carpet but it took a couple of hours. The towels were soaked in blood – and so were the sheets - but I had an idea. There was a twenty-four hour laundry a few blocks away. If I could have the sheets and towels washed before the morning, nobody would know they'd been used.

I parked the pickup in a dark place where I removed the sheet from the body and added it to the others. I put them in a bag and walked the block to the laundry. There were a couple of customers using the machines, the type of weirdos who would wash their clothes in the middle of the night. I didn't want to go in, but I had to risk it. Getting the blood off the sheets was vital.

I lowered the baseball cap over my face before approaching the entrance. I was sure they would know what I was doing the moment I walked inside, but the other customers barely looked up from their own machines. One was a hairy stoner sitting with his eyes half-closed. Another looked like a serial killer. I was in good company. I chose some machines away from everyone else. I put the sheets in and put them on full cycle with plenty of washing powder. It would take about an hour.

I considered waiting, but I decided to use the time for getting rid of the body. Not far from the edge of the town was a deep forest. I drove out into the forest for ten miles. I thought about just ditching the body somewhere off the road, but there was a flashlight in the glove compartment and a spade in the back of the truck. It was far better to bury him. I chose a place behind some trees, not visible from the road. Digging a hole was exhausting, but I didn't dare rest until it was done. It wasn't as deep as I would have liked – I would have liked it to be a thousand feet deep – but a shallow grave would have to do. Dragging him a second time was twice as hard. My arms ached like they'd been torn from the sockets. I buried him inside the tarpaulin so it would stop wild animals digging up his bones. I felt sick as I covered him with soil. I tried to make the ground look untouched before leaving.

I still had to do something about his pickup truck, but I didn't know what. All I knew was I had to return to the laundry. The weirdo customers had gone when I went in to collect the towels and sheets. The washing powder had done a good job. I could not see any stains. I put the sheets in the dryer and waited for them to be dry before taking them out. I drove back to the motel.

I made the bed and then messed it up as if two people had had a good time last night. I took a critical look at the room. I could not tell someone had died in the room – there was no blood visible anywhere - which was exactly what I wanted.

Now I had to just figure out what to do with the pickup truck.

I thought of driving it somewhere remote and ditching it, but then how would I get back home? Instead, I parked the pickup in the lot of a local bar, where it could stay for days before anyone would notice it. I left it unlocked, with the key in the ignition, praying a thief would find it. I hated leaving it there but I could think of nothing better.

Walking home, I dumped the baseball cap and jacket in a garbage can. At four in the morning, the streets were spookily quiet. I was the only fool around. I jumped each time I saw headlights, but

I avoided being seen by staying on the side streets.

My house was in a suburban neighbourhood. Lana had parked my car on the drive. I almost wept with relief as I entered my house and closed the door behind me. Then panic set in. I wished I'd done everything differently in a thousand ways, but it was too late now. Any mistakes I'd made could not be erased. What if the police found something? Had I left fingerprints anywhere? The horror of the night caught up with me. I retched violently into the kitchen sink everything I'd eaten yesterday.

*

"Miss Gretsky?" someone said.

I didn't realise that was my name for a few seconds. Then I jerked back into reality like I'd been slapped awake. One of my ninth grade students was asking the question. I was supposed to be teaching but I'd been staring out of the window thinking about last night.

"Are you okay, Miss?"

"I'm fine, Gerry."

Gerry and the rest of the class kept staring at me. Something was wrong, but I didn't know what. Then I noticed the time. The lesson was over but I'd not heard the bell. I was really out of it due to lack of sleep and the memory of what I'd done to help my sister.

"Okay, class dismissed." They headed for the door. "Remember the homework."

As soon as the classroom was empty, I opened my bag and took out my cell phone. My hands were shaking. I called Lana. She answered immediately. She sounded odd on the phone. Tense. We didn't mention Ken.

We agreed to meet after school.

*

It was a balmy autumn evening suitable for romantic trysts, not clandestine meetings. Lana and I sat in my car for ten minutes without saying anything. The whole situation did not feel real. My sister nervously smoked cigarette after cigarette despite saying she'd given it up as a New Year's resolution. She was dressed in a powder blue jacket and skirt, an outfit she wore as a realty agent. She didn't look different from normal except for her eyes, which looked puffy and bloodshot.

"Dean was up when I got home," she said. "He asked where I'd been all night. I said I'd been with you."

"Did he say anything else?"

"No."

"Did he seem suspicious?"

"No." She lit another cigarette despite having one already between her lips. When she realised what she'd done, she offered me the cigarette. I shook my head. She smoked them with alternate drags. "I've been worrying all day about you. How did you get rid of it?"

It. She was already distancing herself emotionally. I was suddenly mad at her. "You really want to know?"

She nodded.

"I buried him in the woods."

"I'm sorry."

"For what?"

"For getting you into this."

I sighed. "Forget it. It's done now."

"Susan, what do I say when people realise Ken is missing?"

"You say nothing. You don't know anything."

"I don't know anything," she repeated. She sounded uneasy. "I feel so guilty. I've been flustered all day. I lost a sale because I scared a customer by almost breaking into tears when I was showing a house. I feel like I'm about to explode. Maybe I should tell Dean and the police what happened ..."

"No! It's too late now, you stupid idiot!"

Lana looked scared of me. I had shouted. I was angry. She had no idea what I'd done for her. I felt like slapping her.

"Lana," I said, trying to calm down. "You can't change your mind *now.* I got rid of the stupid body for you. I'm implicated in this as much as you. It's too late for changing your mind now just because you're feeling bad. Ken's dead. It's just a terrible fact we have to deal with. Remember, he did try to rape you."

She nodded slowly. "I know, I know. It's just so hard not talking about it."

"We can talk about it. Anything you have to say, say it to me."

We sat there for maybe an hour. Eventually Lana noticed the time was getting late. She wiped her eyes and re-applied her makeup. "I feel a little better having talked to you. I knew you would take care of everything. My big sister. I can't tell you how grateful I am. Anything you want, just ask. I owe you the biggest favour."

We hugged goodbye.

*

For the rest of the week, I watched the news and read the newspapers for anything about Ken. There was nothing. I began worrying the police had found him and were keeping it a secret so they could trick me into returning to the grave. I was dying to know if he had been discovered. The temptation of checking the grave was almost unbearable. I got as far as driving my car to the entrance of the forest before turning back. I wanted to know if Ken's disappearance had been mentioned to the police yet. It must have been, I thought, because he had a family. Lana did not know any more than I did, as she had no legitimate reason for asking Dean about his foreman, so I tried to forget about it, like I'd told Lana. But it was impossible to do it. That long night was the only thing I could think about. I had bad dreams. In one dream Ken was a zombie trying to kill me. I slept with the light on after that. And I started wondering if Ken had actually been dead when I buried him. What if he had been badly wounded but alive? What if I'd buried a living man? No, no – it was crazy. He was dead. Wasn't he?

I needed to check the grave.

But I rationally knew it wasn't a good idea.

I fought the urge by going to the local gym. It was the first time I'd been since my ex-boyfriend Joshua gave me a year's membership as a birthday present. (It was his way of encouraging me to lose a few pounds. We broke up because he was always criticising my body.) I worked out like an adrenaline junkie for three hours every night after school. It helped me resist the temptation. Just.

On Friday, I had dinner with Lana and her family. I didn't feel like going, but it was something we did every couple of weeks. It might have aroused suspicion if I did not show up at their home.

Lana and Dean lived in a beautiful house built by Dean's

company. Everything about it was perfect, like the glossy pages of an interior-decorating magazine. The dining room was more spacious than my entire house.

During dinner, Dean mentioned Ken.

"Here's something weird," he said. "He's disappeared like something out of the Twilight Zone."

"Really?" I said. "What do you mean?"

"Nobody's seen him since Tuesday. He didn't come in on Wednesday. I thought he was sick or something, but I phoned his house and nobody's seen him. His wife Grace contacted the police. They found his car parked at a bar with the keys still in it, but no sign of him."

"That's strange," I said. I looked at Lana. Here eyes were bugging.

"It's a real pain. Ken's a good foreman. I can't understand where he's gone."

"What do the police think?"

"I don't know. They seemed as baffled as everyone else."

Let's hope it stays that way, I thought, but I had a bad feeling it would not.

*

Another week went by. I taught my classes just like normal. Pretended everything was okay. Mid-week a story appeared in the local paper about Ken. It was entitled "Missing Man Mystery." According to the story, the police had not learnt anything new. However, the story featured a photograph of Ken with his wife and daughters. It had been taken on vacation last year in Florida. They looked so happy it made me want to confess all.

That Friday morning I found a white envelope in my mailbox with just my name on it, no address. It had not been stamped like the rest of my mail, which was mostly junk and bills. It looked like it had been typed on an old typewriter with a fading ribbon. I had a bad feeling about it even before I opened it and read the single sheet of paper inside, also typed. I stared at it, the words searing my brain.

I had to see Lana straight away.

She was in her office on the phone to a client when I came in. The expression on my face told her enough. I closed the door and slumped in a chair, holding the envelope. She quickly ended the call.

"What's wrong?" she wanted to know.

"Did you get any strange letters?"

"No – why?"

"I got this in my mail." I handed the sheet across her desk. She read it silently, mouthing the words. I knew the contents by heart already, having read it a dozen times.

We know what you and your sister did. We saw it all.

Bring $1000 to Century Park on Saturday at 18:00.

Wait on the bench by the lake.

Pay or pray – it's up to you.

The Watchers.

"Oh, God, no," she said. "We're being *blackmailed.* Who do you think it is? How could they have seen it all?"

"I don't know," I said.

"Could it be the police, trying to trick us?"

"Maybe," I answered. "If it is, there's nothing we can do about it, though. I think we have to assume it's not the police, but a genuine blackmailer."

"I don't get it. Why did they contact you, not me?"

"They must have found out I live alone – so they sent the blackmail note to me to ensure the wrong person didn't read it first. It's the smart thing to do. Also, the amount they want is not outrageous, so they know we can afford to pay it. Of course, the thousand won't be the only money they want. It will just be a first instalment. They'll want more. A lot more. They'll probably want regular payments to keep quiet. That's how blackmailers work."

"You seem to know a lot about blackmailers." She made it sound like an accusation.

"I've read a lot of crime novels."

"What should we do?"

I thought about it. We were powerless unless we could find out the identity of the blackmailer. I thought of a plan, but it would have to be carefully executed. There were so many things that could go wrong I dared not even think of them. "I'll go alone to the rendezvous. Meet the blackmailer. We might need to make the first payment. Can you get the money?"

"Yes, but I can't afford to pay forever, Susan."

*

I sat down on the bench at five minutes before six. An old man was reading John Grisham. He looked up at me. I stared back. I wondered if he was the blackmailer, but he got up and walked off after thirty seconds. I probably scared him with my stare. I looked around as I waited.

It was a warm evening with plenty of time remaining before the sun went down, though the shadows were long. The lake looked golden in the sunlight. There were several people walking or jogging by on the path circling the lake. There were some kids playing baseball. The blackmailer had chosen a discreet but also populated place. There were several exits via paths into the woods. I watched everyone as they approached the bench, half expecting them to stop, but they did not. I kept looking at my watch. It was after six. The blackmailer was late. That was to be expected. The blackmailer would want to keep control of the situation.

A jogger was coming around the lake. He was wearing a grey jogging top with a hood covering most of his face. He was white, in his twenties, but I could not see much more because sunglasses hid his eyes. He had long greasy black hair and acne scars. He sat down next to me and looked around nervously.

"Where's your sister?"

"She couldn't make it. Who are you?"

"Shut up. Don't ask me questions. I'm here for the G. Do you have it or what?"

"Are you a cop?" I asked.

"No," he said. "Do I look like a lousy cop?"

"I had to ask," I said. "You wrote me a blackmail note, but why should I give you money?"

"Why? Because I've got evidence that'd put you in jail. That's why."

"Evidence? What evidence?"

"Don't play games," he said. "I've got a tape. It's real interesting."

"I don't know what you're talking about."

"Yeah, right. I suppose you was nowhere near the Two Hearts Motel last Tuesday? I suppose your sister didn't kill Ken, the guy the police are looking for? You didn't help her get rid of the body? It's all on VHS, baby."

"I want to see this so-called tape before I give you money."

"No way. All you've got to know is the tape could put you both away for a real long time. I've made plenty of copies of it so don't even think about trying to mess with me. Anything happens to me, my lawyer's been instructed to open a safe-deposit box with the original in it. If you don't want the cops getting a copy, you'll give me the money *right now*."

"Okay, okay." I reached into my handbag, taking out a paper bag. "Here."

Looking around agitatedly, he grabbed the paper bag and counted the money inside. He looked pleased with the total. "This is the way it is, lady. I want another G next month. I'll contact you on the Friday where to drop it off. You show up with the money or the tape puts you in jail." He grinned coldly. "I'm going now. Don't try to follow me. My associates will be watching."

He sprinted away, looking back a few times to assure himself I had not moved. I waited until he had disappeared before standing up. I hoped Lana had been able to track him through the binoculars. I returned to my car before switching on my cell phone and calling her. She answered immediately. She was breathless.

"I'm following him," she said. "He's leaving the park via the south entrance. He's still on foot. I'll call you when I know more."

*

I met Lana in a café an hour later.

"Well?" I asked. "Did you find out where he lives?"

"No. I lost him," she said. "He jumped on a bus. I'm sorry. I tried to follow him."

I swore. I had been hoping she would have been able to follow him home so we would know his identity. "Don't worry. There's always next month. We can try again. Anyway, I recorded the meeting. You want to hear what he said?"

Lana nodded. I opened my bag and took out the tape I'd made of the conversation. She listened to it on headphones.

"He has a tape – but how?"

"I don't know, but at least we now know what he has against us. If only we had the tape, the blackmailer would have nothing. Then it would be just his word against ours."

*

That night I lay awake, thinking. I could not sleep. I got up and went for a drive. I ended up parking not far from the Two Hearts Motel. I walked there. I could see into the brightly-lit office from across the street. There was a young man behind the counter with long black hair. It was hard to tell from a distance, but it looked like he had marks on his face.

"The night manager," Lana said when I told her. "Are you sure?"

"Fairly," I said. "I would have to see him up close to be sure, but I'm eighty percent positive. He must've remembered seeing you with Ken. He probably saw my car arrive later. That's how he figured out who we are."

"So, what do we do now?"

"I'm going to spend the day finding out his name and where he lives. Tonight I'll break into his place while he's working and search for the tape – if it exists. He could be lying. But I need to know what evidence he really does have. His power over us is the fear of what evidence he's got."

"That sounds risky," Lana said. "I don't want to break into his home. I'm not doing that, Susan. I'm not doing it!"

"I'll do it by myself," I said. "It's probably better if you don't get involved, anyway. I know how to pick a cheap lock – I read about it in a book. I'll be very careful."

"Don't do it," Lana said. "You don't want to make him angry. Maybe it's best if I just keep paying the money? I can do that. It's probably safer to just keep him happy."

"Listen. I won't disturb anything. He won't even know I've been there, I promise. I'll just look for the tape. Without the tape – if there is a tape – he can't blackmail you. It's just his word against ours. You have an alibi for the night, remember? Me."

"No, Susan. I'll pay the money. Forget about it. Don't look for the tape."

Lana begged me not to do it until I agreed, but I lied. The thought of being blackmailed for the rest of our lives made me angry. I needed to know if the tape really existed.

That morning I made discreet inquiries at the motel into the name of the night manager. His name was Gregor Arnoslov. He worked the nightshift from nine until nine the next morning. There was only one G Arnoslov listed in the telephone directory. He lived in a brownstone tenement building three blocks from the motel. His apartment was on the third of six floors, number 308. Anyone could enter the lobby by getting buzzed in, but getting into his apartment would be harder, despite what I'd told my sister.

During the afternoon, I learnt how to use the tools necessary for committing my second crime – a set of lock picks. I practised opening the locks in my house until I was good at using them. My own house locks were quite easy to unlock once I'd practised. I promised myself I would buy some good deadlocks to replace them. I hoped Gregor Arnoslov had no better locks than my own as I headed for his apartment after it got dark.

There was no light on in his apartment, which was a good sign. Just to be sure he was out, I buzzed his number. There was no answer. While I was standing there, a woman came up the steps with some shopping bags. As she entered the lobby, I sneaked in after her.

I hurried up the stairs to the third floor rather than the elevator. The corridor looked empty. I approached apartment 308, taking out the picks. Luckily, the lock was cheap and unlocked in about a minute. I slipped on some surgical gloves, then entered the dark apartment. I closed the door behind me before switching on my flashlight.

I didn't have to look long. There was a TV and VCR beside a vast collection of videos and DVDs. I found a tape was already in the VCR, labelled "SEC TAPE TUE". I pressed PLAY and watches as a grainy image appeared of the parking lot of the Two Hearts Motel. It had not even occurred to me there was a security camera there. The tape had been stopped a few seconds before I came outside, dragging the body towards the pickup truck. I'd thought I'd been so clever but had not considered looking for cameras.

I sensed someone or something in the room. I spun around. There was someone standing in the darkness of the bedroom doorway. They turned on the light.

"Lana?"

My sister grimaced. "Susan! I'm so glad it's you!"

"What are you doing here?"

She hesitated. "I lied about losing him the other day. I followed him here, but I didn't tell you because I thought I could talk to him myself. I wanted to explain how Ken died, hoping he'd stop the blackmail if he understood the truth. But things didn't quite work out the way I wanted. I think ... I think you'd better come in here."

Slowly, Lana walked back into the bedroom.

Reluctantly, I followed.

"He didn't care that it was an accident – or that Ken tried to rape me. He was just angry I'd found out where he lived. He said I'd have to pay extra. He wanted me to sleep with him. I refused. He slapped me and dragged me onto the bed. I grabbed the lamp. I hit him back. I think I smashed his skull because he rolled onto the floor and stopped breathing."

I looked at the body. A broken lamp was near him.

"He's been dead for a couple of hours," Lana said. "I've been sitting on the bed, wondering what to do. I didn't dare call you. I was too ashamed. But now you're here, anyway, can you help me.
One more big favour ... "

Starlight

The man was waiting outside the lecture room when I came out with my film class. He was wearing an Armani suit and Rolex, holding a briefcase, smiling a little too hard. "Lawyer" was written all over him. They were the only people who wore ties in Los Angeles. As my students drifted away for their lunch, I was left alone in the hall with the stranger.

"Excuse me," he said. "Are you Laura Kenyon?"

"Yes?" I said.

"I've been looking for you. My name's Whitford. I'm a lawyer, but don't hold that against me, please. I'm not here with a subpoena."

Whitford looked as old as my father, who had celebrated his fiftieth birthday in July, but he had kept himself in better fitness. His hair was peppered grey, cut short. His teeth looked straightened and capped. They were too white to be entirely natural. He reminded me of the actor Ian Holm in his seminal performance in *Alien*.

"I'm here because I read your books. Your publisher told me you'd be here." He offered his hand to shake. It was warm and smooth, the nails perfectly manicured. "My client wants to hire you to ghost-write her autobiography."

"Your client?" I said. "Who's that?"

"Claudia Besson."

He watched my stunned reaction. He had to be joking or mentally disturbed.

I knew a lot about Claudia Besson. She had won an Academy Award for Best Supporting Actress. During the 1940s, Claudia Besson had not only been a beautiful film star but a sublime actress.

I loved all of her seventeen movies, even the badly scripted or poorly directed ones. Her on-screen talent had radiated out of every frame. In her time she had been as famous as Marilyn Monroe. Any film student would have heard of her. I had written a book on her life and career, but I had never met her for one very good reason. She had died before I was born.

*

The strange man's words left me speechless and wondering what to do. He was clearly deranged in some way, perhaps schizophrenic. I wanted to get away from him before he did something dangerous. I looked around hoping to see someone – anyone - but the corridor was deserted. The building was utterly silent. There was probably nobody else in the building during the lunch hour. He had chosen the perfect time to approach me without witnesses.

Whitford was smiling even harder now. I thought I glimpsed something crazy behind his eyes. I decided to humour him. "So, she's your client?"

"Yes," he said.

"That's ... interesting."

"I'm not mad," he said abruptly. "You're thinking Claudia Besson died in a car crash in 1951. I *know* that. That's what she wanted the rest of the world to think, but she's alive. She's a good friend of mine. A very good friend. I would do anything for her, which is why I am here today."

I nodded while thinking of ways to escape him. The exit doors were at least thirty feet away.

"She wants to meet you, to discuss writing her autobiography,"

Whitford said. "I'm to bring you to her – if you are interested. Everything will be explained after you meet her, I promise."

"You want me to go with you now?"

"No, no. I couldn't expect that. You have a busy life, I know. I'll give you some time to consider my offer – say, until Saturday?"

"Why Saturday?"

"You can spend the whole weekend getting to know her. In the meantime, I'll leave you my card. I hope you will call me back."

He handed me a white business card with his name and telephone number on it:

Whitford Reece

Attorney-at-law

90210-555-3710

The area code was familiar to anyone who had watched TV: it was the code for Beverly Hills.

"Oh, one little thing. Miss Besson doesn't want her privacy invaded by the media knowing she is still alive – not yet, anyway. That's a secret she would rather keep between us for now. She would really appreciate your discretion. Thank you. Goodbye."

Whitford bowed politely like a Japanese businessman, then he walked out of the building, leaving me dumbfounded.

Was she really alive? I had so many questions, questions I had not asked Whitford because I was only thinking of them now. The whole encounter felt surreal. Was it a sick joke? Everyone who knew me knew how much I would have loved to have met Claudia Besson. I was probably her biggest fan. I had a website dedicated to her memory. Was one of my ex-boyfriends setting me up?

I looked at the card. Whitford Reece? Come on! That didn't sound like a real name. There was no address on the card, which made me more suspicious. I needed to ask him some questions before he was gone. I quickly followed him out into the bright sunshine, but he was nowhere in sight.

*

For the next few days, I kept the card but did not call the number.

I had become obsessed with the work of Claudia Besson when I was a little girl. My grandmother first introduced me to her films. She had been a makeup artist during the 1940s. She had met the movie stars and liked to tell me what Hollywood was like back then. As a hobby after her retirement, she had collected thousands of classic movies from that era, Hollywood's Golden Age. She screened movies in her basement, which she had converted into a small theatre, complete with red velvet seats and a projector. My grandmother had bought the projector from a closing down cinema. When she was babysitting me, we would watch her movies and eat popcorn like we were in a real cinema. There was something magical about sitting in the dark, watching black and white movies being projected onto a big screen. Her favourite actress had been Claudia Besson, whom she had known personally, having done her makeup on two movies. "I felt redundant doing her," my grandmother used to say. "She was already perfect when she came in. She was the most beautiful woman I had ever seen." We had watched her films over and over, each time experiencing something new. Her characters had all been memorable, vivid, real. Sometimes I had dressed up my grandmother's old clothes, pretending to be her. My grandmother and I had acted out many of her famous scenes until I knew the lines by heart.

My grandmother died when I was nine, but I never forgot how exciting it was to be watching those old movies and pretending to be Claudia Besson.

Later, I often wished I had been born in those days, but the closest I could be was to write my doctoral thesis on the subject and have it adapted into a book. Claudia Besson had been born in 1922, the third child of two poor Swedish immigrants. Her original name was Lena Nordenberg. Lena had been a startlingly beautiful child, inheriting her mother's natural blonde hair and teal blue eyes. She had grown into a tall and graceful teenager, the star of several high-school plays, much to her mother's delight, though her father had not approved of her acting. He was an alcoholic who had often beaten her. She ran away when she was fifteen. She came to Hollywood, where she got a job as a waitress at a restaurant across the street from a studio. A director noticed her and offered her a small part in a film. He changed her name to Claudia Besson because it sounded French and sensual. That first role led to others, more substantial. She made over twenty films, some of which were underrated classics. She won her Academy Award for her role in an adaptation of an Arthur Miller play. Then, just as her star was rising, she had the fatal car crash on a lonely desert road. Of course, all of her biographies ended in 1952 with the crash – including my own. There was a lot of speculation about what caused the accident – but as wild as the conspiracy theories were, none suggested she might have survived.

The story of her death was as famous as the story of her life, if not more famous. It had happened on the night of the wrap party for what turned out to be her final film, The Blue Echo. The producer Maxwell Greenberg had invited everyone involved to a party at his Beverly Hills home. There she was seen drinking several glasses of champagne before slipping out of the party long after midnight. Despite being drunk, she drove herself home in her new MG, a vehicle she had only owned for two weeks. The MG careered off a narrow road, smashing fifty feet below on rocks.

I had seen the notorious black and white photographs of her crushed, burnt-out vehicle. Her charred body had been behind the wheel, a blackened skeleton with grinning teeth staring out of an eyeless skull. Strands of her long, platinum blonde hair, stuck to her scalp, had been the only part of her not destroyed in the fire. The gruesome nature of her death had guaranteed her a place in Hollywood Legend as much as Jane Mansfield's decapitation, James Dean's crash and Marilyn Monroe's mysterious overdose. Claudia Besson was remembered as much for her demise as her brilliant but tragically short acting career.

There had been a thorough investigation into her death, which had been ruled an accident. The local police had checked the dead woman's dental records against Claudia's before pronouncing her dead. Her relatives had also confirmed her identity. There had never been a single rumour about her being alive.

I had always believed she was dead.

But now?

Now I was having doubts.

Dental records could be swapped. Witnesses could be paid off. Photographs could be faked.

There was only one way to know the truth.

*

Early on Saturday morning, a black BMW with tinted windows drew up at my house. The driver was Whitford Reece. Like a chauffeur, he insisted on carrying my bags to the car and putting them in the trunk. Then he opened a rear door for me. It looked awfully dark inside. I felt nervous about getting in the car with him, having told nobody where I was going. He had not even told me where we were going! I hoped I was not doing something incredibly stupid. Getting into a car with a complete stranger seemed like something only an idiot would do in a horror movie like *The Hitcher*. I would never hitch-hike for that reason ... but I was willingly allowing a stranger drive me somewhere. For all I knew, he could be planning to take me out into the desert to be raped and murdered. I hesitated.

"Is something wrong?"

"No," I lied. I climbed in. The BMW was cool. The tinted windows made it look like twilight outside. He closed the door after me. It made a hefty clunk. I wondered if had locked automatically, trapping me. I was now in his car exactly where he wanted me. I deserved to be killed for being so naïve.

Whitford went around and climbed into the driver's seat. He started the engine. I looked back at my house as we pulled away. I prayed I would see it again.

We were soon on the freeway.

"Where are we going?"

"I can't say."

"Why not?"

"Miss Besson values her anonymity. If you knew where she lived, you might be tempted to reveal it to others. Speaking of which, do you have a cell phone?"

"Yes – why?"

"I must insist on taking it temporarily." He turned around with his hand out. "I've been instructed to take you back home if you refuse."

I did not like it, but I opened my handbag and gave him my Nokia. "Don't damage it."

"I'm only turning it off," he said. I watched him place it in the glove compartment. The next thing he said was polite but alarming. "Now, if you don't mind, please slip this over your eyes."

It was a blindfold.

*

"We're here," he announced, hours later.

I had spent the time in darkness, listening to music on the BMW's CD player. At first I had been scared about wearing the blindfold, but when nothing happened after ten minutes I'd managed to relax (a little) sufficiently to let myself (almost) fall asleep. The BMW provided a comfortable ride. I was glad the ride was over, though. Tears stung my eyes as I removed the blindfold and looked at my surroundings.

The BMW had parked on a cliff in front of a large white-painted house. The wild ocean roared against the cliff, huge breakers exploding against the rocks along the coastline. There were no other houses, cars or people anywhere in sight. There was only the white house, gleaming in the sunlight. I was no expert in geography, but I suspected we were somewhere near Big Sur. There were miles and miles of beautiful coastline just like this along Highway 1.

Whitford stepped out and opened the door for me. It was good stretching my legs and breathing in the salty air. Whitford led the way up to the front porch while I looked for some indication of the address. There was a mailbox but I could see no name nor number on it. The front door was the same. Whitford opened it with a key, inviting me inside.

We entered a hall lined with vivid oil paintings of the Big Sur cliffs and ocean. They were by an accomplished painter.

"Miss Besson did those," Whitford informed me, with some pride. "Painting is a hobby of hers."

Whitford led me to a broad staircase sweeping up to the second floor. We stopped at a door. He knocked gently.

"Come in!" a woman called out.

We stepped into a light and airy bedroom. It smelled of strawberries. Large windows revealed a stunning ocean view. An old woman was lying in a four-poster bed, propped up by several plump and luxurious pillows. I had been wondering how I would know if the woman really was genuine who she claimed – until she turned to face me. Her eyes were teal blue, eyes that had captivated audiences across the world. They radiated a special light, drawing me to stare dumbstruck. An echo of the young film star remained in her despite her hair being pure white.

I was meeting *the* Claudia Besson.

"Don't stand on ceremony," she said in a voice I recognised. It was lyrical, sensuous, deep. It was a voice demanding attention, as powerful as the most gifted singer's. "Come in, my dear. Sit down next to me." An Edwardian chair was by the bed. "Whitty, be a dear, bring our guest something to drink."

"What would you like?" he asked.

"Just coffee," I said.

Whitford backed out of the room, leaving us alone. I sat down, not knowing what to say. She was studying me. It made me more self-conscious than usual. I smiled awkwardly and looked down, but could still feel her eyes on me. I forced myself to look at her. She had a copy of my book her hands.

"Laura, I loved your book," she said. "It helped me refresh my memory of the good old days. I could feel your love of cinema on every page."

"Thank you," I said.

"This wonderful book is also the reason why I chose you. After I read your book, I felt like I knew you personally. I felt I could trust you with my secret. Have you told anyone about me?"

I shook my head.

"Thank you. For the last fifty years, I have lived like a normal person. Nobody around here knows me as Claudia Besson, the famous actress. I have been living under my old name, Lena Nordenberg. Only one person ever recognised me – Whitford. He has an excellent memory for trivia like the real names of movie stars. He put two and two together after he saw me browsing in a local bookstore. He's been my friend since then."

"Can I ask you some questions?"

She smiled. "I'm counting on it."

"What happened that night?" I asked her. "Who was found in your car?"

"That was Rose Stewart. She was an assistant to Maxwell Greenberg. She drove me home that night because I was drunk. Maxwell made her do it even though she had no experience driving. She was a young girl, just obeying his orders. She didn't know the road ... the poor girl. The crash killed her instantly, but I was thrown clear. I remember waking up, seeing the car on fire. I was badly injured. I passed out and woke up in hospital a few days later. Nobody knew who I was – except for Maxwell Greenberg. He was frightened he would be sued by Rose's family for making her drive me home, so he paid off the local police and arranged it so 'Claudia Besson' died in the accident. He even had someone swap my dental records for hers. I went along with it when I found out because I had no choice. You see, I could never be Claudia Besson again."

"Why not?"

"The accident damaged my spine, making me paraplegic. Nobody in Hollywood would hire a cripple in a wheelchair, believe me. I left Hollywood behind, becoming Lena again. I changed my appearance and moved to a small town without a movie theatre, where I could re-invent myself. I went to college and studied to become a drama teacher. I taught generations of kids how to act, until my retirement. Since then, I've lived here by the ocean, painting and writing."

I heard Whitford's footsteps behind me. He had brought some coffee and sandwiches on a silver tray.

"Whitty, I think it's time for another," Claudia said, suddenly wincing. He was at her side in a heartbeat, taking a bottle of pills out of his pocket, given her one to swallow with a glass of water. She swallowed the pill and lay back for a minute until the pain had gone.

"Are you okay?" I wanted to know.

"No," she said. "I'm dying."

"What?"

"I have cancer. In a few weeks, I'll be dead, but first there is something I'd like to do. I want to give you something, Laura. There are some things in my study. Whitty will show you the way. Excuse me, I need to rest for a little ..."

*

Whitford showed me into a large wood-panelled study filled with antique furniture. "Miss Besson would like you to read her writing."

A thick manuscript stood on an oak desk. I estimated a thousand pages.

"What is it about?"

"Her life," he told me. Then he stepped into the hall, shutting the door.

I approached the desk, taking a seat. I switched on a desk lamp and pulled the heavy manuscript towards me. I picked up the first page and read it. It was good. Very good. I read on and discovered she had written her complete autobiography, warts and all. It must have taken years and years to write it. She had left out nothing significant, answering all of my questions. I read the manuscript in one sitting, putting down the final sheet several hours later, hardly aware of the time passing. I looked at the window and saw it had gone dark outside.

I stood up, puzzled. She didn't need a ghost-writer. Her manuscript was excellent. So, why did she need me? It certainly wasn't to be her ghost-writer. I was going to look for Whitford, who was certain to know the answer, when I noticed something in a cabinet across the room.

I gasped. No. It wasn't ...? Yes, it was. There – in among as display of photographs – was her Oscar. I stepped closer for a better look. From a distance, to a layman, it could have looked like a sports trophy, but I instantly recognised her Academy Award. Margaret Herrick, a librarian for the Academy of Motion Pictures Arts and

Sciences, had thought the gold statuette looked like her uncle, Oscar, a name that had quickly caught on. I stared and stared at the Oscar, enraptured by it. It was beautiful.

I knew what I was going to do next was wrong, but I could not help myself.

Slowly, I stepped up to the cabinet and opened the glass doors. Reaching out, I felt my hands trembling. I almost expected an electric shock when I put my fingers around the base of the Oscar, but it just felt cold. I lifted it out and held it in both hands as I had imagined doing if I had won one. I felt the iconic power of the statue, the pinnacle of recognition for achievement in the film business. I wished ... I didn't know what I wished, but I felt strange, holding an Oscar. I also felt a little guilty for taking it out of its case without permission. After a minute or two, I returned it to the cabinet, somewhat reluctantly.

It was then I became aware of Whitford. He was standing in the doorway, watching me shutting the cabinet.

He smiled. "Yes, I like to do that, too."

I blushed. "I'm sorry."

"Don't be. I should have shown you it, anyway. She's awake now, wanting to see you again."

*

"I don't understand something," I said to her as I entered her bedroom. "You don't need a ghost-writer – so why am I here?"

"I'm sorry for misleading you," she said. "If I had told you the real reason, you would have thought me insane. First, I wanted you to read my book, so you would know what I was offering."

"What are you offering?"

"My memories."

I frowned. "What do you mean?"

"When I die the only thing left of my life will be that manuscript, which tells you about me, but doesn't show you. As a writer I'm sure you've heard the advice that is better to show than tell?"

"Yes?"

"Well, I want to do that for you, Laura. Have you heard about the memory experiments performed on rats? No? Some neuroscientists trained some rats to run through a maze. They then removed parts of the rats' brains, implanting the biopsy tissue into other rats, ones that had not seen the maze before. They discovered the rats could run the maze without seeing it before - just as if they had remembered it. The new rats had the memories of the first ones. Those experiments showed it was possible to transfer memory. That was decades ago. The technology has moved on. I have found a neurosurgeon willing to perform the operation on me, transferring my most important memories. I will die in the process, but my memories will live on – in you. Imagine what it will feel like to remember what it was like to win an Oscar. Books and movies can't convey what it feels like. You have to experience it for yourself. When I read your book, I felt your passion for your subject. You're in love with the old Hollywood. You want to experience it. Let me give you that gift. Let me give you my thoughts. What do you think?"

I thought she was a dying woman desperately seeking a way of cheating death. "I want to help you, but ..."

"You don't believe me?" She sounded amused. "I didn't believe it myself, until I read the research. It will work – but nobody has dared do it on a human subject. There are risks, but I wouldn't ask you to do it if I thought you would be harmed. Whitford has already made sure you are a compatible donor. He has a friend who hacked into your medical records. You have the right blood type so you won't reject my brain tissue."

Whitford was standing by the door, nodding. "The neurosurgeon is the best in his field. All he needs is your consent."

I stared at Claudia. "You're serious?"

"Deadly," she said.

"What if I say no?"

"Then you're free to leave. Whitford will drive you back to your home."

"What would you do then?"

"I'd try to find someone else before my time runs out. If I'm lucky, I'll find someone willing to have the operation."

"But it took months to find you," Whitford said. "She'll die before we find another person, Laura. You have to say yes. I'm begging you."

"Don't put pressure on her," she said to Whitford. "The decision is yours, Laura."

I sighed. "Can I have some time to think about it?"

*

Her obituary was in the *LA Times* a few weeks later. I read it out in a class to my students. They were all interested in it because the story had been in the news since it broke. The obituary stated Claudia Besson had been living under a false name for over fifty years. Her real identity had been discovered only after her death, when a friend found a manuscript in her house, proving she was the famous movie star. Her body had been cremated and scattered into the ocean. It was expected her autobiography would be a bestseller. All of the profit would go to the family of Rose Stewart.

"I was lucky enough to meet her before she died. She gave me something in her will, which I have brought in for you all to see today."

My class stared as I opened my handbag and pulled out the Oscar.

I remembered when I had held it for the first time, standing in front of an audience of thousands, their faces staring up at me as I made my acceptance speech, tears of joy rolling down my cheeks. I remembered. I remembered.

Now it was time to pass that memory on.

Disconnected

When they turned the street corner, Alison knew they were lost. There were two BT phone boxes under the sycamore trees, shaded from the sweltering sunlight of the Indian summer, but no sign of a large redbrick house. Alison and Hailey paused in the relative coolness. Alison looked up and down the road, looking for the Eddington Road, while Hailey pulled a pack of cigarettes from her cut-off jeans and lit one, blowing blue smoke halos into the road.

"Smoke?" she said, offering one.

"No thanks." Alison could not see Eddington Road. A sign for Theaston Avenue was on the stone wall running the length of the street. Private houses hid behind the walls, not the student flats supposed to be around there somewhere. She jumped as a grey squirrel darted across the road and into some bushes. Alison opened her A-Z and stared at the ring of red Biro ink around Eddington Road.

"This is Theaston Avenue, right?"

Hailey nodded.

"I can't find Theaston Avenue anywhere near Eddington Road. I think we got the wrong bus from the station because I'm completely lost."

"Great. So what are we going to do? I haven't seen a single person to ask directions. No cars. No buses. Nothing. It's Deadsville, Arizona."

"I know, I know." Alison opened the nearest phone box. "Okay, we call the landlord, what's-his-face -"

"Nigel Brentwood?"

"- and ask him how to get there." The phone box was pleasantly cold after the long walk. Hailey squeezed in behind her. Alison gave her a look.

"I want to listen," Hailey said.

Alison lifted the receiver. The line hummed tunelessly. "Do you have some change?"

"Spare change?" Hailey said. "Or the regular type?"

"Ha, ha. Have you?"

Hailey rumbled in her Laura Ashley handbag. Alison grew bored waiting, but she could not complain, since she had no money at all until her grant cheque cleared. She already felt guilty about borrowing the train and bus fares from Hailey. It was lucky they were going to the same university, studying the same subject - Law - and had known each other since Secondary School, or the disastrous events of the day would have proved too much. A six hour train journey was one thing, but the unusual weather had made it a nightmare. For September, the weather was unbelievably hot and sticky, testing her temper to the limit. There was nothing like a long train journey in 90° Fahrenheit heat to get the blood boiling. Just when she'd waited too long - how much stuff did Hailey have in her handbag? - Hailey found her purse.

"Aha! Here you go, girl," she said.

Alison put ten pence in the slot and dialled the number. "It's not ringing."

"Give it time to connect."

"It's not ringing. There's just the sound the phone makes. Eeeeeee."

Hailey tut-tutted. "Let me," she said, with an air of superiority Alison considered rude. Hailey pushed past Alison. The door closed, leaving them squashed face to face. As Hailey's naked midriff pressed against Alison's T-shirt, she could feel the navel ring there. Hailey tried the phone. As if she could work magic on the telephone system. Her eyebrows made a tight V. "This phone's well knackered. Try the other one."

Alison pushed the door and grunted. "Won't move."

Hailey added her weight. "You're right. It's stuck."

Alison tried again, feeling her cheeks flush as she strained and sweated. The door resisted as if blocked by a brick wall. "This is ridiculous!"

Hailey put her back against the opposite wall and used both legs as a lever. She looked as if she were squatting on an invisible toilet, her face reddening, the cords on her neck standing out, teeth bared. The half-burnt cigarette dangled from her lips, which she spat out. "Try this with me."

Alison copied her, pushing the door with all her leg strength, using one leg to kick and kick while the other provided support.

Nothing happened.

The door was stuck.

Alison could feel a growing panic, a sudden claustrophobia. *I'm never going to get out of here. I'm never going to get of here.* Pushing, she was breathing harder and faster, unable to get a decent breath. *I'm going to spend the rest of my life trapped in a phone box.* She kicked at the glass, but it was modern sort of box with Plexiglas. The glass absorbed the impact with a quiver, bouncing back into shape undamaged. After a couple of minutes, she was exhausted, and so was Hailey.

"We ... have to .. think ... of another ... plan."

"I ... agree."

Alison faced the phone and dialled 999. Then the operator. No reply. "Worth a try," she said. "Of all the phone boxes in the world, we have to be stuck in this."

"If we yell loud enough maybe someone will hear us."

So they yelled.

And yelled.

"Hold on," Hailey said. "I don't think anyone can hear us. These booths are soundproofed against traffic noise."

"Sound travels under the gap at the bottom."

"Right. I forgot. There's normally a gap of about six inches at the bottom to let air in."

"And urine out."

"But look!" Hailey's shout stunned Alison. "The glass goes all the way to the ground."

"What?" Alison hunched down. Hailey was telling the truth. The glass did go all the way to the ground. They were sealed in. She examined the door. The gap between the door and the box was filled with glass, glass which clearly could not have been there earlier because the door had opened easily. "Maybe the heat has melted the glass into the door frame?"

"This isn't a real phone box," Hailey said. Her voice was up an octave. "There's something wrong with it. I can feel it."

Though Alison did not want to admit it, she could feel it, too. There was a palpable atmosphere inside the box, something prickling her senses. It was the same feeling she got when someone was staring at her from behind. On a hunch, she reached for the Yellow Pages, but the phone book was solid, looking like paper but something harder. She could feel it throbbing under her fingers. Alive. The discovery was like an electric shock up her arm. She pulled her hand away but her fingers could still remember the feeling. "Jesus! You're right."

Once it had been said, Alison could see the slight differences between the phone box and the *real* phone box outside. "This street doesn't need two phone boxes. I think this is some kind of creature copying the actual one in order to lure people inside."

"Why?" Hailey's wide eyes showed she probably knew the answer, but wanted Alison to voice her fears.

"Food," Alison said. This was one time she would have been grateful to see Jeremy Beadle step out from hiding, to tell her it was all a *joke*. "I think we're inside its stomach."

"You're scaring me."

"I'm scaring myself," Alison admitted. "I think - I think this creature must suffocate its prey. The door is like its mouth. You know, this area used to be forest a hundred years ago, and I'm wondering if this creature was a chameleon-like species. Maybe it can't move quickly, so it disguises itself. Then humans came along and destroyed its natural habitat and it had to move among us. It must have adapted itself to live in full view of humans. It learned to copy a telephone box. If there were witnesses around it would have acted like an ordinary, broken phone - who knows how many of them are all over the country and no one ever bothers to report them. Just think of the number of people who go missing each year -"

"No," Hailey whimpered. "I don't want to die. Someone's got to save us."

The phone box creaked. They both screamed at the same time and hugged, watching the walls in case they moved inwards. The walls did not.

"I love you," Hailey said.

"I love you, too."

"No, I mean I *love* you."

Alison froze. Now was not the time to discover her best friend was a lesbian. She extricated herself from Hailey's embrace. "*You* love *me*?"

"Yes, I'm a lesbian," Hailey said.

The word was out. "Oh."

"I just thought I'd tell you, since we're probably going to die in here. Suffocate or something. Anyway, I'm glad I told you. You don't know what it's like to love someone you know is not interested. Why do you think I chose the same course as yours? I guess I was hoping I could somehow convert you off boys." Hailey looked away. Her shoulders trembled. Alison could see her reflection was crying. She still could not believe it.

"But you went out with Tom and Mike and Gareth?"

"For my parents," Hailey said. "I was really seeing Jenny."

Blonde, blue-eyed Jenny? Jenny with the big boobs all guys found mesmerising? She was a lesbian as well? This new layer to Alison's best friend's secret life was a revelation almost dwarfing their predicament. To be trapped in a living phone box with a lesbian. Twilight Zone time. Suddenly the distance between them was uncomfortable. "Look, I admire your honesty." She gently put her hands on Hailey's shoulders. "I have no problems with you being a lesbian, and I hope we can stay friends after this is over, but right now we have to figure out a way to get the hell out of here while we are still breathing. So you've got to hold up."

"Right. S'okay." Hailey sniffled tears. "God, just promise me you won't tell my parents about me, will you?"

"I promise. If we survive this everything that happened today should be forgotten."

"BUT IT'S GOING TO KILL US!"

"Hailey, you have to calm down. If we panic this creature will win even faster because we'll use the air up quicker."

"Air quicker ..."

"Have you anything in your handbag we could use to make a hole in this thing?"

"My cigarette lighter."

Hailey flicked on her lighter and pressed the flame against the door. The glass started blackening. Alison urged it to burn the creature, force it to open its mouth. The orange and blue jet licked the glass. It was accompanied by the smell of burning bacon. A vibration passed through the box.

It was feeling pain.

Yes, feel pain you evil SOB.

And the glass buckled outwards, stretching like cling film. Hailey chased it - but the glass formed an elongated tunnel to get away from the flame. Soon Hailey's arm was fully stretched beyond the original limit of the box. Alison hoped the lighter would burn a hole and the creature's skin would burst like a balloon. Hailey's face was set with grim determination, a wildness born of fear and hate.

"Nearly got the evil -"

Away from the flame, the glass was moving towards Hailey's arm.

"Pull your hand back -"

"What?"

Alison grabbed Hailey's clothes and yanked her backwards - just as the glass closed on her arm. "Hey! Hey! It's got me!"

The transparent flesh had Hailey's arm in its vice-like grip. Without oxygen the lighter died in her hand. Now it had Hailey where it wanted. Alison pulled her friend, trying to loosen the hold. She could see the creature applying pressure to Hailey's arm, hear the bones cracking and juices bursting out. Hailey screamed and thrashed about, while the phone box crushed her arm at its leisure. Now her arm looked like a strawberry swizzle-stick, a tube of blood, all too visible in the glassy substance.

"No! Please! Nononononononon ..."

A wet thunk separated her arm from her shoulder. Arterial spray showered up and down and sideways as she collapsed into Alison's arms, warm blood soaked her clothes. Hailey was in shock in seconds, unconscious. The square of ground was awash in her blood. Alison removed her own jacket and tied the sleeve around the injury in her best attempt at a tourniquet - but in a couple of minutes Hailey died. When someone was dead, Alison realised, it didn't matter what their sexuality was, they were dead. Alison curled up beside her, afraid to move. Hailey's eyes were open, staring sightlessly.

The phone box sounded as if it was swallowing her arm. Alison could see the red mulch spreading out, the thin crimson lines like a spider's web. The web expanded from the main source of pulped tissue until all sides of the box had fed, then the web faded as Hailey's arm became part of the thing. The glass popped back into shape. The phone box was a phone box again. The bloody lighter fell at Alison's feet, rejected by the digestive process.

After seeing the creature's morphing skill at work, she had little doubt that it could have killed them both within seconds of the trap closing, but for some reason it had chosen to keep them waiting. Only Hailey's attack had provoked it into acting.

"What's the reason?" she muttered. "Don't you like to eat in daylight?"

That could be it. If it started eating in daylight its camouflage could not conceal its activities for long. It was a nocturnal eater. Maybe that was just part of the explanation. Perhaps it liked to eat its victims slowly? Maybe it could not eat a whole person in one go? If its normal diet consisted of smaller creatures - squirrels, mice, cats - a human would be a week's worth, a binge. And now it had two of them, it probably did not know what to do. It was obviously not very intelligent, and she hoped that would give her breathing space to devise an escape route. Even here, in the middle of a suburban ghost town, someone would come along eventually. She prayed. Right now the creature was probably wondering if it should kill her as well as Hailey.

Alison did not want to provoke it into action, but she picked up the lighter. There was still some fluid inside. It could come in use later, if there was a later. She felt in Hailey's pocket for her cigarettes. Alison wasn't much of a smoker, a strictly social smoker, but now seemed a good time to change her habits. The nicotine would calm her down, help her calm down. She smoked a cigarette, then pressed the butt against the phone box, hearing a satisfying sizzle.

"How does that feel?"

The phone box stayed silent.

An hour passed. No one walked down Theaston Avenue. The box was as hot as hell, and Hailey's body began to smell. The air was foetid. Just when she thought no one even lived on the street, she saw an old man. He was walking a little terrier.

She banged her fists on the glass, shouted and waved. The old man looked at her, shook his head and walked straight past *as if nothing had happened.*

Light bled from the sky.

At six o'clock it was dark. The real phone box was lit from the inside, but the fake box stayed in darkness. Alison could hear it shifting in the shadows, but could not see what it was doing. There was hardly any oxygen left in the air, and she was feeling sleepy. Then a car's headlights illuminated the box for a moment and she went crazy trying to attract the driver's attention. Fumbling the lighter, Alison set fire to her friend. But the flame died, starved of oxygen. She saw the thing absorbing Hailey, coating her in a slime. The car swept by and disappeared, leaving Alison alone again with the phone box. The box was losing its shape, becoming something rounder and ill-defined. The roof lowered inexorably. The walls closed in. Suddenly the phone cord snaked around her neck, lifting her bodily off the ground. The receiver closed over her mouth, wet and cloying, like the kiss of an old relative.

Eeeeeeeeee.

In the morning, there were three phone boxes in a line.

ABOUT THE AUTHOR

John Moralee writes crime and horror stories, often mixing the two genres together into dark suspense fiction. He lives in the UK, where his short fiction has appeared in magazines and anthologies including The Mammoth Book of Future Cops, Crimewave, The New Writer, The Asylum Within, Hideous Progeny: A Frankenstein Anthology, Acclaim, the British Fantasy Society's magazine Peeping Tom, and the Fish Short Story Award book Scrap Magic and Other Stories.

Many collections of his short fiction are available as e-books. They include The Bone Yard and Other Stories, Bloodways, Afterburn and Other Stories, Blue Ice, The Good Soldier and Other Stories, Thirteen: Unlucky For Some, Under Dark Skies and a science fiction collection called The Tomorrow Tower.

His début crime novel is a Rhode Island-based mystery thriller called Acting Dead.

Printed in Great Britain
by Amazon

40887803R00159